honestly ben

BILL KONIGSBERG

ARTHUR A. LEVINE BOOKS
An Imprint of Scholastic Inc.

Library of Congress Cataloging-in-Publication Data

Names: Konigsberg, Bill, author.
Title: Honestly Ben / Bill Konigsberg.
Description: First edition. | New York : Arthur A. Levine Books, an imprint of
Scholastic Inc., 2017. | Companion to: Openly straight. | Summary: Ben Carver
returns for the spring semester at the exclusive Natick School in Massachusetts
determined to put his relationship with Rafe Goldberg behind him and concentrate on
his grades and the award that will mean a full scholarship—but Rafe is still there,
there is a girl named Hannah whom he meets in the library, and behind it all is
his relationship with his distant, but demanding father.
Identifiers: LCCN 2016008865| ISBN 9780545858267 (hardcover : alk. paper)
Subjects: LCSH: Gay teenagers—Juvenile fiction. | Homosexuality—Juvenile fiction. |
Identity (Psychology)—Juvenile fiction. | Preparatory schools—Massachusetts—Juve
nile fiction. | Fathers and sons—Juvenile fiction. | CYAC: Gays—Fiction. |
Identity—Fiction. | Sexual orientation—Fiction. | Preparatory schools—Fiction. |
Schools—Fiction. | Massachusetts—Fiction.
Classification: LCC PZ7.K83518 Ho 2017 | DDC 813.6 [Fic]—dc23 LC record
available at https://lccn.loc.gov/2016008865

10 9 8 7 6 5 4 3 2 1   17 18 19 20 21
Printed in the U.S.A.   23

First edition, April 2017
Book design by Nina Goffi

For Chuck Cahoy, always. I may not have known you as a teenager, but your voice gave birth to Ben, and I am forever grateful to you for that. And everything else in my life.

1

According to the swim instructor at the Gilford gym, I had the worst buoyancy of any human he'd ever seen.

My brother, Luke, and I got one lesson each as our Christmas present, mostly because Luke wanted to learn. I wasn't so sure I needed to add swimming to my life, as I'd gotten along just fine without it for seventeen years. Also, it was three degrees outside, so the idea of being in a bathing suit, even inside, was not appealing. I offered my lesson to Luke, but he wanted us to do it together, so I gave it a try.

The instructor, maybe two years older than me, had a thick beard, like you could hide a full-grown blue jay in there. "You don't have to be afraid of the water. All people somewhat float. It's Archenemies's law," the guy said, and I resisted the urge to correct him by saying, "Archimedes." When you attend a fancy boarding school, it's best not to be a know-it-all on your winter break.

He got the class to kick our way to the deep end while holding on to kickboards, and then he took them away and we all clung to the pool's edge as if we were hanging over the Grand Canyon. He modeled treading water, which looked like riding a bike, except if you fall off, you drown. He showed us that if we somehow fell to the bottom, we could use our arms and legs to propel us upward. Then, one at a time, he told us to let go of the edge.

"You'll see how your natural buoyancy kicks in, and your fear will just melt away," he promised.

I was at the end of the line, and while some took more prodding than others, each person took a deep breath and let go. Just as he predicted, everyone sunk a bit and then rose up until the crowns of their heads poked to the surface. Then they thrashed around in some approximation of water treading until their mouths were above the blue, gasping for oxygen, and the instructor helped them reach the side again.

Luke went before me. He's about seventy pounds skinnier, and he did fine. He didn't even thrash that much on his way back up.

"Wicked awesome. Just like riding a bicycle," he said, his legs pedaling water even after he reached the edge.

This was ironic for him to say and not of great solace to me, as we were both taught to ride a bike by our dad, who took us to the top of a gravelly hill near our farm and told us to sit down, stop our whining, and start pedaling. Mom had four gashed knees to nurse that night, and she was not assuaged when Dad shrugged and said, "It's how my father taught me."

When it was my turn to tread water, I did what the guy said. I let go.

I sunk directly to the bottom of the pool in three seconds flat. My butt hit the bottom, I bounced up maybe a foot, and then I re-sunk.

Like a stone. Like a thick, Czechoslovakian stone.

There was something almost comfortable about sitting on the pool floor, even with all the chlorinated water I'd swallowed and the lack of oxygen down there. Like for a simple moment, nothing was pulling at me. I was just Ben-at-the-bottom-of-the-pool, and I opened my eyes, saw the light blue world around me, and thought, *Yes. This.* A part of me actively chose not to push myself up to the surface.

Then I felt the instructor's frenetic arms under my armpits, and I launched myself up with my legs, and we drifted the six or so feet back to the surface.

"What are your bones made of?" he asked, once his gasping for air subsided and I was safely clinging to the side again.

I wiped the water from my eyes. I have learned from a lifetime of being a Carver that questions don't always require a response. Science classes taught me that my bones are made of collagen and calcium, the same stuff as other people's bones. The only difference is that I am large—like six foot two, two hundred fifteen pounds—and I am Czech.

We are a dense people.

My mom's specialty is Czech dumplings, the densest food known to man. They're flour, milk, mashed potatoes, and eggs, made into a loaf and boiled, and their general purpose is soaking up gravy. One could build a well-insulated shack out of them.

I am convinced that in many, many ways—buoyancy included—I am a Czech dumpling.

I mentally checked out of the lesson after twenty minutes, when I found myself unable to do the simplest things in water—breathing, kicking—and my thoughts dove into the same dark abyss they'd been in for much of the day.

That morning, my dad came into our room while Luke was in the bathroom and sat down on my bed. I smiled, still feeling warm from Christmas, five days before. Our family is big on tradition, and our Christmas tradition is waking up, bundling up in lots of clothing, and getting in Dad's brown Ford truck. Mom gets to-go cups from our store and fills them with steaming hot chocolate, and we huddle in the truck, me and Luke in the back, Mom and Dad up front, our breath and the steam from the drinks crisply visible. Dad drives slowly through the roads of Alton for an hour or so, and we *watch the crops grow*, as he likes to say. There's something perfect about the silence, all of us together, witnessing the pristine, snow-filled fields *out there*, while we're safe and warm *in here*.

It's not fancy, but it's always in those moments that I most feel like a Carver. We're quiet, but we're together. And then we go home and Luke and I open our present, which is usually a "simultaneous," which means we open them at the same time, and we usually get the same thing, as we did this year with the swimming lesson.

Call it simple. But yeah, I kinda love our Christmas.

But when I smiled at Dad as he sat down on my bed this morning, he didn't smile back.

"Got your report card yesterday," he said.

"Oh." My heart dropped.

"Benny," he said. "How did that happen?"

I sucked in my teeth. "That" was a C plus in the first semester of BC calculus. Prior to last semester, I'd been a straight-A student, but this past fall I got a little sidetracked by my new and suddenly exciting social life at boarding school. Suddenly I was a straight-A student with one C plus that stood out like a sore dy/dx. I'd gone from possible valedictorian to also-ran.

"I know," I mumbled, averting my eyes. "I'm sorry."

He shook his thin, grizzled face at me. "That's not good enough, Benny. You know what this world does with a C-plus student? It spits him out. You need to fix this."

I didn't say anything. What was there to say? It was my fault. I hadn't done my best.

"I'm disappointed in you," he said. "I thought you were better than that."

I felt my rib cage expand and tighten, and I thought: *Maybe I'm not better than that?* And then my brain went on this little ride.

I screwed everything up. I'm so stupid. I won't stand out to colleges now. I won't get in anywhere good, and I definitely won't get a scholarship, and what kind of future does a brainy kid from a poor New Hampshire farm family have? Would we even have enough money to send me to community college? Shit shit shit.

My dad was staring at me, like he was waiting for me to speak. He's not big on emotional outpourings or anyone getting upset, so I swallowed that all down.

"I'm sorry," I said. "I'll fix this."

He shook his head and walked out of the room, and I closed my eyes and felt about three inches tall.

The worst thing was, he was right. I'd let him down. I'd let myself down. Dad worked so hard, and when I'd gotten a scholarship to Natick, he'd been proud. It was a sacrifice to not have me on the farm, but for an education and a chance at college? It was worth it, he'd said. And now I'd gone and possibly screwed everything up. And for what? For Rafe Goldberg? Jesus.

Rafe Goldberg. That was a name I'd be happy to forget.

When we finished the lesson and got changed in the locker room, Luke enthused about how wicked rad swimming was. I smiled and said, "Exceedingly rad."

After, as I drove us home to the farm across the frozen tundra in Gretchen, my old Chevy, and my brother talked nonstop about video games he gets to play at the Tollesons, I re-played the scene for the millionth time. Three weeks ago, my dorm room. Rafe in tears. Me? None.

"It just kind of snowballed," Rafe said, wiping a tear away. "It's tough to tell someone something when you don't tell them right away."

Ya think? Is there a lesson there, maybe?

These flashbacks were happening a lot lately. Like I was hovering over the scene, watching it from the ceiling. The judge, maybe. The jury. Rafe's jury. You don't befriend a guy, make him drop all his defenses, and then, when pretty natural feelings develop, you don't go, *Oh, by the way. Back in Boulder? I was openly gay. Have been for years. Used to do school talks about it. Oops, probably should have told you.*

Here I thought we were two explorers, charting some brave new world together. Turns out he'd already explored it and was just pretending. How wrong is that? I felt my blood pressure start to rise.

I hate you, Rafe Goldberg. With a fiery, burning passion that makes it hard to focus on anything else.

"Hey, Ben. Is it weird if I . . ." Luke leaned way back in the passenger's seat. It creaked.

"Weird if you what?" I was glad to be brought out of my mind-rant. The sky was monochromatic gray in that inimitable New Hampshire way, like God never wanted you to forget the somber feel of the landscape.

"Never mind."

"Tell me."

Luke rocked his body forward and put his head in his hands, inches from the glove compartment. He scratched at his scalp. White flakes fell to the floor. He snowed.

"What if I like a girl, but . . ."

"But what?"

I moved to the right lane to let an asshat in a red Mini Cooper speed past. Luke and I were pretty close, but he wasn't one to ask big, personal questions. None of us Carvers were.

"What if she's fat?"

I cracked up a bit. "Who cares?"

"Everyone calls her Bulldozer."

"That's rude."

"Her real name is Julie, and I saw her crying by the fence at recess. The thing is, I always liked her, kinda, so I went up to her and asked if she had the math homework, and she gave it to me."

I laughed. "So you made her feel better by asking her to give you her homework?"

Luke shrugged. "I had the homework done. I just didn't know what else to say to her."

"That's actually pretty nice."

"I dunno. So now I always ask her math questions, 'cause she's pretty good at math."

"Sure."

"I just don't know what to do next. And is it weird that I want to talk to her? I mean, everyone will make fun of me."

"It's not weird. You like who you like. Don't worry about other people and what they think of you," I said. "As for how? Ask her a question about her."

"Like what?"

"'Where do you live?'"

He snorted. "I know where she lives. She lives in town."

"I don't know. What she likes to do? Does Mom know that you like a girl? Dad?"

"No, thanks," he said, and I laughed. I remembered being a fourteen-year-old Carver once, with all sorts of questions and no one to ask, except the Internet, which isn't the same as asking an actual person who will talk to you about the answers. One spring morning I couldn't take not knowing anymore. All these things happening, all these questions. I got up my courage and went out to where my dad was fixing a loose floorboard in the barn. I stood there watching him work, my arms crossed tightly across my chest and my eyes trained on a loose hay bale. Finally I said, "At what age did you get hair on your legs?"

Dad whacked a nail with his hammer and said nothing.

I sucked in my teeth. "At what age did you start to think about girls?"

"Looks like rain," he said, not looking up. And then he whacked the nail again, even though I could tell it was already in all the way.

To this day, Dad has never had that talk with me.

"I know," I said to Luke. "They aren't so good for the big talks. If you ever need to talk . . ."

He shrugged and looked out the window.

"You're a good brother," he said after a while, and I felt a pang in my chest.

"You too."

I loved my family. We got one another. They knew who I was. My dad can be a little demanding, but there are nice moments too. When you work on a farm for a living, you don't have a lot of time for chatting. Sometimes less is more, like with Luke and me. That little conversation we'd just had was worth a thousand late-night talks with Rafe, and the proof of that was that just two months of sharing my deepest emotions with Rafe had led me *here*.

I thought about sitting on the bottom of the swimming pool, and how in that moment it had felt like I'd be completely okay to not be here anymore. To not be anywhere. Which doesn't seem right, because it was one betrayal by a guy, and in the grand scheme of the universe, that doesn't amount to a parasite on an ant on the butt of an elephant. But at that moment in the pool, I sure did think it would be okay to cease to exist.

And that just didn't make sense.

I mean, I was Ben Carver, and I had so much. I was lucky enough to go to the Natick School on a full scholarship. If I kept my head down and got my calc grade back up, I'd be the first in my family to go to college, and then graduate school. The plan was to be a college history professor by twenty-five. And sticking to the plan was way more important than the fact that I wished I had someone I could talk to about the Rafe thing. About everything, really. About sitting at the bottom of the pool.

Because I can't do that. When you're Ben Carver, telling someone that for a fleeting moment you thought you loved a guy? Or telling someone you thought it might be okay to not be alive anymore? Those are big fucking deals. They're atomic bombs. And I don't drop atomic bombs on people. Rafe does. I don't.

2

When the announcement came over the loudspeaker that I needed to go to the headmaster's office, I thought: *Maybe they're putting me on academic probation?*

It was the first morning of classes after winter break, and as I hurried across the empty quad to the administration building, all bundled up in my brown hooded jacket, part of me realized how crazy that was—one C plus wasn't exactly probation-worthy. Another part of me couldn't stop my heart from pounding because I was sure I'd done something bad.

I'd never been to Headmaster Taylor's office. Swank. I sat in the waiting room, which was all wood paneling and high ceilings and sculptures. It even smelled manly, like the aftershave lotion my old roommate, Bryce, used to put on before parties.

The secretary told me the headmaster would see me, and I stood up and slowly walked toward his door, trying to get my heart to stop pounding in my ears. I opened the door.

"Benjamin Carver," Headmaster Taylor said, a little too buoyantly. "My man."

"Hello, sir," I said back.

It was rumored that Headmaster Zachary Taylor was a descendent of the twelfth president of the United States, which was why they had the same name. I had always meant to research that to find out if it was true. Taylor was the kind of guy who would shake your hand real strong, and flash you a perfect-toothed smile, and call you "my man," and tell you that his door was always open.

His door was generally never open.

"Sit down, sit down," he said. "How are Richard and Marlene?"

My parents. "Um, they're fine. They—"

"Right, right," he said, and my throat got tight. I realized this was going to be bad news. You don't greet a kid so kindly unless it's something bad. "So I called you here with some news."

I could barely move my neck to nod.

"Tell me, what do you know about Peter Pappas?"

My mouth dropped open and my arms went numb. Peter Pappas was a Natick student in the 1960s. He was an all-around great guy, a student athlete who had enlisted in the Vietnam War voluntarily after his junior year. He was killed in service, and now a major scholarship award was named after him. Each year, it was given to a junior who was also considered an all-around great guy. Last year, Kyle Guidry had won it, and he'd given a speech in front of the whole school.

"Um," I said. "I know quite a bit, actually." I could barely breathe. No way.

He laughed. "That doesn't surprise me in the least. Your teachers say you're studious to a fault, that you take an interest in just about everything."

"Thank you, sir," I said, but I was thinking: *But what about my bad math grade last semester?*

"Congratulations, Ben. You're this year's recipient of the award!"

11

"Me?" I said.

"Yes, you, good sir! Congratulations!"

I stared at his desk. It was like I was waiting to wake up from a dream or something. I'd never won an award before. And this one, this was a big deal. Huge. It came with a scholarship for college. Oh my God. A college scholarship!

I felt a wave of some foreign feeling sweep through my chest. "Thanks!" I said. "Thanks. Thank you."

Taylor gave me a tight-lipped smile and ran his hands through his graying hair. "You are very welcome, sir. We don't take this lightly around here. Your teachers and your coach all had glowing things to say about you, and it simply can't be denied, Ben. Everyone likes you. You're a gifted young man, and you have a very bright future. The foundation was quite pleased when they heard us talk about you."

You can't cry in moments like these, but it felt like a definite possibility. I felt dizzy and light and giddy, like my body didn't know how to react.

"Thanks," I said again. "Thanks."

"Now, it's provisional. The foundation has certain requirements that must be met throughout your time at Natick. For that reason, we will alert a runner-up. I don't anticipate a problem, but I want to make sure you're aware. You must abide by the code of conduct and remain among the top ten percent of the class in terms of GPA." He looked down at some papers in front of him. "Now, I saw that last semester, you took a dip in calculus."

"Yes, sir. But I'll do better this semester. I promise."

"Good. I think you'll want to stay above a three-point-seven to stay in the acceptable range."

I nodded and nodded, and in that moment, I promised myself I wouldn't take on anything new that could get in the way of focusing on my studies. Nothing could be more important than that.

"Also, the foundation was really impressed with your activities. As long as you keep playing baseball and doing Model Congress, I think you'll be fine there."

"Yes, sir."

He smiled at me again. "The assembly will be the Friday before spring break. You'll give a speech, and then you'll receive the Pappas Foundation's four-year scholarship. Now, it's a partial scholarship, and I know you may well need more aid, but you wouldn't be the first Natick student to pair it with another scholarship or grant. You'll focus on that next year with your advisor."

"Thanks," I said again. "This is amazing."

"Your speech should pay homage to Pappas. You should also share a little bit about your life plans and goals. Kyle did such a nice job last year."

I nodded. I remembered the speech. It had been very good.

"Good man. We'd love it if you invited your family down from New Hampshire. And a large wooden plaque with your name and your picture will be placed in the hallway of the main building, next to all the other winners."

Me. A plaque with my name and face. I felt full. That's what I felt. Full and deeply grateful. I didn't want to get weird, so I just said, again, "Thanks. Thank you. Thanks."

He gave me a hearty handshake, and after I left the office, I nearly sprinted across the quad, feeling ticklish, like parts of my body I'd never felt before were all now very awake and alive.

The Pappas Award recipient. Me.

Back in my room, I called my parents.

"Mom," I said. "I won the Peter Pappas Award."

"Oh. What's that?" she asked.

"It's a scholarship. Well, it comes with one, for college. Partial, but still. It goes with an all-around student award they named after this guy who died. It's a . . . kind of a big deal."

"Oh! Well! Isn't that nice, Benny!"

"Yeah," I said, laughing. "Imagine that! I never won an award before."

"That's terrific, Benny. Let me tell your father."

My throat got tight. I knew she'd tell him, obviously, but I wasn't sure if I could take it right now, him telling me to not get a big head.

My mother said, "Richard! Ben won a big award!"

I braced for the letdown.

"You don't say?" I heard him say. "Let me talk to him." He took the phone. "What's this, Benny?"

"I, um, won this award. It's not, like, a huge deal, but . . . it'll pay for some of my college. I mean, there's a scholarship. It's called the Peter Pappas Award. Named after a guy who volunteered to fight in Vietnam and died there. He was a great all-around kid, very popular, good athlete, good student. Good guy. They'll put up a plaque with my name and face on it, I guess."

I heard a noise that I hadn't heard too much in my life: my dad chuckling. "Well, I'll be," he said. "Ben Carver, award winner. I am so damn proud of you, Benny!"

I couldn't help it. I gasped, and then I turned it into a cough, as if the gasp had been me clearing my lungs. I just couldn't remember my dad ever saying that before. But I sucked my feelings down and said, "Thanks. Thanks. I guess they want you to come for the ceremony. It's the Friday before spring break? If you can, I mean."

14

"Well, I'm sure we can get some help here on the farm and get on down there, sure," he said.

"Maybe you can stay over? Stay in a hotel?" I surprised myself. I never suggested anything that would cost my dad money, because I knew he'd tell me that he wasn't made of money. But for once I wasn't in control of my mouth.

"Well, then. Maybe," he said. "Maybe we'll do just that."

I got off the phone with this full feeling I wasn't used to in my chest. I imagined my dad, at the store, telling the Stevensons, maybe, or the Majkowskis. *Yeah, we're heading down to Massachusetts tomorrow. Gonna close the store, even. My boy Benny's getting an award. I'm so proud of him!*

I shivered. *Careful,* I told myself. *You don't want to set yourself up for a fall. Be happy. Just not too happy.*

A pounding on my door woke me from a deep, upright sleep.

"What?" I groaned, rolling my neck to fix a kink in it. It was my first Monday night back at Natick, and after finishing up homework, I'd fallen asleep in the burgundy desk chair Bryce left me when he withdrew from school last semester. I wiped the sleep from my eyes and looked at my phone: 1:44 A.M. On the windowsill outside, several inches of snow had piled high, and I remembered I'd fallen asleep watching the snowstorm.

"Blizzard Bowl, baby!" the voice yelled, and I managed a sleepy smile. It was definitely Steve Nickelson's voice, and this was a great Natick tradition. Once a year, we celebrated the end of the season's first blizzard with a pickup football game at whatever hour the snow stopped. My freshman year, the blizzard ended during class, and we'd simply walked out, no explanation necessary. Headmaster Taylor even played with us. Last year it was a night game, and I liked that one better; there was something delicious about moonlit snowflakes, the way you could see actual grains of snow if you stood under one of the streetlamps lining the path.

"I'll be right down!" I yelled, and I could hear Steve stomp off and bang on the next door. I jumped up, suddenly wide-awake, and bundled myself up in layers. The other kids might have the newest in boot technology and snow pants, but somehow I was never the first one to whine about the cold. *Sometimes old and ratty gets the job done best,* I thought, looking at the olive-green work gloves I'd gotten as hand-me-downs from my dad in ninth grade.

Outside, the snow was knee-deep, and as I stepped into a virgin pile, I felt the sweet chill curl into my calves. After last year's game, Bryce had lent me an extra blanket and we'd drunk hot chocolate in the dark. It still was a few hours before I thawed out. That was how I was built; it took a while for the cold to seep in there, but once it got to my bones, it would stay.

"Yo, Ben!" this kid named Standish called over. He had stringy blond hair, and the probability that he would move to Southern California and be a surf instructor in his twenties was 100 percent. "What up, Blood?"

I tromped through the snow toward the others. "Hey," I said. Each step was work, as I had to dig my already sopping boots out of the pack, then break through the crust of an untouched snow blanket.

"Congrats on the Pappas," Standish said, and I mumbled, "Thanks." Word had gotten out about the award sometime before lunch, and people had started to congratulate me. I wasn't used to the kudos, and truthfully I was looking forward to that part being over.

"Yeah, congrats, dude," this senior named Tommy Mendenhall said. Tommy was shortstop on the baseball team, and last year I'd played varsity third base. Other than some monosyllabic orders on the baseball field, he'd never uttered a word to me before.

"Thanks, thanks," I said, picking imaginary lint off my jacket.

"You ready for some serious baseball?" he asked. "Big year for us."

I smiled. "Absolutely. Can't wait."

I'd been looking forward to the first practice for a month, and now it was about twelve hours away. If you wanted to play baseball here, you couldn't play basketball, because practice began in January, three months before actual games. The reason was the spring break tournament. Each year, Natick was one of the very few northern schools to participate in a weeklong tournament in Fort Lauderdale. The varsity players got to stay at a nice hotel, eat in cool restaurants, and even go to the beach while they were down there. It was one of the reasons our basketball team sucked rocks.

I'd been one of four sophomores to play varsity last year—Steve was one of the others. But when it had come time for the tournament, I couldn't go for financial reasons. It kind of stunk, because when the guys came back, they had all bonded and I felt like an outsider. This year, Coach Donnelly said he hoped to find some funds for me.

"Where'd you go over break?" asked Zack, our left fielder. He was short and looked nearly orange from tanning on whatever rich people's island his folks had taken him to for Christmas.

"Home," I said. "New Hampshire."

"Your family didn't do anything special?"

I stared at Zack. To me, being home with my family is special.

"All right. Good talk," Zack said, turning away from me. The guys were used to me not saying much, and I was used to them giving me a little shit about it.

Steve gave Zack a chest-bump, and the guys started talking about the Boston Bruins. I stretched out my still sleepy legs.

"Carver." Steve came up behind me and hit my back with his forearms.

"Yo," I said.

"We gonna kill it this year?"

"Yes. It's going to be dead," I said, and he laughed. A lot of the guys were dolts — Steve included — but they were my dolts.

Perhaps because it was two in the morning, only the true Blizzard Bowl fanatics had shown up. I was teamed with Steve, Zack, and Mendenhall. We got the ball first. Mendenhall called quarterback.

"Flag, twenty yards," Mendenhall barked my way, and I nodded. Flag meant go straight and then angle out toward the sideline and end zone.

Mendenhall called hike, and that's when we all remembered: The idea of Blizzard Bowl was always better than the game itself. I attempted to run through the knee-high drifts, but it was impossible. We started laughing as the sense memory kicked in. Zack tried to make it look like he was running by exaggeratedly swinging his down jacket–enclosed arms, but really he was walking too. And there was the slight issue of sight, since the brown leather ball could barely be seen except when under one of the streetlamps.

Mendenhall rifled the ball toward Steve, who had run-walked toward one of the lights and yelled, "Throw it here." The ball slipped straight through Steve's hands and landed fifteen feet behind him. It drilled the snow like a diagonal missile and disappeared, and a search and rescue mission commenced, with a guy from the other team finally coming up with the ball plus a face full of snow.

Both teams began to realize that the only way to complete passes was to throw short and toward the sideline where the lights were, and after a while the game degenerated into a game of catch and trash talk about local Natick townie girls.

"You gonna tap that ass?"

"Who? Allie? That trick? Fuck that bitch, yo."

Things tended to get a little hip-hop when all the guys got together, which made no sense, as we were all white and, other than me, exceedingly wealthy. I wondered if we could get a transcript of one of these conversations, and perchance have a social anthropologist sound off on it, or post it on the school website for prospective students, so they could all decide whether they could hang, yo.

That would have been helpful for me, for instance. Because while I can hang, yo, the reason is a little weird.

I'm big.

When you're a big guy, people just assume you fit in. They assume you run things, that you're in control, that you know what to do. I've noticed that if I don't say anything, people will continue to assume these things about me. Because I am athletic, because I have broad shoulders—farm work, by the way, not the gym—other guys salute me wherever I go. I get reverential nods.

I appreciate that it makes my life easier. But it also means that people don't really get me. They don't know what's up in my brain. I think, maybe, when you're a big guy, it's assumed your intellect is not as important as whether you can throw a ball.

We soon tired of digging for lost footballs and gave up on the game. I was walking with the others toward the dorm when some familiar laughter grabbed my attention. I could barely see, as the lights were now well behind us all, but I could hear it, about twenty feet to my right. It was the inimitable, melodic, high-pitched giggle of Toby Rylander, matched with the thundering chortle of Albie Harris. I stopped.

"You coming, Carver?" Mendenhall yelled.

"Go on without me," I said, bending down, pretending to tie my boots, which were well under the snowpack. They kept walking.

My sort-of friendship with Toby and Albie was part of the

brain-dead Rafe haze I'd been in the previous semester. Toby and Albie were such a weird duo; it was as if they spoke an alien language. And while they could be amusing, they were also annoying. The first time I drove somewhere with them, I distinctly remember this one time, as we were pulling out of the school parking lot, when Toby, wearing a fake mustache, announced he was a crime reporter. In the end there were way more fun moments than weird ones. But that friendship was in the past, with the rest of the Rafe wreckage. It belonged there.

Yet I moved toward them as if on autopilot, and soon I could make their shapes out in the moonlight. I could barely see what they were doing, but it appeared they were clearing a circle, building a huge wall of snow all around them. Then I saw an indentation in the snow, on the opposite side of their snow wall, and I realized that of course there weren't just two of them. There were three.

My pulse went rogue on me. Wild, crazy, strange, nonsyncopated beats. I felt my heart soar, and then plunge, and then soar again. I hadn't been pulled toward Toby and Albie; subconsciously it was Rafe I'd wanted to see, and that was just crazy.

I slowed my pace but continued walking, and sure enough, there was Rafe, illuminated by the moonlight and the light of the snow, all bundled up, about six inches below the powder surface. He was making a snow angel.

He was wearing the same bright red jacket and black hat he'd worn when we'd gone skiing in Colorado over Thanksgiving. I flashed on Rafe skiing in front of me, his legs moving from side to side like a pendulum while his upper body stayed totally still. On the long chairlift rides, his visible breath dissipated into the cold mountain air, while everything around us felt crisp and clear and right.

It had been one of the happiest days of my life.

But that was then. Now my insides were all messed up about it, and I knew if I let myself feel even a little bit of that it would be a lot, and I didn't have room for a lot anymore. It might break me in two, and I was a big guy, and big guys who play baseball don't break in two. I wished I could just disappear.

"Snow angels have no place in an igloo community," Toby said.

Rafe kept making his arm and leg motions. I could hear them scraping the snow. "Maybe igloos have no place in a snow angel community," Rafe yelled.

"Snow angel community. There are no communities of snow angels. There are flocks. Everyone knows that." This was Albie, who was currently carving a pile of heavy snow into bricks.

I shifted my frigid legs, and it made a sound, and I silently cursed my stupid, thick body. Toby looked over, and it took a moment for him to see me, but then he gave a tiny, tentative wave, the kind of wave you give someone you're not sure if you're friends with anymore. We hadn't spoken since Thanksgiving, when everything blew up.

"I think there could be communities of snow angels that have yet to be discovered," Rafe said, hoisting himself up from his angel shell with his arms. That's when he saw me standing there, maybe fifteen feet away.

Rafe smiled, a questioning smile, like, *Can we be okay, please?*

No. Yes. No. I didn't know.

Part of me wanted him to burn for putting me through everything I'd felt since then. The sleepless nights; the need to talk to someone when there was absolutely no one, *no one* who would understand. And another part of me? No way no how did I want Rafe to think I hated him. I wasn't sure what I wanted, but my mouth naturally curves down into a frown, and I didn't want to frown at Rafe. So I flickered my mouth just a bit, and Rafe's face lit up into a tentative smile, but then I adjusted back into what I figured was a neutral expression, and his face unlit.

"Hey, Ben. Congrats on the award," Albie said, and I nodded. "We need builders," he added, looking at me, and I realized that Rafe must not have told them about what had happened between us. A part of me wanted to reach out and hug him for protecting me, but the bigger part of me, the thick part that sinks in water, stayed totally still.

"So cold," I said. "I'm gonna . . ."

"Sure," Rafe said, his voice soft, and I had to turn away because I couldn't stand anyone looking at me when I felt the way that voice made me feel. All mixed up inside and not in control and not like a Pappas Award winner, not in the least.

The voice was coming from my closet.

It was hours after the Blizzard Bowl, and in the deep winter night, the radiator rattled and hissed. The wind whistled against the windows, and the muffled voice wafted through the frigid, lonely darkness.

Ben.

Even in that strange, disorienting place between sleeping and waking, my brain recognized the irony of hearing my name whispered from a closet. Still, I could not discern whether I was in the midst of a recurring nightmare, or if the idea that this had happened before was simply part of my current dream.

Ben.

The hoarse, gravelly whisper made my hair stand on end, and in my dream state, the voice became dissonant musical notes hovering around my head. Then they chased me across Natick School's quad. The voice, saying just one word, but meaning so much more. Telling me the thing I least wanted to hear. Telling me this thing with Rafe wasn't over, and it wasn't going to go away. It was inside me still, and it was very much alive. It was like Frankenstein's monster, following me, pursuing me, taunting me. Damned AP literature. Mary Shelley wouldn't let me sleep.

In the dream my body picked up speed and sprinted across the quad, yet the voice just got louder and more insistent. And then I was back in my bed, and the voice was saying words, more words than just my name. Words I could understand. Words that pissed me off.

Come out, Ben. Come out.

I thrashed in my bed, buried my head under my pillow, held my breath, and tried to squeeze the thoughts from my brain.

But the damn voice.

Ben, come out. Come out, Ben.

"Fuck!" I muttered, aware I was talking in my sleep.

I'm in the closet. Um. You're in the closet.

My eyes flashed open. I sat up. There was no way I had created those words. Was there? I looked out the window. Still not morning. Checked the clock. 4:15. I'd been asleep maybe an hour. A sliver of light from the moon cast a purple glow on my desolate room. I listened. Nothing.

The radiator clattered like it was clearing its throat. Could that have sounded like words? Was my brain so crazy that it could make up phrases out of sounds?

I sunk back under the sheets and turned onto my side, curling my legs under the red wool blanket my mom had knitted for me and allowing its heat to sink into my still-chilled bones. My heart was pounding from the strange nightmare.

The world was quiet again, aside from the wind. I lay there staring at what was left of the moon, feeling uneasy about everything. If I had been back on the farm, all this snow would mean plowing. Here that wasn't my problem, yet that didn't really make me feel much better. I had other concerns, and I kept my eyes open and watched the night slowly fade into morning.

And then the silence was broken.

"Come out, Ben. It's an option. Consider your options, Ben."

This was no radiator talking. These were words, and they were definitely coming from my closet. I leapt up and grabbed the first object I could find, a history textbook that had lived on my desk all break long. It was large and heavy with the history of the world. I poised myself outside the shut closet door, hefting the book over my head as if it were a weapon. My voice trembled.

"What the hell? Who the hell is in there?"

"Um, go back to sleep, Ben. Never mind—"

I yanked the door open. A skinny boy with spiked hair was sitting on the floor in the center of the closet, cradling his head as if to protect it.

"What the fuck, Toby?" I said. I yanked him up, half by his hair, half by his shoulder.

"Ow. Sorry," Toby stammered as I threw him onto the floor in the center of the room.

"Are you out of your skull? What the hell are you thinking?"

"Sorry," Toby said, raising himself up onto his elbows and flipping over. He rubbed his knees. "I saw you going to the bathroom." I looked at him funny. "I mean, I saw you heading to the john, so I just took that as an opportunity to explore your closet."

I sat down on my bed and rubbed my eyes, incredulous. "Did you really just . . . What the . . . ? And did you really tell me to—"

Toby put his hand up like a stop sign. "Relax. I'm the only person Rafe told about your gayness. I swear. He needed someone to talk to."

I punched my mattress, and it took everything in me not to roar. "I'm gonna kill Rafe. I'm not gay, by the way. Not gay. Got it?"

Toby flinched. "This is really not going the way I had hoped."

I looked at him and saw a scrawny idiot, and I remembered, just for a moment, that he was Toby. Who did stuff without thinking, all the time. Who'd never mean to hurt a fly. "Just so I know. How exactly did you expect this would go?"

"I'm subliminalizing. I did it with Albie before break. I'm pretty sure I got him to stop eating Cocoa Puffs. I just figured, like, I'd offer you some suggestions while you slept, and then sneak out, and, um, subliminally, you'd, like, get the message."

"As I said, I'm not gay. Not that it's any of your business." I couldn't help it. I said the gay part quieter than the rest.

"Oh, okay. Right. I, um."

"I'm not, okay? That was a one-time thing. Never, ever again. Because, apparently, if you make a stupid, moronic mistake once, you wake up with a psychopath whispering, 'Come out, come out' from your closet."

"As I said, in retrospect, I might have made a different choice."

I laughed despite myself. "You think? Do you promise to never, ever do that again?"

"Scout's honor."

I lay down and looked at the ceiling. "Shit."

"Sorry again." Toby stood up. "We miss you, by the way."

I shrugged. "That'll happen."

"It's not the same without you. You have to forgive Rafe. You have to. We want you back."

I shrugged again. A lot of people wanted a lot of things. Didn't mean they got them.

Toby spoke again. "You feel like talking about it?"

I laughed. "Um. It's four thirty in the morning."

He repeated his inflection exactly. "You feel like talking about it? Because, I mean, I kinda need to talk to someone too."

And you chose me? What about Albie? What about Rafe? Why would Toby pick me out, of all people?

I stared up at the ceiling, and I thought about what it would have been like, over break, to talk to a friend. A family member. If Uncle Max had still been alive, and I could have unburdened myself without ruining my life.

That was the biggest difference since Rafe. The lack of talking about stuff. I missed it.

But on the other hand, look at what all the talking had got me. What good had any of it done? My brain felt like it was getting squeezed in a vise, and my chest felt like it could pop.

So the idea of talking to Toby at four thirty in the morning about my feelings?

"Get out of here," I mumbled, putting my hands over my face. "Go away."

5

It was the first Thursday night of the second semester and I was doing my homework at my absolute favorite Natick getaway: the Bacon Free Library. Bryce and I used to joke about it being a library free of bacon, and he'd do commercial voice-overs for me ("All the same great library taste, now ninety-nine percent pork-free"), but truthfully it was one of the only places in the world where I felt at home. When I really wanted to be alone, I drove here and climbed a rickety old staircase up to the quiet loft area. I always had it all to myself.

I started with calculus, because now the stakes were high if I wanted to keep my scholarship. I was curious to know how lost I'd feel.

Very, it turned out.

L'Hopital Rule
If

$$\lim \frac{f'(x)}{g'(x)}$$

has a finite value or if the limit is ±∞, then

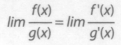

$$\lim \frac{f(x)}{g(x)} = \lim \frac{f'(x)}{g'(x)}$$

I found myself reading the rule over and over. Using derivatives to determine limits. Okay. But what did that mean? I tried to break it down, working hard to stop focusing on the fact that this rule was named after a French hospital, until my brain felt like it was melting. Was it possible that I couldn't process this kind of abstract material? And worse, a lot of future engineers in the class were probably not having as much of a problem as I was.

After I trudged through calculus homework, I prepared for the next day's English lit class. We were reading Tennyson's "All Things Must Die."

> *The stream will cease to flow;*
> *The wind will cease to blow;*
> *The clouds will cease to fleet;*
> *The heart will cease to beat;*
> *For all things must die.*

It was amazing how something so somber could make me feel uplifted. *All things must die.* The finite, to me, was a thing of beauty. There was a start and an end. Someday we'd all be history, and if I was going to be history then, it meant I existed now.

Sometimes I wasn't so sure of that.

I was focusing on re-reading that section when I heard what sounded like muttering coming from around the corner. When it continued, I exhaled loudly, hoping the sound would make the person stop. But every few seconds, the noise was there, and then there was shuffling, as if someone couldn't quite find a comfortable position. It started to annoy me, so I crept around the corner for a peek.

A girl, maybe about my age, sat in a chair facing away from me, with one leg kicked up on the desk in front of her. Her head was splayed back so that I could see the rise of her forehead and her brown hair flowing behind her. She wore a black jacket, and a large, black scarf had fallen on the floor behind her. The black-booted foot that was still on the floor tapped away, and once in a while she'd bounce her whole leg and wiggle her torso like a fish on the floor of a boat. The movement suggested agitation, and finally she kicked up her other leg and rested both on the desk in front of her.

"You're not even . . ." she muttered.

At first I thought she was talking to me, but then I realized she was muttering to herself still. I didn't want to get involved, so I backed away toward my seat. My coat rubbed against a shelf of books.

She sat very still. "Is that a person?" she asked.

"Sorry," I said. "Just investigating the noise."

She kicked her legs off the table and spun to face me. Her face looked to me like maple syrup tasted. Not the color. Just the sweetness of syrup. Her eyes were large, wide, and a pretty shade of green. Her long, narrow mouth curved up at both ends. She looked more curious than defensive.

"Are you okay?" I asked.

She laughed, not meanly. "Well, I'm alone in a library loft talking to myself, so I suppose I'm not stellar."

The lilt in her voice intrigued me. She seemed like the kind of girl you'd meet in a loft in a barely used Massachusetts library while reading Tennyson poems about the finite nature of man. If that wasn't a type before, now it was.

When I didn't say anything back, she said, "I'll be okay, thanks."

"Good," I said, frozen in my tracks.

"Normally I'm intrigued by awestruck boys, but I'm just not there right now," she said, and her voice was so earnest that immediately all my butterflies fluttered away. "What's your name?"

"Ben," I said. "Ben Carver."

"Hannah," she said. "And good girls don't give their last names out to boys who might cyberstalk them on Facebook. Good boys might want to avoid that too." She smiled a bit, and when she did it was amazing how still the rest of her face stayed. It was like a Mona Lisa smile.

"Not on Facebook," I said.

"You still in high school?"

I nodded.

"Where?"

"Natick."

She rolled her eyes. "Oh, wonderful."

"Sorry."

"You don't look like one of them."

"I'm basically not," I said. "I'm here, aren't I? You see a lot of other Natick boys skulking around the stacks reading Tennyson?"

She laughed. "I do not. I know Natick boys. One in particular, and he was a highly regrettable person."

It was my turn to laugh now. "Many of my classmates are indeed highly regrettable."

She wiped a wisp of brown hair from her eyes. "Mine too."

"Ah. Lonna Grace, I assume," I said.

Lonna Grace was our sister school in Wellesley, about five miles away from Natick. The jock guys referred to the school as Lonna

Dyke—which was not clever—and basically viewed it as a breeding ground for lesbian feminists, but I knew the truth: It was another rich kid school. The lesbian population was likely about the same size as the gay population at Natick.

She nodded. "Girls can be so awful," she said.

"Boys can be awful too."

"Yes, but this is like a special brand of awful reserved for teenage prep school girls. Someone who shall remain nameless named Rhonda Peterson wrote, 'Hannah munches rugs' on my door in indelible pink magic marker. Very original, no?"

"Yikes," I said, thinking, *Please don't be a lesbian. Please don't be a lesbian.* In all the dances I'd been to in my two-plus years at Natick—and we had two a year—I'd never had a single connection as good as this one was already.

"I mean, it's not even the rug munching thing that gets me; I can handle that. It's that Rhonda actively took the time to stand there and write her malicious thoughts on my door. Exactly what kind of issues does a girl like that have, and why is it that I constantly get shit on by people with issues?"

Wind out of sails. Oh, well. My posture relaxed. "Do girls make fun of you for being a lesbian all the time over there?"

She ran her hand through her wavy hair. "Oh, I'm not a lesbian. I wish! Men are so fucking lame. Present company excluded. I think."

I stood there, beginning to feel awkward.

"You wanna sit?" she asked.

"Um. Okay." She pointed to the ground in front of her. It was weird, but I sat down there anyway, at her feet. "So, Hannah. Do you come here a lot?"

"Ugh," she said. "Bad pickup line from the last century."

"Sorry. I'm not used to this."

She smiled that Mona Lisa smile again, and I had to look away because she was so — raw, maybe? She seemed to wear everything right there on her face. I was not used to it.

"This?"

"Um. Meeting girls — um. Pretty girls — at the Bacon Free Library."

She pursed her lips. "Are you used to meeting ugly girls here?"

"I'm not used to meeting girls, period. I mean, I'd like to, but. Not girls, like, multiple, but it would be nice to — oh God. Stop talking, Ben," I said.

She laughed, and her laugh was melodic and childlike, which was funny because she didn't talk like she was young, exactly. She seemed a little bit like an old soul, which I liked. But I liked the young laugh too. "Oh, good, you're quirky," she said.

I looked at the ground. "I don't think I've ever been called quirky before."

"Well, there's a first time for everything. I like you. Maybe you could be my manic pixie dream boy."

I swallowed. "Um. I actually have no idea what that means."

"That's like a boy in the movies who is quirky and kind and makes the female heroine feel better, then disappears."

I crossed my arms over my chest and quickly uncrossed them. "You want me to disappear?"

She bit her lip in a slightly flirtatious way. "I don't know yet."

"Um. Okay," I said.

"Okay," she answered, and she smiled at me, and I looked away again because she was so beautiful.

"I don't want to disappear," I said softly.

Her face flushed a little pink. "Duly noted."

I felt my face heat up too. Was this really happening? A girl who was interesting, smart, beautiful, easyish to talk to, and possibly interested in me? I could be okay with that. And then I thought about my grades, and how I had promised myself not to get involved in anything that would get in the way of studying.

But was man supposed to live by studying alone?

"This is my favorite time of year," I said. "When you have to bundle up in lots of clothing. I love the cold."

"You are talking about weather," she observed.

"I grew up on a farm. We tend to be a little weather-obsessed."

"You grew up on a farm and you go to Natick? You must feel like a misfit."

"Yes. Exactly. Um. Thank you for getting that," I said.

"You're welcome."

"You feel like taking a walk sometime, and not talking about the fact that it's cold?" I asked.

"What would we talk about instead?"

Your eyes, I thought, and I'm so glad I didn't say it. "You."

She smiled. "I'm in."

"Yeah? Good. I'm glad. Can I call you?" I asked.

"You can," she said. "Let me text you my number."

"I don't text," I said.

"What decade are you from, Ben Carver?"

I shrugged, not wanting to explain to her that on our cell phone plan, texting costs money, so it's understood that we won't do it. "The nineteen fifties," I said.

She pulled out a pen, wrote her number on a piece of paper, and handed it to me. I carefully tore the paper in two, wrote my number on the empty piece, and gave it to her.

"Cool. I could get into knowing a guy from the fifties. Maybe we can go to a sock hop."

"Sock hop it is," I said.

6

I wish dinners at Natick were more formal.

It's true. There's something delightful about the idea of dressing up for dinner and sitting in assigned seats in the dining hall, like back in the days of yore, or at Hogwarts. We'd sit in neat rows in high-backed wooden chairs, we'd speak in low, polite voices about the day's doings while proctors walked by taking attendance, and everyone would dab the corners of their mouths with cloth napkins. That would be perfect. Even better if everyone spoke with a proper English accent. We'd be like people in history.

Instead, I sat with the baseball team, which was about as un-Hogwartsian as it got. If my plan was to basically stay on the surface this semester, not get too entangled or deep with anyone, sitting with these guys three times a day was definitely a way to achieve that. Not a lot was expected of me in terms of talking.

On Friday afternoon of the first week, I got carried away reading about James Polk's presidency and Manifest Destiny, and by the time I looked up, dinner was half over. I ran over to the cafeteria, but the team was just finishing up their food.

"Carver!" Mendenhall yelled, a huge smile on his face, as I approached the baseball table with my tray. "What up, dude?"

"Hey," I said.

"We were just talking about the Schroeder incident," he said, and I guffawed. Schroeder was a senior last year and a total hothead. He called everyone a pussy and made constant jokes about date rape. Mendenhall, then a junior, had gotten his hands on some habanero powder. The plan was for some other juniors to get Schroeder's attention and they'd coat the inside of his jock with the stuff, but Schroeder was naturally suspicious about people's intentions and wouldn't take the bait. Bryce and I were the quiet guys, and in the spur of the moment, we improvised. Bryce pretended to fall and sprain his hamstring, and while we all crowded around his locker, the guys coated Schroeder's jock pretty good. Bryce made a quick recovery, and when Schroeder got changed, the screams he made could be heard a mile away. The guys were all pretty impressed that Bryce and I had helped.

"Where is Bryce these days?" Mendenhall asked.

"His mom sent him to an Outward Bound program. He's out in the wilderness of Utah."

"Shit, dude. That's intense."

"Yeah," I said.

"I heard they're holding a bake sale for you," Zack said. He was wearing an inside-out Celtics jersey.

"What?"

"Zack's an idiot," Steve said. "Donnelly said the school is going to pay your way to Lauderdale. Zack just thought it was funny, the idea of a bake sale for Ben Carver."

I ignored the profound and unfettered privilege involved in the

38

last sentence and focused on the important information instead. "Really? They're paying for me to go?"

Steve shrugged. "That's what Coach said."

"Wow. That's so nice."

Steve stood to bus his tray. "You coming out tonight, Carver? Blowout in town. Joey Warren kid. Gonna be off the chain, dude," he said. Joseph Warren High was the public school in town, located right across Dug Pond from us.

For a quick moment, I thought about Hannah's smile and wondered if she'd be at the party. But no. She'd feel about as out of place at an event like that as I always did. Anyway, I'd already decided: I'd do meals but not parties. I was tired of being the designated driver, the doofus sitting in the quiet room pretending to have fun. "Nah, got work to do," I said.

"All work and no play, dude," Mendenhall said.

"I know, I know."

"Suit yourself. More pussy for us." This was Mendenhall again, and I was relieved when they all headed out. I was not one to quantify pussy.

I pulled out my history text and put it next to my tray, happy to have company that wouldn't ask me questions. Then I started on the mammoth salad I'd put together with the tail end of a pile of wilted lettuce and whatever vegetables were left on the buffet. I got through my entire salad while reading about the Dred Scott decision, and then I felt a light tap on my left shoulder.

I turned around. It was Toby. I'm not great with clothing, but it seemed to me he was wearing a green blouse, cinched around his tiny waist with a big black belt. I scowled, remembering his visit to my closet just a few nights earlier.

"Eek," he said. "Not the reaction I was hoping for."

"Any more subliminal messages for me?"

He gave me a toothy smile. "Nah. A more liminal one." He turned and waved his hand.

"No," I said, when I realized who he was summoning, and I stood up so quickly that I almost knocked my tray off the table. I steadied it, and when I turned around, Rafe was standing in front of me, his arms behind his back and his head bowed slightly.

"Hey," he said.

"Hey." My head felt tight, like my brain was too big for my skull.

Toby looked at Rafe and then at me, and then back and forth at both of us. "Well? Come on. This is ridiculous. Spit it out."

Rafe turned to Toby and flapped his hand backward at him. Toby backed off. We stood there, just me and him in the cafeteria, and my thick brain began to buzz.

"I know I kind of already said this, but. I just . . ." He seemed lost for words. "Shit. Apology," he said. "Sincere apology."

I laughed. He had caught me off guard, I guess. "So now you just have to say the thing you want to do, and that will suffice?"

"Yeah, sorta kinda."

"Shit," I said. "I'm so tired of being mad at you." Until I said it, I hadn't realized how much I'd felt it. My anger at Rafe had become my roommate, and I wanted it gone.

"I'm tired of you being mad at me too. For the record, I was never mad at you."

"Well, why would you be?" I said, narrowing my eyes at him.

He shrugged. "Can we just have a truce?" he asked.

I took a deep breath. My brain suddenly didn't feel tight anymore. "I feel like we already have a truce," I said. "I've placed my imaginary Maginot Line, and there is an uneasy accord along the Western Front."

"Oh, Ben," he said, and the gentleness of his voice made me look away. "Wait. Am I Hitler in that analogy?"

I hadn't thought of it that way. "I guess."

"So you made the Jewish guy Hitler. Nice."

I laughed, and so did he.

"Tell those guys to get lost," I said, pointing at Toby and Albie, who were staring at us from a nearby table. "Walk me back to the dorm. Let's see how well our diplomats do in a postwar meeting."

"Those baseball guys must adore you," Rafe said, and I laughed again, because aside from maybe a little with Hannah, it was the first time I'd used my actual sense of humor since the last time he and I had hung out. We could reach an accord. We'd have to. I wanted my friend back.

Rafe made a hand signal that connoted, *It's okay to leave the cafeteria, I am not in mortal jeopardy,* and Albie and Toby headed out. We gave them about a minute head start, and then we bundled up and went outside.

It was that time of night when you can almost feel the temperature dipping and the wind picking up, when you can spend the entirety of a fifty-yard walk across campus savoring how your legs will feel under the covers as you watch the wind whip through the tree branches outside your window. Rafe walked by my side, and it felt peaceful, more so than I could have imagined.

"How're your folks? How was winter break?" I asked.

"They're good. Claire Olivia created a new holiday on December twenty-ninth called Rafesmas, where she covered a statue of a mule on Pearl Street with stickers she had made with my face on them."

"Sorry I had to miss that," I deadpanned, and Rafe laughed.

"How was yours?"

"Oh, you know. Partays left and right."

"Right," he said. "Of course."

"You're doing the whole GSA thing now, right?" Steve had made a comment about it one day at lunch.

"Yup."

I wanted to say something like, "Good for you," but there was no way to say it without sounding like a jackass.

"Well, I'm glad you're meeting some new people," I said instead, and then I winced, thinking it sounded like I was saying I was glad he wasn't counting on me as a friend.

"It's been good. I've actually been hanging out with a guy."

Something inside my chest seized up. It was weird, involuntary, and surprising. It wasn't like I owned Rafe; he could do what he wanted. But somehow the idea of him hanging out with another guy hit me someplace deep and painful, right above my gut.

"Oh," I said. "Okay. Sure."

If Rafe noticed anything, he didn't let it show. "Yeah," he said. "You know Jeff Frazier?"

I could feel myself gritting my teeth, like there was a vacuum somewhere in my throat and it was sucking my upper jaw into my lower one.

Rafe stopped walking. "You okay?"

Something stronger than me was kicking in. Maybe if I just willed it away, I could pretend it wasn't happening. I tried to focus on him, but he looked fuzzy. In the dark night, he was a mere blur against the dim quad.

"Oh. Yeah. Just. Preoccupied. Homework." I was well aware that five one-word sentences in a row was strange, and I couldn't figure out how to un-strange it. So I said nothing. Then I started walking.

Not fast, because I didn't want to be a jerk, but I figured that maybe if I wasn't looking at Rafe and I started moving, some ideas or words would form to explain away my weirdness.

"What just happened?" Rafe asked, walking behind me. "Are you okay?"

"I'm fine," I said, continuing to build walking speed. I spoke without turning around to look at him. "Just got stuff to do. Another time, okay?"

"Um," he said, and I could tell he'd stopped trying to keep up with me. And I was glad, because I definitely didn't want to make a scene, and it was stupid of me to even feel whatever the hell I was feeling, and there was no way I was going to let him know any of this. No chance.

7

When I finally got inside my room, I exhaled, closed my eyes, and leaned against the door.

Why was I such a freak?

What was this? Why the hell did I give a crap what he did with some stupid guy? I didn't care. He could do whatever he wanted, and it was none of my business.

I went over to the refrigerator Bryce had left behind that I'd put in the closet and grabbed an orange Gatorade. I tossed it from my right hand to my left and shook it up. Then I threw it down onto my bed and stumbled over to the bottom drawer of Bryce's old desk. Under a bunch of file folders was my old, half-empty bottle of vodka. I'd promised myself I would stop drinking last semester, when it started to feel a little bit like a problem. *Screw it,* I thought. *I just need to take the edge off a little.*

We called orange Gatorade and vodka a plastic screwdriver, and that had always been the drink of choice for me and Bryce, and then for me and Rafe. I swigged down a third of the Gatorade and closed my eyes as I got a brain freeze. Then I filled the bottle back up with vodka. I put the top back on and shook it. I placed the vodka bottle deep under my bed in case someone walked in, and then I sat down, waited for the brain freeze to subside, and took a sip of the screwdriver.

I exhaled as the alcohol burned my throat.

Rafe. Damn. I let my guard down for one second, let him back in, and what did I last? Two minutes before I got hurt again?

He'd sure gotten over his broken heart pretty quick. Jesus. I grimaced. Why the fuck was I even thinking about this? Rafe was a guy. I was a guy. A straight guy. For most of the last twenty-four hours, I'd been thinking about Hannah's cute button nose and her sweet red lips. I didn't think about guys that way. Ever. But then last year Rafe had gone and opened up this strange, weird, crazy part of me that had never been there before, and—damn him. Damn.

I took another swig and closed my eyes, feeling the alcohol seep into my bloodstream. There was always this moment in drinking when you could sense the alcohol starting to do its thing.

What was I going to do about Rafe? He could date or whatever anyone he wanted to, and I sure wasn't going to let him know that it upset me, because that was a closed door, sealed off with concrete, never to be opened again. And shit. Had I been too obvious? Why hadn't I just ignored it and kept talking? Why couldn't I just be cool for once?

I took a long swig, and suddenly my bottle was empty.

A piece of white paper slid under my door.

I knew who it was from, and as much as I wanted to ignore it, I couldn't.

Ben,
I'm sorry. God, I say that a lot, huh? I don't know why I always do the wrong thing with you. I don't mean to.

The stupid thing (the stupidest of the many stupid things, maybe?) is that I only said that about Jeff because I was trying to let you off the hook. It was kind of my way of saying, "Don't worry. I'm not into you anymore." I should have known not to say anything. I'm sorry I'm so stupid. I just want to be your friend again. That's all. I promise.

Your sad and stupid wannabe friend,

Rafe

I pulled the note into my chest, and then, when I realized I had done that, I crumpled it and threw it onto my desk.

Yeah, I got it. Rafe was nice. That didn't change the fact that right now, I wanted to be left alone. I had more than enough on my plate, thanks very much.

I went back to the closet for another Gatorade, and I went through the same steps as before, minus the brain freeze this time. Once the bottle was full and shaken, I curled up under the blanket with it, huddling it close like a football, or a baby. Then I slowly pulled the bottle out, opened it, and took a sideways sip, which nearly made me choke. Hard to drink sideways, but I didn't feel like moving. I put the top back on and cradled the bottle again.

This used to be a lot more fun with Bryce. Before Rafe. We'd play two-person Would You Rather, and we'd crack up about how stupid the guys acted at some party, and Bryce would do spot-on impressions of all of them, and when he'd turn it into a full-on conversation between them, I would almost pee my pants, I'd laugh so hard.

Last September we were playing this game called Two Truths and a Lie, and I had broken out a little-known nugget about how the

Nazis co-opted the Harvard fight song and used parts of it for their Sieg Heil march. He thought that was the lie, and the ensuing conversation went from the invasion of Lichtenstein to Rommel to Rommel McDonald House, which he said was a place where they encourage kids with cancer to annex northern Africa.

I thought about disappearances.

In my life I'd been close to three people: Uncle Max, Bryce, and Rafe. Uncle Max had been the only one who got me back in New Hampshire, and he was the one who encouraged me to apply on my own to Natick. He knew I needed to get out of there. We talked about life and ideas and history and literature, and even feelings sometimes, and he was my lifeline. Then, one day a year ago, driving home from God knows where at two A.M. on the Mass Turnpike, he crashed into a guardrail. Luke said he heard that he'd been decapitated. I wish he'd never said that, because now, when I thought of one of the three people in my life who'd ever really known me, I pictured him headless.

Bryce had been assigned at random as my roommate freshman year, and we became best friends fast. He cared about ideas and didn't think it was weird that I liked to go to the World War II museum alone. He told me when he was depressed, and when I broke up with Cindy, my first-ever girlfriend, he was there to talk to. When Uncle Max died, Bryce went to the funeral with me. Then I think being the only black guy at Natick really got to him. We used to talk about race and privilege together, and then one day he stopped talking about it. He'd stare at one spot on the wall for hours at a time. I'd watch him do it. And I should have gotten him some help, but I didn't know what to do. He took a leave of absence and went home to Rhode Island, and he wasn't coming back.

Rafe had been there for me to pick up the pieces. He cared enough to come to my room when Bryce disappeared, and he was funny, and silly, and sympathetic, and there was just something about him that lit me up inside. Maybe it was the silly stuff. I'd never met someone who could get me to do things in the spur of the moment that made me feel so light inside, and I'd never had a friend who laughed so much at things I said. He'd become the friend that made me forget all the other pain, and I'd fallen into the deepest friendship of my life, and I'd opened up to him. Then he'd reached into my chest, grabbed my heart, and stomped on it with his dishonesty, and I had no one — absolutely no one — I could talk to about it.

I took another sip of the screwdriver. The alcohol warmed my nose. I took another gulp, closed my eyes, and threw the covers over my head, and I felt the alcohol flow into my ears, my chin, the nape of my neck.

Good alcohol, bad alcohol, I thought. *This stuff, used recreationally, can ease the pain. You can use it and then stop before it gets to be a problem. Rafe, on the other hand. Bad alcohol.*

I leaned over to the desk and picked up Rafe's note. I smoothed out the paper, grabbed a pen, and wrote on the bottom:

Rafe = alcohol.
Alcohol is bad for me.

I stared at the words I'd written, and then I rolled my eyes and crumpled the note back into a ball. So much for me putting words down on paper. I leaned back into my bed and lay down. Forget studying for the night. I was going to sleep drunk, or whatever this was. Buzzed. When I woke up, things would make more sense.

○ ○ ○

My phone woke me. Disoriented, I looked around. My light was on, my clothes piled on the floor, and I was cradling a nearly empty Gatorade bottle. My head was cloudy. Like drunkish cloudy. I'd never woken up drunk before. It was strange. I scanned for the clock on my desk. It was just 8:37 P.M. Jesus.

I fumbled for my phone. It was Hannah, calling me for the first time. Timing. Wow. Not answering was obviously the smart thing to do, but I was so fucking tired of doing the right thing. She'd understand.

"Alcoholics Anonymous," I said, my voice cracking.

She laughed. "Uh-oh. Are you drinking?"

"Yup." I was enjoying the way the vodka felt in my bloodstream.

"Edgy. Who's there with you?"

"No one," I said, before I could think about it.

"Drinking alone? That's bleak, Ben Carver."

"I got troubles," I said, feeling very un-Ben.

She gave an awkward laugh. "Are you okay? You sound different."

"Yes. No. I don't know, actually."

"You feel like talking about it? Want to meet up?"

I crossed my legs, imagining her here with me right now. "Um. Driving. Can't."

"Of course," she said. "Good thinking. Should we just talk here, then? What's going on?"

"It's really nothing," I said.

"C'mon. Tell me, tell me. What's your problem?" she asked, and then we both laughed, knowing she didn't mean it the way it sounded.

"I don't really have problems," I said.

"Let's play a game. You pretend I would never, ever judge you or whatever you say. Because, actually, I won't. I promise."

All my life I'd done what I was taught as a kid. You don't talk about your problems. You don't bug people with them. You solve them your-self. It seemed like the smart thing to do. "I told you," I said. "No real problems. People are being exterminated in the Middle East. Millions of children in sub-Saharan Africa go without food. Meanwhile, I'm struggling with calculus and, I don't know. A friend of mine who is no longer a friend. It's truly nothing."

She exhaled. "I think that's a cop-out."

"What is?"

"The idea that because things are worse somewhere else, you're not allowed to have issues in your life. That's what people who are try-ing to avoid having normal feelings say. Boo. I think you're better than that."

"Did you just say 'boo' to me? Did you boo me?"

"Well, yeah. I mean. The boy I met at the Bacon Free was smarter than that macho bullshit you just spewed. 'I'm a man and I have no feelings.' I call bullshit."

I felt my throat close up, like the wind was sucked out of my air pipes. I swallowed. "Wow. You just say everything on your mind, don't you?"

"Sometimes."

"Huh."

"Does that bother you?"

"It doesn't . . . bother me, exactly. I'm not used to it, I guess. We're not big talkers in my family. We don't do a lot of booing and calling bullshit."

"Well, I guess the good thing about being a woman who knows what she wants is that I don't have to put up with bullshit if I don't want to. So I figure I'll call it like I see it, and if you want to tell me to fuck off, that's cool."

I laughed. "I've never met anyone like you," I said.

"Is that a good thing or a bad thing?"

"I like you," I said, feeling a little more open from the booze.

"Good," she said. "I think I like you, but I'm probably going to have to, like, hang out with you one or two times to know for sure."

"Um. Okay. Did you just ask me out on a date?"

"Call it what you want," she said. "Wanna meet up this week? Wednesday?"

I closed my eyes and felt the alcohol course through my veins and all I wanted to be was sober so that I could fully enjoy this moment as Ben and not as a drunk person.

"Yes," I said. "Very much yes."

She laughed. "You're so funny, the way you talk. You seem like the kind of guy who is not used to saying things."

"I am that."

"Well, maybe we can be the kind of friends who say things to each other."

"Okay."

"It doesn't hurt that you're insanely hot in a geeky sort of way."

I felt heat throughout my body. "You're hot in a beautiful sort of way."

"Thank you."

"Thank *you*," I said back.

I felt a zillion times better when we hung up, and I put the phone on my chest, put my hands behind my head, and just allowed myself to smile and tingle for a bit. *Yeah, not so gay*, I thought to myself.

That would not happen if I were gay. . . .

I jumped up and grabbed my computer. An experiment.

I had a couple Tumblr pages bookmarked for times like this. Feeds full of hot girls. I didn't go to them. Instead I went to Google and typed in "naked gay guys."

Up popped some pictures.

I stared at them. I studied them. The men were in really good shape. They didn't remind me of Rafe, even though he is in good shape too. Just not like a porn model, I guess.

Down popped something else. Total deflation. It wasn't like I was disgusted: not in the least. I just felt like I was looking at a science textbook.

I smiled. *Yeah. Not so gay after all. One-time thing. One-person thing.*

And then I thought about Hannah, and her maple syrup face, and the mole under her lip, and her wavy hair, and her compact, sweet body, and the scarf covering her up, and how it would feel to have her lying there with me. And I allowed my hand to drift downward, and I smiled again, because it just felt so good. Maybe there was even a little chance that right now, Hannah was thinking of me too.

8

I woke up around three in the morning with what felt like a ferret rampaging through my insides. I clenched my stomach and suddenly I was nauseous too. Something acidic rose into my esophagus. Oh no.

I made a run for the bathroom, my head still spinning from the booze. This. This was why I didn't want to drink anymore. One of the reasons, anyway.

By the time I made it to a stall, I realized, to my dread, that this wasn't some standard reaction to vodka. Maybe it was the wilted salad I'd eaten instead. My stomach rumbled, and I knew that I wasn't going anywhere for a while.

In the chilly, too-public stall, I closed my eyes and prayed for an end. When I'm sick to my stomach, I don't feel that I want to be dead, but that it would be nice to be temporarily not alive, like I could take something and just turn my brain off while this thing coursed through me. It's like all your life force is leaving your body, and I think, *Is my life force shit? Is that what it all comes down to? Is that the fundamental human truth? We're all shit?*

I had no idea how much time had passed or what time it was when I started to hear other students coming and going in the bathroom.

53

This was not a place I cared to have company, especially sick. Was it morning? I tried to remember what the light situation had been when I'd run to the bathroom. No idea.

"Jesus," someone said, and suddenly there were eyes peering into the stall through the crack between the door and the wall. "Carver. Light a fuckin' match."

I tried to hide my face. "Go away," I moaned. "Sick."

"Yo, something died in here," said another voice.

"It's Carver."

I heard Mendenhall's voice yelling, "Zack, get your phone."

"Guys," I moaned. "Please don't."

But soon there was a camera up above the stall, aiming down. I wanted to stand, but it wasn't the right time to stand. My pajamas around my ankles, I tried to hide my junk and my face at the same time, and I hated the world and all the people in it. Everyone was laughing and then my name was being chanted, and I wondered what gene you had to have to chant the name of an ailing person while they were suffering. I just didn't get it. I would never do that to anyone.

"Party in the boys' room," I heard a familiar voice say. "What's up?"

"Carver's sick," another voice said, just as I was realizing the new voice was Rafe's. And then my stomach turned even more, and I felt my gag reflex gurgle.

"What? Stop it. You guys are fucking idiots," Rafe said. "Are you insane? Leave the guy alone."

"Weak," someone jeered.

But Rafe kept at it, telling people to delete the video and get a fucking life and move on, and the voices slowly dispersed. And soon I could sense it was just him and me. I flushed.

"Thanks," I said, feeling barely alive.

54

"Morons."

"Sorry," I said, but he didn't reply, and soon I realized he had left the bathroom.

I closed my eyes and exhaled, thankful to be alone. I owed him one. We were still done, but I definitely owed him. That was a downright decent thing to do.

About fifteen minutes later, I trudged back to my room, feeling weak, dizzy, and a bit queasy still. I opened my door, and there, in my burgundy chair, sat Rafe.

I didn't know what to say. When I looked at him, I remembered what had happened earlier, and I opened my mouth to apologize, but then I saw the crumpled-up letter. With my note on it. Shit. He'd clearly uncrumpled it and read it, and he was staring right at me, and as soon as I thought to apologize, he shook his head and pointed to the bed. On it was a tray with a can of ginger ale from the vending machine and a light blue heating pad.

"It'll help settle your belly," he said, like he was my mom. It was oddly comforting. I walked over to the bed, and he hopped up and picked up the tray so I could get in easily. He handed me the ginger ale, and he said, "Drink."

I took a sip. Ginger ale is about the most calming liquid. I don't know why; it just is.

He plugged in the pad and handed it to me, and I pulled it under the covers. It warmed my midsection, and I closed my eyes and muttered, "Thanks."

"No, I have no idea why Albie has a heating pad either," he said.

I let the warmth radiate through me. "Sorry about . . ." I said.

Again he didn't answer. He gathered up his stuff, made sure I was comfortable, and said, "Call me if you need something."

I was never so happy to be in my bed. My head was still pounding from the alcohol, my throat was raw from vomiting, and every part of my body felt wasted. I fell into a deep sleep, part of me wishing I was back at the bottom of that swimming pool.

A couple times I heard knocking but was too comfortable to answer, and then the knocks stopped and I conked back out again. The sleep was epic; it just seemed to go on and on. Occasionally I had the sense that someone was wiping my forehead with a washcloth, or re-filling a water glass and putting it by my bed, but I didn't know for sure if I was dreaming or awake.

When I next opened my eyes, I could tell it was late morning from the position of the sun. A full glass of water sat on my desk. I looked around the room, and there was Rafe, watching me from the other bed. I took a deep breath and cringed. The room smelled vaguely hospital-like.

"I'm disgusting," I moaned, and he laughed.

"That's what showers are for," he said. "How're you feeling otherwise?"

My stomach was no longer hurting, but I felt drained, that feeling where you just want to lie there and do nothing. I stayed silent until I felt like I was being rude, and then I said, "A little better. I just wanna rest. How many days has it been?"

"It's Sunday," he said. I'd been asleep for twenty-four hours.

"Whoa. That's substantial."

"Forget sub. That's fully stantial," he said. "I was worried about you there. Quite a bug you must've had. You feeling a little better?"

"I guess."

"Cool," he said. "You want anything from the cafeteria?"

"Nah," I said.

"Toast with honey it is."

He put on his boots and his jacket, and I watched him from my bed and felt drowsy comfortable, that feeling when you accept that you'll be in bed and it's okay, the world will spin on without you for a day.

He gave a half wave and said, "I'll be back," and I closed my eyes and tried to put it all together in my head. What it meant. Was the awkwardness over? Paused? Did we have to talk about the thing I wrote on his note? Could we just pretend it didn't exist and move on?

As I felt myself sagging into sleep, I realized it didn't matter right now. He was a friend. The only friend who cared enough to be there for me when I needed it. And I was grateful.

9

I walked into the locker room on Monday before our third winter baseball practice and saw Mendenhall looming over a freshman who was crawling along the slush-covered floor on his hands and knees.

"Dogs sniff everything," Mendenhall said. "Lead with your nose."

The meek-looking boy — a freshman named Peterson — jutted his neck out and sniffed under and around the bench in front of his locker. I shuddered, remembering when the same thing happened to me. Freshman year, I crawled around when they told me to, even though I was bigger and stronger than some of the guys who told me to do it. I thought it was ridiculous, but I wanted to be part of the team.

I looked around the room and caught Steve's eye. He was frowning, and I matched his frown and walked over to him.

"Do we really need to keep doing this stuff?" I asked.

"I'm all for team traditions, but this one I could live without," he answered.

"Carver, you want Spot here to fetch something?" Mendenhall called over to me, pointing at Peterson.

"Um, no, that's all right," I said, now that I was at my locker. "I have everything I need."

"There's gotta be something," he said.

"Nah. I can fetch it myself later."

"Don't worry, Ben doesn't do fun," Zack said.

Mendenhall shook his head in disgust. "Get changed, kid," he told Peterson.

I stared at my locker. *Some fun,* I thought. *Making a kid bark like a dog.* But still. Was he right? Shit. Was I a killer of fun?

Why couldn't I chill the fuck out?

I'm five. Mom has bought me a coloring book and crayons. I've never had crayons or a place to draw before. I have a picture of a dinosaur in front of me, and I am transfixed, using every single color, ones I'd never thought of before. I'm making a Robin's Egg sky with an Outrageous Orange sun, and the dinosaur has Neon Carrot hands and an Electric Lime body, and I am singing. My mom is in the kitchen, cooking, and she is singing along to a song on the tiny radio she keeps on the white Formica countertop next to the sink. "I Like It, I Love It" is the song, and I'm happy, and my dad comes in to the kitchen and sees me drawing and he grabs the coloring book away and says, "If you have so much time, why don't you go clean out the llama pen?" And he jerks open the back door. I look at my mom, and she looks sad, and my first thought is, "Dad made Mom sad." Dad comes back with a metal bucket and shovel, I go outside, and as I shovel up llama crap I think, I shouldn't have been having that much fun. You're not supposed to. There's work to be done. We're Carver men. We work. We work hard.

I'm nine. We're out at a restaurant for our yearly dinner out, waiting for a table. They're playing some kind of polka music, and I start moving up and down a little bit. Luke laughs. I do it some more. Luke laughs more. Dad grabs me by the arm and pulls me out of the restaurant. He pushes me up against the wood shingles of the wall and looks me directly in the eye. "You look like a fool. You will not embarrass me, hear?" I nod and nod until he releases me.

I'm seventeen now. And I can't remember too many times in my life I've gone along with other people's idea of fun. Usually I just sit on the sidelines, like at parties when everyone is drinking and having a blast. The most fun I ever had was last semester in an apple orchard, when Rafe and Albie and Toby and I decided we were a gang and then got kicked out after a massive apple fight. I wanted to get back there. How do you get back there, when your factory setting is *killer of fun*? Did I have to become my dad?

I was still getting over my weekend of food poisoning, but practice itself went well. I enjoyed indoor practice. You got truer and faster hops off the laminated floor of the gym, and I'm pretty sure there's nothing I like better in this world than cleanly fielding a grounder. Keeping track of where the runner is while I focus on the ball, keeping my glove down, squaring up my body, the fluid motion of the ball hitting my glove, my right hand retrieving it, the two steps and throw, like a perfect, un-criticizeable little dance. I don't know where I got it from; Dad was not an athlete. He thought sports were a waste of time. Luke had never been on a team because he had to work the farm after school, and that was my story too, before Natick. I'd only been playing for a couple years.

Coach Donnelly hit a chopper between me and Mendenhall at short, and I ranged to my left, anticipated the high, quick bounce — ear level for me — reached out, gloved the ball, stopped my momentum midmotion, pivoted toward home plate, and rifled a bullet to our catcher.

"There you go, Carver, midseason form," Donnelly shouted, and I kept my head down and circled behind Walton, the backup third baseman, who would get to field the next one.

60

Then it was time to take a few swings. A lot of the other guys tried to slam the ball into the basketball bleachers at the far end of the gym, which was probably about fifty feet short of a normal fence anyway. *Big deal, you hit a can of corn to left,* I kept thinking, watching Steve do it five straight times. When it was my turn I focused on going the other way. By going to right field, I could start to gauge my timing and work on staying back and making hard contact, which I did on about half my swings.

"See how our best power guy isn't swinging for the fences? Take notes, gentlemen," Coach Donnelly said from the mound after I took my last hack. "That there is humbleness. That there is what you aim for. Humbility."

"Dude is humble," Mendenhall said, and a bunch of the other guys said, "Yup."

As I waited for my second swings, I saw that Mendenhall had two ninth graders, Clement and Zander, off to the side. I heard him say, "You wanna be varsity someday, right?"

He was holding jockstraps over each of their heads. I winced. A guy named Morris had done this with me and Bryce. We were told that if we wanted to show that we were team players, we'd put jockstraps on over our shorts. I remembered how Bryce had looked at me with this powerless expression. We both knew that this was some sort of stupid prank meant to embarrass and demean us, but what were we going to do? The mesh crotch looked stupid with nothing to bulge it out, and the seniors pointed and laughed all that practice.

I wanted to say something, to tell Mendenhall to knock it off, but more than that, I didn't want any trouble. So I didn't say anything. I simply watched as the two boys threaded their legs through the leg holes of the jockstraps. Donnelly seemed oblivious to what was going on, and I wondered why he would ignore such behavior.

I glanced over at Steve, who was up after me. He was watching the stupidity too, and then he must have felt my stare, because he turned and looked at me. I rolled my eyes, and he did too. Then he shrugged and smiled the way kids who have grown up with powerful dads and just about no struggles tend to smile, with perfect, privileged teeth. I mirrored him, knowing that my left front tooth was slightly uneven, and that I would never, ever look like Steve.

After practice, Donnelly called a team meeting, and as we assembled on the floor in the center of the gymnasium, he began talking about the importance of teamwork.

"You know what teamwork is? Ask the poor Russians working in the Gulag. The Russian leaders, they used teamwork to create a situation where the poor were the underclass and had to toil while the leaders did nothing. That, kids, is the result of teamwork."

I was pretty sure even Stalin himself would be turning over in his grave with that one.

I realized that I hadn't said a single word all practice. Not one. I looked around. Had anyone noticed? Probably not.

"So now it's time to pick a captain," Donnelly said. "Nominations?"

This guy named Reagan's hand shot up. "I nominate Mendenhall."

"I accept," he said, and someone began to clap as if he'd already been elected.

A kid named Rodriguez yelled out, "I nominate Marcus." Marcus was a senior outfielder who batted leadoff. He said, "I accept."

Then Steve called out, "Carver," and I snapped my neck in his direction. *What?* I was a junior. No junior had ever been captain, at least as far as I knew.

He raised an eyebrow at me, and I glanced over at Mendenhall. He was glaring at Steve, and then me. It got quiet, and after about ten seconds of silence, I realized it was my line.

"Um, I accept," I said, and I purposefully didn't look at Mendenhall. I knew that he would not be pleased that I was trying to subvert the natural order of things. Seniors lead. Juniors follow. I studied the gym floor.

"Anyone else?" Donnelly said, and when no one else was nominated, he asked us all to say a few words.

Mendenhall stood and said, "I'll go first," and I realized it hadn't even occurred to me to take charge like that. I was just going to wait until Donnelly called on one of us. Maybe I wasn't the right choice for captain, anyway.

Mendenhall's speech went something like this:

"Respect is everything. You don't get anywhere in life jumping in line when it's not your turn. I've been on this team since my freshman year. Every year, a senior takes on the role of captain, and every year, we line up behind him and play as a team, and we gel on and off the field. Having a captain who hardly ever talks — never mind. The point is, you know who is born to be a leader and who isn't. Vote for a leader who can lead the team."

When some people clapped, I felt punched in the gut. He hadn't so much as advocated for himself as maligned me. And all I'd done is said, "I accept." I sucked in my teeth and swallowed.

Marcus went next. He went on about what a real leader is, but I wasn't really listening. I was focused on what I would be saying in a few minutes.

Then the guys were all looking at me, so I slowly stood, surveyed my teammates, and took a deep breath.

"Playing on this team has been an honor," I said. "I learned so much last year as a sophomore, and, I suppose, I . . . think there's something to be said for quiet leadership. For walking softly and carrying a big stick."

"Carver is hung," a junior named Rollison said, and as much as I felt like turning purple, I took a deep breath and laughed a little with the others.

"C'mon, boys," Donnelly said.

"Not that kind of big stick," I said. "What I want to do is lead us in an honorable way. I want us to thrive on the field, and off the field I think we can — do better. When I was a freshman — well, all of us. When *we* were freshmen, we were put through an initiation process that's supposedly a noble tradition here at Natick. I love traditions. I believe in them. But I don't believe in humiliation as a tactic. And yes, it happened to us, so now it's supposed to be our turn to dish it out. But where does it end? What do we gain as a team by humiliating our teammates? Let's stop the whole initiation thing. Let's be the group that restores honor to the baseball team. And also, let's just have a great year. Win some games. That's what we need to focus on. Thank you."

I sat down, my head buzzing. There was silence, and then, slowly, there was applause. More, maybe, than the other guys had gotten. I wasn't sure. I gulped and studied the floor in front of me.

The candidates had to leave the gym while there was a vote. I followed Mendenhall and Marcus out, and when we got to the hallway, Mendenhall turned on me.

"That's a bunch of bullshit," he said. "You better not win."

I didn't respond. There was nothing to say.

"You don't fuck with Natick tradition just because your pansy-ass feelings got hurt as a freshman. You take it like a man. It's how we become men, Carver."

I stared him directly in the eye, but I said nothing.

He laughed. "Men speak up," he said. "You'll never be one because you don't."

The door opened and we were invited back in. I looked around, and the first thing I saw was a big smile on Steve's face.

The final vote had gone ten to nine to three.

"Congratulations, Ben!" Coach Donnelly said. "You're our new captain."

As my face heated up, the first thought I had was, *I can't wait to tell Dad.* My second was, *This is going to look great on my résumé.*

"Bush league," Mendenhall muttered as he bumped past me on the way to the locker room, and any guilty feeling I was harboring in my gut went away. "You made a powerful enemy today."

And I thought: *What are you, a supervillain? Who says shit like that?* Tommy Mendenhall, perchance. I didn't say that, though. Instead I said, "It was close."

He flipped me off.

Excited about my new position, I called home.

"That's great, Benny," my mom said.

She handed my brother the phone, and he said, "Broseph."

"Hey," I said. "Guess who's captain of the baseball team?"

"You're captain?" he said. "Cool."

I heard my dad's voice in the background. "Tell him not to get a big head about it."

The first meeting of Model Congress occurred on Tuesday afternoon. I'd joined the club my freshman year, as a way to expand my résumé for college applications. My uncle gave me the idea. I also really enjoyed pretending to be a congressman and making political arguments. It was the kind of thing I'd envisioned myself doing when I applied to Natick, and while the social aspect hadn't been that exciting—I didn't hang out with the guys outside of the club—I'd always enjoyed the events. I'd been given permission to miss Tuesday baseball practices, at least until games started in April. Any Tuesday game would take precedence over the club.

Mr. Sacks was a cootish old guy with more hair on his hands than he had left on his head. He wore a beige suit jacket every day, and he loved to talk about the "damn liberals" and how they were ruining the country. Everybody pretty much loved Mr. Sacks and his codger-y ways; even the liberal kids thought it was fun to rile him up, and he seemed to enjoy a good riling.

"Well, looks like we got the usual suspects," he said as the twelve of us sat down. "We do best when we don't get to choose our topics, I think, so that's what we'll do. Any questions?"

Mitchell Pomerantz raised his hand. "What if I really, really want to argue something?"

Mr. Sacks adjusted his thick glasses. "What is it that you really, really want to argue, Mr. Pomerantz?"

"Fracking."

"For, or against?"

"Are you kidding me? Against," Mitchell said.

"Of course," Mr. Sacks said. "As a kid who doesn't yet support himself, why would you worry about gas prices or energy independence? No skin off your nose."

"So we should rape the environment?"

"There you go again, misusing the word 'rape.' Just like a lefty to throw that word around and devoid it of meaning."

"'Devoid' isn't a verb, Mr. Sacks," Mitchell countered.

"Correcting my grammar won't get a bill passed. How do you propose to argue against lower gas prices? Anyone?"

I smiled. This. This was why I came to Natick in the first place. A club where kids could talk about current events and plead to write bills? That wasn't about to happen in Alton, but here I could do it to my heart's delight.

Mr. Sacks had smiled at me when he saw me walk in. I think he liked me, probably because I kept my political beliefs to myself. I wasn't an ideologue, as he would say. At a congress in Boston just before break, I'd successfully argued in favor of school vouchers. After, he'd tried to get me talking about politics, but I didn't bite. Better to keep people guessing about my real beliefs.

When no one responded to Mr. Sacks's request for an argument against lower gas prices, he told us that he'd written twelve issues on pieces of paper and put them in a hat. We could choose which side of the issue we wanted to argue once we'd picked a topic from the hat. He passed it around, and I thought about what subject I'd like to argue. Legalization of marijuana would be fun, but so would how best to handle terrorism.

"DREAM Act, crap," said Tucker Collins, and Mitchell said, "Trade ya. I got Iran."

"No trades," Mr. Sacks said. "I'm taking you out of your comfort zone. You get what you get, and that's it. Okay?"

The hat got to me, and I reached in, felt around, and pulled out a thin piece of paper.

It read, "Religious Freedoms Are Under Attack by Gay Marriage Advocates."

My face turned a little red, and then I stopped myself from feeling embarrassed. It was an interesting issue, one I could research and come up with a cogent argument against.

We all shared what we got, and then Mr. Sacks asked us to pick a side. I didn't worry about anyone's response when I said, "Against." He wrote our names, our topics, and our positions on the board. Then he stood at the board for a few troubling seconds, this impish smile almost hidden by his mustache, and I realized what he was going to do. *Damn it,* I thought.

He erased the word "pro" next to the line on Tucker Collins's topic, and he wrote "con" in its place.

Groans all around, and that got Mr. Sacks to show some teeth, a rarity with him.

"I said I'd be taking you out of your comfort zone. I meant it. We're all going to argue the opposite side of our issue."

"But you said we could pick our side," Tucker said.

"I lied," replied Mr. Sacks. "It's Model Congress, after all. Can't believe everything a congressman says."

Jesus, I thought. *How am I going to argue that religious people's freedoms are under attack by gay folks?* I couldn't even imagine how two guys getting married could be seen as an attack on someone else's civil liberties. That just didn't make sense.

After Model Congress, I went to the school library to look up Peter Pappas. I'd had it on my to-do list ever since I'd heard about the award, because I was going to have to give a speech about him. The online catalog had two hits from the *Natick Newsman,* the school paper. The first was a profile of him as the captain of the basketball team. He was a tall kid, with a wide, toothy smile, and the article said he was from Dorchester, a suburb of Boston. While at Natick, Pappas lettered in four sports, and he won the top award at the Massachusetts state Model Congress, beating out kids from twenty other schools. After impressing judges at the state competition, he got a job working for a congressman the summer before his junior year.

I photocopied the article and then looked up the other piece. It was written two years later, after he'd been killed in action in Vietnam. My heart dropped as I looked at the same picture of Pappas. When you know a lot of history, you get a lot of facts about war casualties, but it's not at all the same as looking at a picture of a kid your age, who once stood where you stood, and thinking about how the very last thing he saw was likely some sort of explosion.

I copied that article too, and I wondered what I could possibly say to do him justice. A guy who believed so deeply in a cause that he voluntarily went to war, and died for that belief.

That was a level of commitment I'd never be able to understand, and I wished there was something out there I felt so strongly about I'd willingly die for it.

11

"If you could have dinner with one person from history, who would it be?" Hannah asked as we sat down on a freezing wooden bench in Warren Park. It was Wednesday after practice; the sun was beginning to set. The park she chose was more like a playground, with a sandbox and swings and a jungle gym area surrounded by benches, but who cared if it wasn't the most romantic spot ever for a first date? Not if it meant getting to be with Hannah.

"Probably Winston Churchill. Maybe Abraham Lincoln," I said. "Churchill, I guess."

"What would you talk about?"

My legs were cold, so I stood and began walking. "I guess I'd ask him how it felt to be the one person most responsible for the Germans not annexing all of Europe."

"Wow, you really are a history geek."

I stepped onto a wooden merry-go-round. It creaked under my weight and tilted almost all the way to the ground. "Guilty as charged."

She got up and stood on the other side, not quite balancing the weight but doing enough so the thing could spin if we wanted it to.

"Who would you choose?" I asked.

"Probably Dian Fossey."

I stumbled over to the center, where there was a round metal bar. I grasped it and pulled, and the merry-go-round moaned into action. "Who?"

Hannah quickly stepped to the center and helped me turn the thing. I watched the world slowly spin, and I felt like the evening could just float by in this pleasant way.

"Get with the program. You don't know Dian Fossey? She lived with the gorillas in Africa? *Gorillas in the Mist*?"

I shook my head momentarily before I realized how dizzy that made me with us spinning. I closed my eyes. "I didn't know you cared about gorillas."

"I'm fascinated by animals. Did you know that every time a disreputable zoo poaches a gorilla from the wild, up to ten gorillas die?"

"Really? How does that work?"

"A lot of them die during the hunt to take one alive. Gorillas will fight to the death for their children. They aren't so different than humans, really. Human parents would do the same. Well, not mine."

My wrists were tiring from spinning us, so I stopped and the world slowly came to a standstill. "No?"

She scowled. "I went to use my dad's computer over Christmas break, because mine was out of power and I couldn't find the cord. And there's this Google message chain between my dad and some chick named Marnie. All gross stuff. Can you believe it? *Marnie*?"

"The name is what upsets you?"

"I just think, like, if you're going to fuck up your life and the life of your family members, don't do it for a *Marnie*. Jesus."

I did a walking gesture and she nodded. There wasn't much of a place to walk, so we wandered over to the sandbox.

"So I told my mom about Marnie." Hannah stomped on the hard, cold sand, leaving a sneaker mark. "She wholesale freaked out. Dad came up to my room and laid on the heaviest possible guilt trip, with this whole 'I made a mistake, but you compounded that mistake' shit. I stayed in my room for thirty-six straight hours after that. Suffice it to say it was not a stellar Christmas."

"That's rough. Where are you with it now?"

She jumped up and down on the sand a few times, and then leaned down, took a fistful of sand, and shaped it into a sand ball. "Well, it was three weeks ago, so not that different."

"I just mean —"

"No, I get it. And it is better than it was that first day. It's just a betrayal. I don't think I'll ever really get over that."

"Wow."

"So, like, just know that if you become my boyfriend, don't go and find yourself a Marnie. Just tell me."

"Whoa," I said.

"I'm just saying. Don't ever lie to me. It would not be amusing." She threw her sand ball, raised her hands to the sky, and spoke in a weird authoritative tone. "Hannah establishes healthy boundaries with new friends."

I laughed. "Been a thing in the past?"

"Yeah. To the tune of tens of thousands of dollars in therapy."

"You really say everything that comes to your mind, don't you?"

"I grew up in a family where no one listened to me. I learned to say everything, like if I threw it all out there, maybe something would stick. I was what psychologists would call a precocious child."

"How do you know all this?"

She climbed up some steps of a jungle gym structure, and she sat on a deck under a gazebo with her legs dangling down a slide that was about my height. I stood by her side, my chin at about her thigh level. She let go, and she stuck to the frozen metal. We laughed together.

"Whee?" she said.

"Whee."

"They put me in therapy when I was six, so . . ."

"What the hell does a six-year-old even do in therapy?"

"Play with dolls, mostly. The therapist watches. And even though I was six, I swear there was a part of me that was like, 'Go ahead and watch me play with dolls, you freakazoid perv.'"

I laughed.

"What's going on with you?" she asked. "I've been doing all the talking."

And I like it that way, I thought. This was a fascinating girl. I couldn't imagine saying half the things she'd just said to me, and I hoped I wouldn't have to.

"Not much. I got voted captain of the baseball team on Monday, did I tell you that?"

"You did not," she said, raising an eyebrow. "That's . . . information."

"Is that a bad thing?"

"No! It's . . . kinda sexy actually. You're a sensitive jock."

I winced.

"What?"

"Oh, it's nothing. Labels. Not a huge fan. It's fine, but. I mean, I do Model Congress on Tuesdays. Does that make me a geek?"

"No, I totally get that," she said, and she rubbed her pant leg against my cheek, which was a totally new and not entirely unpleasant sensation. "I won't label you again, I promise."

"And I won't label you either."

She bit her lip, grabbed the sides of the slide, and pushed her way down. "I kind of hate that I said that, anyway. It's like, I say you're a sensitive jock, and now you're going to have to prove that you're not too sensitive."

"What? What are you talking about?"

"Oh, you know. Gender roles. Misogyny is so pervasive that the idea of being associated with female behavior freaks guys out. Even good guys like you. And I think that it says something interesting about men that they love women so deeply and yet hold them in such low esteem."

"Hmm," I said. Hannah was really smart.

"Nothing?" she said. "No response?"

"I just sometimes have to think about things before I respond," I said. "You said a lot and it's interesting and deserves some thought."

I could feel her smile as she stood up from the bottom of the slide. We walked in silence around the perimeter of the playground. I didn't think I was a misogynist. I mean, guys on the baseball team definitely said things, and while I didn't always speak up and tell them to stop, never for a second did I think it was okay for them to speak that way about women. What would Hannah think if she knew I didn't stand up for women at practice sometimes?

"So what about your family?"

"Eh," I said.

"Eh?"

"Not interesting," I said.

"Can I be the judge?"

I shrugged. "We live up in New Hampshire, in a very rural area. My dad is a farmer. My mom minds the farm store attached to our house."

"Oh, that's adorable!"

I shot her a narrow-eyed look. "Gee, thanks."

She made a cute face. "I'm sorry."

I walked toward the jungle gym, remembering what it was like to climb on one. There was one at the elementary school playground back in Alton. One time I touched one of the metal bars without my gloves in the thick of winter, and it left a red mark that lasted a week.

"You don't respond sometimes," she said as we got about a foot from the monkey bars.

I exhaled. That was like my dad. I didn't want to be like that. Wrapped up tight like in Saran Wrap, like I couldn't breathe. But how do you battle your biology? Was this just who I was? Could I change if I wanted to? "I don't always know what to say."

"Why do you have to know? Can't you just say things without knowing if they're the right thing to say?"

My lips tightened. This was what I didn't always like about talking to people. Because they tell you that you're doing it wrong, and I hate doing it wrong. And I don't know how to do it right sometimes.

"Sorry," I said.

"For a baseball captain, you sure are sorry a lot."

"Sorry," I repeated. I put my gloved hands on the top of the bars and leaned backward with all my weight. It gave me a good stretch.

"Well, at least we found the limits of your ability to communicate." She said it in a tone like she was done with me, and a shiver went through my body.

I pulled harder at the bar, leaning back even farther. "I'm not always great at talking, okay? I have to really trust someone first."

She put her hand on my shoulder. "I get that. I really do. You're an introvert."

I shrugged. "Yeah, I guess."

"I'm, like, both. Extrovert and introvert."

"Yeah?"

"Yeah."

I closed my eyes and inhaled frigid wind. "It's just. The 'adorable' thing. My life is not adorable. I grew up in a place called Alton, and in the summer it's all these rich folks. And we run a farm store, and people come in and they're always telling us how adorable we are, like puppies. But we're human beings, you know?"

"Sorry," she said, and I could hear a little hurt in her voice.

"It's fine," I said.

"No, I get it," she said, and she reached up to the top bar, jumped up a few inches, and hung from it.

"I don't know why that's such a sore spot for me. It just is."

"Well, I guess it would be hard to go to such a rich kid school and not be rich."

I put my gloved hands in my pockets. "Nobody seems to understand what privilege is."

She dropped down from the bar, grabbed my elbow, put my hand on my hip for me, and slipped her arm around mine. She started walking, so I did too. "I know I can't prove it to you and there's nothing I can say that won't sound ridiculous, but I'm not a snob. I need you to believe me."

"Thanks." I took in her beautiful profile. "I believe you."

She pulled me close. "I think you're amazing, Ben."

I swallowed hard. Being told you're amazing shouldn't be a challenge, but it was one. Because now I'd have to say something, when in reality the only thing in my brain was a voice saying, *Don't get a big head about it.*

I rubbed my ear against my jacketed shoulder and tried to undo the knot in my chest. It felt like someone was twisting the life out of me.

"I—think you're amazing too." I moved my face toward hers. Her breath was sweet.

"That's true, I am," she said, and then she made a face. "Way to take a compliment by making a joke out of it, my psychologist would say."

I laughed. "I do that too." I bent down and kissed her softly on the lips. She kissed me back, but when I felt her lips trying to open mine, I pulled back. "Let's save it for next time."

"You," she said, her eyes wide. "You are a different boy. You sure you're not gay?"

There was a part of me that was rock hard at the moment. "I am more than usually certain of that."

She grinned.

12

There was a refreshing lack of boys crawling around like dogs before our Thursday practice. Apparently my promise to change the culture of the team had meant something to the guys, because I hadn't seen any of that since I'd become captain three days ago.

I went to my locker and got changed, nodding to a few teammates. I allowed the sights and sounds of the room to melt away as I got myself mentally prepared for practice.

I had a few things on my mind that weren't leaving me alone. One was Hannah. She was unlike any girl I'd ever met. She said stuff I wouldn't dare to say, ever, and she made me want to be better than I was just to be worthy of her. That stuff about misogyny was deep in a Bryce way. And that button nose. So, so cute. She might not fully get me yet, but if she was patient enough to get past my stupid defenses, she definitely was the kind of person who at least might understand me. I wanted that. I needed that. And the kiss. Such a warm, sweet kiss. I had been thinking about her so much last night that I almost didn't finish my calculus homework, which was not advisable. I'd had to do the final problem in class while Ms. Dyson started collecting papers on the other side of the room.

Two was Rafe. He'd nursed me back to health all weekend, but we hadn't really talked yet, even after he'd seen what I'd written about him, which was terrible and unfair. The day before, I'd seen him and Toby walking ahead of me, across the quad, toward Albie, who was about twenty steps ahead of them. Rafe whispered something to Toby and Toby laughed. Then Rafe sprinted ahead. Albie turned around and put his hands up, like he knew what was coming.

"Please don't tackle me," Albie said, and I felt myself smirking, because it was so — them. Silly. Irreverent.

"My name is Rafe and I'm a compulsive tackler," Rafe yelled out, and Toby yelled back, "Hi, Rafe!"

"Please don't," Albie said again, bracing himself.

"I've been compulsively tackling for about two years now," Rafe said, and he sort of leaned on Albie, who stumbled toward a snow bank.

"This is one of your more annoying idiosyncrasies," Albie said as he slowly tipped over into the snow bank, like a huge tree that had been chopped down.

"Yay!" yelled Toby, skipping toward them. "A tackle! A tackle! Yay!"

I chuckled out loud, remembering the incident, as I tied the laces on my cleats. Never in a million, trillion years would I do that to someone. So why did it make me laugh so much to think about it? And how could I become friends again with Rafe, if I wanted to? And did I want to?

And yet. Every time I thought about Jeff Frazier, my head pounded, like I wanted to tear his limbs off or something. Which was deranged, given that I was clearly straight and beginning to have an exceedingly fine girlfriend.

Weird. I was just plain weird, and it was a good thing no one had access to my innermost thoughts.

At practice, a freshman took a ball off his cheekbone. It caromed off his shoulder and into his face, or else he'd have a broken cheekbone, but still, having done that before, I knew it hurt like hell. The kid kept his head down, but I could see him wince at the pain, so I yelled out, "You okay?"

He averted his eyes and nodded.

"Stop being a pussy!" Mendenhall yelled.

Playing tough, I realized. That was part of the game.

As practice went on, I thought about misogyny, like Hannah was talking about. How boys made other boys crawl and bark like dogs, and how we pressured each other to be a man all the time. What did I think a man was? To me, my dad was a man. He had no emotions ever, at least that he shared. And that wasn't who I wanted to be, yet I still admired him for it. Which was so strange.

I thought about how kids mostly knew not to use the word "faggot" now. Like how Rafe was out, and people were basically cool with him and knew not to say certain words. But we still called things that were weak "gay." What was that about?

I stayed in the zone and fielded grounder after grounder, and this thought came to me: *It's all about gender.* We were an all-boys school. Really, in some ways, it was an all-boys world. Telling someone to stop being a pussy was telling them not to be a girl, as if being a girl was bad. And saying that something weak was gay was saying that straight was better, and gay was weak, and weak equaled effeminate, and effeminate equaled female.

There had to be a way to fix that. To be better than that. To be more than my dad turned out to be in that regard, with his command over my mom, for instance.

"Pull up your girl panties and get back in there," Mendenhall was yelling at a freshman who had bobbled three straight grounders at short. The kid was muttering to himself, clearly mad at his inability to do better, and I realized I could say something.

I opened my mouth to speak, but no words came out. I shut my lips and swallowed.

What good would it do? Am I really going to fix the mammoth problem of misogyny in America by being a killer of fun with my baseball team?

A grounder came to me. I could hear the sizzle of the ball off the bat. It was a hard one, two bounces, just to my left. I got in front of it but somehow misjudged the hop off the gym floor. It got me right in the shin, and I muttered, "Damn," and hopped around.

"Your tampon fell out," Mendenhall yelled over from short, and a bunch of guys laughed. And there wasn't a chance I was going to talk back after flubbing a ground ball.

Crap.

Clearly I was a puppet captain. I was Ngo Dinh Diem, the team was Vietnam, and Mendenhall was President Eisenhower.

13

Dinner with the team on Saturday evening of Martin Luther King Day weekend began with a particularly nonriveting story about exploding cars. Mendenhall was clearly an automobile aficionado. He knew the difference between a Hemi and a V8, and while I generally did not care for stories about my beloved things blowing up, he did.

"We're gonna track you down and take you to the blowout," Zack said to me. At first I thought he meant like a car blowing out, or a tire, but then I realized I'd zoned out and he was now talking about a party.

I smiled and shrugged.

"You gotta hang," Zack said.

"Maybe," I said.

I begged out of dessert, and I found myself smiling again as I walked solo across the quad toward the dorms. Pappas Award winner, team captain, and yet basically accepted as a recluse. I wasn't sure why, really. How could a guy be a leader and a follower? A leader leads, like Mendenhall. He speaks up. Me, I barely said a word, and they seemed to like me anyway.

How lucky was I?

And at the same time, I thought, nothing anyone on the baseball team had done or said in the past two weeks had made me laugh. I hadn't done or said anything that made any of them laugh either. Beyond Hannah, they were pretty much the entirety of my social life, and it was—excruciatingly boring.

Should I just go to the party, maybe?

I really didn't want to; the misogyny at practice two days earlier was still bugging me, and it wasn't like the dinner conversation wasn't full of that stuff too. But I did want to do something. Hannah had already begged out of plans because she had this choir performance.

I got a weird idea. *What the hell,* I thought. I could apologize to Rafe for what I wrote on his letter and clear the air, which was the right thing to do. I could blame alcohol, and anyway I wasn't going to drink anymore, that was certain. It was a Saturday night, and maybe keeping my head down was a good plan, but I could use a little laughter too. I hurried up the stairs to the second floor and knocked on Rafe and Albie's door.

Rafe's expression was an odd combination of confused and hopeful when he saw it was me.

"Hey there," I said.

He motioned me into the room with his head, and I followed him in. Albie was sitting on his bed, reading a science textbook.

"So, what's up?"

Rafe raised an eyebrow. "Not much," he said unenthusiastically.

This wasn't going the way I'd hoped. I looked from Rafe to Albie and back, trying to communicate that maybe we should talk somewhere in private.

Rafe shook his head. "Nah, I don't think so. Anything you have to say to me you can say in front of Albie."

"I really don't think I can," I said.

"Surprise yourself, Ben. For someone who is all about being himself, you sure edit yourself a lot."

My throat closed up. "Whoa," I said.

"Yeah, whoa," said Albie, not looking up. "A little harsh there, Rafester."

"You crumpled up my note. You haven't said a word to me in a week. Just say what you have to say," he said, his arms crossed over his thin chest.

I looked over at Albie. Whom I trusted, but. I really wanted to have this conversation with Rafe only. What if Albie didn't know about . . . ? And then I stopped that thought, because of course he knew.

"Oh, man," I said, looking at Albie. "You know . . ."

"Well, I am friends with Toby, so. And I'm roommates with Rafe, who is the other half of this drama. So yeah, I know things."

"Shit," I said.

Albie said, "I have two friends in this school. Who the hell am I gonna tell? I don't give a shit. I'm Albie Gaga. All the gays —"

"I'm not *gay*," I said, my voice sharp and low.

"All the gays and the gay-adjacents flock to me," he said.

I took a deep breath and turned to Rafe. Then I gritted my teeth and made myself say the words even though Albie was there.

"I shouldn't have written that about you. I was drunk. I'm sorry. You're not . . . alcohol. Okay?"

"Someone needs to put that in a country song," Albie said.

"Shut up!" Rafe and I yelled simultaneously.

Albie pantomimed zipping his lips, and then he gathered a couple books and left the room.

"I hate that I acted that way," I said, once Albie was gone. "I don't know why you mentioning Jeff made me want to pummel him."

"I guess I should be flattered. I should be, but I'm not," Rafe said, and I could tell he'd softened up a bit by the way his face looked less tense.

"Do you accept my apology?"

"Fine. Sure. Yes," he said, and he stuck out his hand and I shook it, and it sort of felt like we were getting divorced, which was bizarre.

"If we're gonna be friends, I think we just need to come up with some sort of agreement not to talk about other people."

"That's so weird," Rafe said.

"So you would want to hear about it if I was dating a girl?"

He shrugged. "I could handle it."

"I'm dating a girl," I said.

He looked into my eyes and immediately looked away. "Okay. Cool."

I kept looking at him, waiting for him to look me in the eyes again. He didn't.

"That's not weird?"

He sighed. "It's a little weird, yeah. But what can you do? I'll call Claire Olivia and ask for the final ruling. But for now, we'll be like gay friend–straight friend exes. Okay?"

"Sure," I said. "I think that works."

"Well, we're going to Boston in a bit. You coming?" Rafe asked.

I wasn't sure we were done, because it seemed a little easy. But I nodded yes, because, well, I was so damned tired of doing nothing, and doing it by myself.

I sat behind Albie in his light blue 1993 Toyota Celica as he drove east toward Boston. Toby, whom I still hadn't quite forgiven for hiding in my closet, was in the passenger's seat, and Rafe sat next to me in the backseat to my right. When Toby turned around to speak, I noticed he was wearing black eyeliner.

Toby said, "Why is it that in every book, the new kid always gets the girl? There's always a new kid in town, and they show him running his hand through his voluminous hair in slow motion, and the main female character swoons and in the end they wind up together? Why is the new kid always such a tramp?"

"In the movie *Clueless*, the new kid was gay," Albie said.

Toby said, "Gay tramp."

"I assume that comment was vaguely aimed at me and that you were trying to make things awkward?" Rafe asked.

"It doesn't take a rocket surgeon to know that. Duh," Toby said.

"Rocket surgeon?" I asked, and Rafe shook his head.

"Anyway, I'm giving up sex," Toby said. "I've got other things on my brain."

I thought back to when he'd come to my room to subliminalize me; he'd said he needed to talk. I wondered what was up.

"Isn't it more like sex is giving you up?" Albie asked. "You don't have a boyfriend, Toby. You haven't abandoned sex; it's abandoned you."

"You should know," Toby pouted, crossing his arms across his skinny chest.

"Ooh, good burn," Albie said.

"Anyway, I would still be giving up sex if I had the choice. Because it's not normal, you know? I mean, is it logical to want to stick your thing in — well, either the baby place or the sewer place or the food place? That's all so weird."

"I think Robinson hurt you," Albie said. "I think sex is perfectly normal in a very — *don't think too much about it* sort of way."

Toby looked out the window and pouted some more. "I think sex is something that happens between two clowns in the privacy of their overcrowded car."

It took us about forty-five minutes to get to Faneuil Hall, which is an old marketplace in front of a meeting hall in downtown Boston. It was an unseasonably warm night for January, and the area was inhabited by a truly diverse group of people. A vendor wearing African garb sold colorful handbags, a Japanese woman was doing an up close photo study of a statue, and a white homeless lady was feeding breadcrumbs to a large gaggle of ducks—which was odd given that it was winter, but then again the last week or so had been relatively mild. The trees throughout the square were still bright with Christmas lights, and old-fashioned lampposts surrounded the actual hall. I'd never been there before, so while Toby ran around showcasing what he called his Nice Tourette's—"I love your hair," he'd blurt out to a stranger; "You're a beautiful flower"—I studied the Samuel Adams statue. Sam loomed high above us on a granite pedestal, his arms across his chest in a very self-satisfied pose. The inscription read, "Samuel Adams 1722–1803—A Patriot—He organized the Revolution, and signed the Declaration of Independence."

As I looked at Sam Adams, Rafe came and stood next to me. I was thinking about how frightening it would be to start a revolution, without the hindsight that it would be a success. How much did you have to believe in something to heed that call to action? It was hard to fathom.

I glanced over at Rafe. He was staring at the inscription. For a long time.

"It makes you think, doesn't it?"

He looked over at me. "What? Oh, yeah. No, I actually was thinking about something else."

"Ah," I said, crossing my arms like Sam.

"You actually were thinking about the Revolutionary War, weren't you?" he asked.

I stifled a frown. "Well, yeah."

"And that is why you are Ben, fascinating intellectual jock dude, and I am Rafe, who is none of those things."

"Yeah, real fascinating," I said as I walked over to the front of Faneuil Hall. Rafe followed.

"You kinda are," he said. "Who's this girl?"

I shook my head. "Didn't we just say we weren't going to do this?"

"I think you made her up to make me jealous."

"I didn't, Rafe. I wouldn't. Fine. There is a girl."

"Okay. Cool. I can handle that."

"Sorry," I said.

He rolled his eyes in a way that said, *What can you do*, and I laughed a little.

"Congrats on the award, by the way. And the captaincy."

"Thanks," I said. "I can't believe it."

"I can," he said.

I said, "By the way: Is Toby wearing makeup now?"

Rafe nodded. "I noticed that too."

"Huh. That's — different."

"Toby's different."

"He is that," I said.

Toby ran over and saved us from the awkwardness of our conversation. "Okay, game time," he said. "Best photobomb of the night wins a hot chocolate at Sparky's. Losers team up to pay."

I shook my head, hard. "Nope."

"Oh, come on," he said. "Don't be such a pooper of parties."

I took a deep breath and bit the side of my lip. *Killer of fun*.

Rafe looked sideways at me as if to gauge my reaction. "I'm in," he said.

I looked around the square. Indeed, photos were being taken all over the place. And this crazy thing happened. I thought, *Maybe this is another apple orchard? A place where I could let loose for once?* For one moment, I forgot my lifelong mantra: *We're Carver men. We work. We work hard.*

I wasn't quite sure how Faneuil Hall was like an apple orchard exactly, since forming an apple-related gang was surely not in the cards here. But I'd never have fun if I didn't try.

"Fine. Whatever."

Albie surprised me by yelling, "Me first, me first!" He skulked around the square for a few moments, then snuck in behind a couple posing about five feet in front of a statue of a chubby man in a suit. Albie leered at the camera like a serial killer from behind their backs. I had to laugh. It was going to be hard to top that one.

Rafe went next. He was less graceful, running through a shot with his arms up just as the flash went off.

Toby yelled, "Now me!" and ran off in search of a photo to bomb. He strutted around the perimeter of the square, looking so suspicious that people stepped away from him. Then he sprinted back toward us. Just to our left, by the benches, a group of tourists were posing for a picture. Toby ran behind them and tried to do the Karate Kid pose, his arms in the air, poised to attack, as he stood on one foot.

That's when I heard the crunch. It sounded like a combination flutter-scrunch-*quack*, real quick like. The tourists jumped away, and the woman taking the picture snapped it. I will never see that picture, but I imagine it was a perfect shot of Toby standing on one leg, his arms high and wide, looking down at the duck whose foot he'd just stepped on.

The woman yelled, "What the?"

Toby picked up his foot, and the duck fluttered away a few feet.

"S-s-orry," he stuttered.

"What the hell? Who does that?" she continued, her hands on her hips.

"Seriously," one of the posing guys said.

"I'm . . . in a contest," Toby managed.

Meanwhile, several other members of the duck gaggle had amassed next to their injured comrade. More ducks flew in to join them.

"Asshole," the photographer said, and the three of them hurried away.

"Watch out!" Albie yelled.

The gaggle of ducks had formed something of a circle around Toby, and they were pecking the ground.

"Yikes," Toby said, just as the first duck quacked out a frantic war cry and charged. It pecked at his leg, and Toby flinched. As he stumbled back, we heard another squeak. He'd stepped on another one.

Now they came at Toby from all sides, squawking and quacking wildly as their beaks pecked at his legs. He stood there, clearly confused about how to respond to a public duck pecking. When a duck rose up to his crotch level, he backed up but stumbled and lost his footing.

The fall was painfully slow: a hand to brace his fall, then butt, then arm. Once Toby was on the ground, the ducks surrounded him, pecking at his face, his Adam's apple, arms, crotch. He didn't have enough hands to cover all the places they could peck, and when he did manage to guard something, they went for his hands.

"Ow ow ow," he yelled.

I stomped hard on the ground, hoping to disperse the ducks. A couple did fly off, but most stayed. I wasn't about to let my friend get beat up by a bunch of ducks. I waded into the circle and reached down for Toby's hand, but as I grasped it, a duck stabbed me in the wrist with his bill. "Damn it," I said, and I did something I never thought I'd do.

I punched a duck.

I didn't mean to punch it. I was just frustrated, and the duck was there, and I punched.

It felt . . . small. Like something that shouldn't be punched by a human. It looked at me like he was thinking: *No, you didn't just do that.* Somewhere far away, I could imagine the ASPCA folks mobilizing against me. It made several of the ducks hurry away, but some others—perhaps the protective mothers?—squawked and attacked me. I got pecked in the shins, the hands, the biceps. But I managed to lift Toby up, and we four ran the hell out of there, not needing to remain at Faneuil Hall as the guys who got their asses kicked by a gaggle of waterfowl.

We only stopped running when we got to Tremont Street. I looked back, wondering if the ducks had followed us. They hadn't run a quarter of a mile, no, and as I watched Albie, bent over and breathing hard from running maybe two minutes, I started to laugh. Really hard. Like years—or at least weeks—of pent-up energy. Thank God laughter is contagious, because soon they were all laughing with me. Even Toby, who had visual proof of duck-related injury in the form of several welts on his face, which looked especially freaky in combination with his eyeliner.

"C'mon, Ben, your turn," Toby said, and I walked over and gave him a hug.

"I think you win," I said.

The ride back was much less weird than the ride there, with lots of laughter about stupid stuff. I looked down at the few sore spots on my wrists and realized that in this case, they were totally worth it.

14

On Tuesday night, I was busy learning about transference and denial for psych class when there was a knock at my door. Somehow I knew who it was.

"Duck!" Rafe yelled when I opened it.

"Har har." I stepped aside and let him in.

I was mostly over the embarrassment of being taken down by a dozen angry ducks in front of a bunch of strangers this past weekend. I still had a couple of bruises on my wrists; they looked like purple semicolons. But I was otherwise fine, so long as the baseball guys never, ever heard about what happened.

"Talk about fowl play," Rafe said.

"I said: har har."

His face was all scrunched up like he was thinking really hard. I said, "I know you think besmirching me is hilarious, but can we move on, please?"

I saw the moment it came to him, and he turned to me with this inimitable Rafe expression of wonder, the one he gets when he surprises himself with what he thinks is a funny idea.

"That must have been very . . . unpheasant?"

That one cracked me up, it was so stupid. "Okay, a point for that one. And no more, please."

He sat down on the bed that he'd adopted last term after Bryce left, and I sat down on mine, facing him. A pang of something came over me. Memories? Not specific, exactly. Just of how it felt to have Bryce or Rafe close by all the time.

We didn't say anything for quite a while. I watched him look around the room, and then, when he looked at me and smiled, I grabbed my psychology textbook and placed it on my lap as if it were a shield.

"What'cha studying?" he asked.

"AP psych."

"Ah. You like it?"

"Meh."

"Why'd you take that?"

"AP credit," I said. "But also — I don't know."

"What?"

I scratched my left eyebrow. "I guess it's kind of like philosophy. It's a study of the brain. Or I thought it would be. Instead, it's a lot of stupid stuff I don't care about."

"Welcome to high school."

"I guess. Oh, wait. This part cracked me up." I flipped through the textbook to the graph I'd just been studying. "They have an actual graph where, like, they explain the unhealthy ways people deal with anger. Check this out." I read: "You are mad at your mother. Possible reactions: Displacement. 'I'm not angry at my mother; I'm mad at my dog. Bad dog.'"

Rafe laughed.

I continued reading. "Projection: 'I am not angry at my mother; she is angry at me.' Sublimation: 'I am not angry at my mother; I just need to arrange these pennies in perfect stacks of twenty.'" I looked up. "I just think that's all a little too neat, you know?"

Rafe kinked his head to the side. "What do you mean?"

"Like, you put everything into this little box. If I'm pissed off and I don't act it, it's not like I'm doing one thing. I'm probably, you know, doing a little bit of this, a little bit of that."

"That makes sense," he said. "What did you do when you were angry at me?"

I clutched my book tight. "Eh," I said.

"It's okay," Rafe said, jumping up and pulling the burgundy chair into the middle of the room. Then he sat down, crossed his legs, and rested his chin in his hands like a shrink might.

I rolled my eyes. "You are really not going to analyze me."

He affected a weird German accent. "It sounds as if vat you're saying ees that you have fear of being analyzed, ya?"

I laughed despite myself. "You could say that."

"Tell Dr. Freudberg. Vat ver you theenking ven you ver mad at that Rafe fella?" By the end of the sentence, he'd morphed into Irish.

I laughed again, crossed my legs and then uncrossed them. I looked at him and said, "You really want to go there?"

The nod started as if he was in character as Dr. Freudberg, but I could see also that he was serious, that he wanted to know, and that it was okay; I could tell him.

And I could. That was the surprising thing. All these months of staying away from the deep stuff, and here I was, about to dive in. I'd been so sure I'd never have this conversation with Rafe, ever. But it was okay. It just was.

"I was — pissed," I said.

"Okay. That much I knew."

I sighed. "I was pissed because of, yes, the lying or whatever you'd call it. Withholding. But it was more than that too. It was like, suddenly I had a boyfriend, who was gay, and I was WAY not ready for that."

Rafe nodded, and he didn't say anything.

"I guess I made more of it about the lying. Not that it didn't bug me, because it did. But a lot of it was that I was freaked out. Do you get that I have totally, honestly NEVER had a serious thought about a guy before? And then you. You just came into my life, and I don't know what happened. Something. But. It was real, you know?"

A tear fell from his right eye and trailed down his cheek.

I looked down at my mattress and continued. "It was real. So. I thought we were both in this place together, this new place, and that was a beautiful thing. But you weren't really there—"

"I was, though," he said, interrupting me. I looked up, and he wiped a tear away.

I raised an eyebrow and waited.

He wiped his eyes again. "I was there. You don't get that it was new for me too. Yeah, I've always known I liked guys, and that part is different. But you don't get that you were my first too."

"What about that other guy?"

"Clay? Are you serious? I barely knew him. I could hardly have a conversation with him. I fooled around with him because he wanted to, and he was there. I tricked myself into thinking it was more, but it was basically—he was there."

"Huh," I said. "That kind of makes you a slut, doesn't it?"

He jutted his neck out like he couldn't believe what I'd said, and he exhaled when I smirked.

"Until you, Ben, I'd never had any feeling that felt like, you know."

My windpipe shut down, and I closed my eyes.

"You okay?"

I took a deep breath and forced myself to open my eyes and look at Rafe. "Sorry, the boy said. I'm not freaked out about this. I'm freaked out about my dog. Bad dog."

Rafe laughed and flexed his feet like he was about to stand up, and I realized he was going to come over to me. I crossed my arms. *Nope. You have Jeff. And not ready for that, even if you didn't.* He seemed to get the message; he un-flexed.

"Can I ask you a question?"

"Sure," I said.

"Are you really straight? Or bi, or whatever? Is there really a girl?"

"Yeah. Straight."

"It's not, like, denial? In the GSA we joke that bi guys are just gay guys who aren't ready to admit it yet."

I tightened my arms around my chest. "Do you really think that?"

"I don't know. I don't, I guess."

"The girl's name is Hannah. She is a real person. I like her, okay?"

He clasped his arms around his legs. "Okay."

"And. Is it okay to talk about this? I mean. Jeff and all."

"It's fine," he half whispered.

"Here's the thing. I'm glad we're talking again. But you really can't ever, ever lie to me, or withhold any information. Never. Seriously."

"I promise. I will never."

His face was so earnest, and I noticed that my arms had uncrossed and there was this feeling in my chest like I was breathing for the first time in a long time. Part of me wondered again if this was a type of intoxication, if Rafe really was like my alcohol, because this feeling of peace came over me, and it reminded me of the first taste of a plastic screwdriver, how it enters the bloodstream and you just go, *Ahh.*

I'd have to watch out for any sign I was becoming addicted.

Rafe smiled at me, and for the first time since maybe Thanksgiving, I smiled back.

"So let's play a game," he said.

"Scrabble?"

"What? No. The game is called Let's Clear the Air. If we're gonna be honest with each other from here on out, let's get every little thing out from last semester."

"I don't have any little things," I said, but I felt my jaw tighten and realized that wasn't true.

"Of course you don't," he said. "I'll start. You, sir, are a terrible dancer."

A giggle came out of my mouth and I covered my mouth with my hand, a little embarrassed to have made such a small-person noise. I knew he was referring to the time he told me about frolicking, which he apparently used to do with Claire Olivia, which should have been a major clue that Rafe was gay. Cindy and I never *frolicked*, which apparently meant putting on cheesy music and dancing like a crazy person, *letting it all fly free*, as he said. We did it in my dorm room one night, and it was fun, just to let go a bit. He was right; I was a terrible dancer. We Carvers are not a dance-y people.

"And you had clearly never, ever played a game of football in your life," I said. "You catch like you think you have flypaper on your hands and the ball will simply stick to it."

"You had monkey breath that night we—you know," he said.

I turned beet red in the face. "What?"

"Sorry."

"Why didn't you tell me?" I scanned my memory for signs that I could have had bad breath with Hannah. How embarrassing.

"Are you kidding me? You think I cared about that?"

"I would have," I said, and I studied the white sheet on my bed. It was crumpled, and I ironed it out with my palm.

"It was fine, Ben," he said. "Really. I was interested in you, not your breath. It wasn't that bad, anyway. Just a tiny bit monkeyish."

"Maybe we should withhold some things," I said, continuing to iron out the sheets with both hands.

"I'm really okay if we don't," he said. "You're Ben. The greatest person in the universe."

"Um. Hi, Jeff?"

He shook his head. "This is different than that," he said. "This is — us, Ben. We're friends. And Jeff and I are really just friends too."

"Okay," I said.

"And admit it. You're the greatest person in the universe."

"Yeah, right." He didn't answer right away, so when I was ready, I looked up.

He was looking at me in this unnervingly close way, and again, the vacuum pull from inside my throat seemed to close up my windpipe.

"You don't really get how great you are, do you?"

"Okay," I said, looking down again. "Let's —"

"Tell you what," he said. "I'll keep knowing you're the world's most awesome person, but I won't say it. Or maybe I'll, like, say another word, just so I don't WITHHOLD anything from you."

I rolled my eyes.

"Porcelain."

"Huh?"

"I'll say porcelain."

"Why porcelain?"

"First thing that came into my mind?"

"Because of the time I was sick? No, thanks. Next word."

He laughed.

"I think it should be an adjective, at least," I said.

"So you're okay hearing how great you are, so long as I simply use an adjective?"

"An unrelated adjective," I said. "And yes."

Rafe smirked. "Magenta."

"Magenta? Isn't that a noun? And could you pick something less gay?"

Rafe shook his head, the smirk still on his face. "It can be both. And nope."

"Fair enough," I said, feeling more at peace than I had in over a month. "Magenta is acceptable."

15

The next night, Hannah asked if I wanted to go to a movie over the weekend, and at first I said yes, and then I called her back and said maybe we should just take a walk again.

"Ben, is this, like, a money thing?"

I didn't answer right away. My dad gave me a hundred dollars as spending money for the semester, which was fine because I rarely needed to buy anything. But a single movie could cost me 15 percent of my cash supply, which would have to last until June.

"It's really okay, Ben. I can pay. It's the twenty-first century, my parents are loaded, and I would rather not spend two hours out in the bitter cold, okay?"

I exhaled slowly. "I hate this."

"You need to stop worrying about that. I don't care, okay? You're not some asshole who's putting one over on me; you're this nice guy I'm getting to know, and I want that."

"It's gonna take me a while to get used to that," I said. "Thanks."

On Saturday afternoon, we saw some French film at the West Newton Cinema about a man who lives alone by the sea and befriends a young, fatherless boy. I found it interesting, but Hannah all-out sobbed at the last scene, when the boy's mother takes him away and the man stands, staring out at the ocean on a cloudy day. I grasped her small hand and she squeezed mine, and when her crying continued, I turned and gave her a light kiss on the side of her neck. She didn't turn her head or react in any way, and then I spent five minutes telling myself how stupid I was for assuming she wanted me to kiss her neck while she was in the midst of an emotional moment. I should have let her have some time. I shouldn't have brought attention to the fact that here she was, crying, and here I was, not crying.

When the movie ended and the credits rolled and people got up all around us and headed for the exit, we sat there, holding hands. At first I didn't dare glance over at her, afraid. Then, when the not looking got to be too much, I turned my head.

Her profile was so beautiful. I wanted to protect her from whatever it was that was making her cry, from whatever this movie brought up in her about being alone or being abandoned. I didn't know what it was, but I knew I wanted to fix it.

She turned toward me. Her eyes were still glassy and red, and she sucked in her upper lip. I sucked mine in too, and I held my breath, trying to figure out what I was supposed to do next.

I didn't have to, as it turned out. She leaned in and kissed me, and her lips parted so I separated mine too, and the tip of her tongue found mine. Electricity ran from the bottom of my feet to the top of my scalp, and I couldn't hold the feelings in my body anymore, so I put my arms around her and cradled the back of her head in my hand as I pulled her face into mine. She gasped when I did it, and she opened up her mouth wider, and I felt like I could devour her, and I did, there in the movie theater. I kissed her and kissed her until my mouth was tired and the guy walked into our row with a broom and dustpan.

I pulled away and we held each other's gaze.

"Where can we go?" I asked.

"I don't know."

"Do you want to?"

She nodded, hard, and I resisted the urge to kiss her some more.

"Is my car too much of a cliché?"

"It's a cliché for a reason. It works."

"I wish I could bring you back to my room, but—"

"No, I totally get it. Expulsion isn't worth it."

"It almost is, though."

We walked, arm in arm, down the empty street in the wintry night. I wanted to warm her up with my body. I wanted to make everything perfect for her.

When we got to Gretchen, we paused and had an awkward moment as we lingered between the front door and the back. She looked at me and I laughed a little, and she laughed back some.

"C'mon. Let's warm you up," I said, and I opened the passenger's side front door.

I turned the heat all the way up, and we sat there bundled in our coats, waiting for the air to warm.

"When you said, 'Let's warm you up,' I thought you were going to open the back door," she said.

"That felt too . . . something."

"I get it."

"Yeah. Plus, I can warm you up here too." I reached over and took her gloved hand in mine and squeezed. She squeezed back. "What made you cry so much in the movie?"

Hannah didn't say anything for a bit. "You're a different sort of guy," she finally said.

The word "magenta" entered my head. Ever since Rafe had given me that word five nights ago, it was kind of hard not to think about it.

"Am I?"

"You are. You actually want to know who I am, for one."

"Is that so weird?"

"In the world of creepy Natick boys, in my limited experience? Yes."

I laughed. "Sorry to hear that."

"Well, there's something to be said for purely physical, but I like that you ask questions."

"Cool."

"So to answer—are you sure you want to hear this?"

"I really do," I said.

"One summer when I was about nine, we spent the whole time in Truro. It's on the Cape. It was a great summer. We would go to the beach during the days and my dad and I would do this thing we called 'Walk and talk,' which I guess isn't that unusual, but for me it was. I'd never had alone time with my dad, and we talked about everything. This was pre-Marnie bullshit, of course. We'd walk, hand in hand, and he'd tell me about all the different kinds of birds we'd see, and we'd look for perfectly smooth rocks, and I'd tell him all about what happened last year in school with my best friend at the time, Lacey Walker, who was the first girl to get breasts and her period, not that it matters in this story. Every day, Dad would stand up next to the blanket while we three were lying there, me and my mom and him, and he'd say, 'Walk and talk?' And I'd jump up and grab his hand and we'd go.

"That's about the happiest memory I have, those lazy, long days on the beach with my dad. And then the end of the summer came, and his vacation ended—I guess he took August off, maybe?—and I pleaded with him not to go, because I wanted more, you know? More

103

time with him, because all he did-slash-does is work, like eighty hours a week, sometimes more, and I remember crying and screaming, 'Dad, don't go, Dad, don't go.'

"And he shook his head and got in his car and drove away, and I remember screaming my head off, and my mom, I think it hurt her feelings, because she just went into the kitchen and clammed up, and I remember sitting on this picnic table on the beach, which was like fifty feet from the house, and just sitting there for hours, looking at the ocean and wondering what it would be like to have a father who was around more.

"I guess that's first-world problems, eh?"

I turned toward her. "Aren't you the one who said 'boo' to me when I said my problems didn't amount to much because they were small compared to other problems?"

She fought off a grin. "Nailed," she said. "Nicely done. It's just . . . It makes me feel bad to whine to you about my summer-long beach vacation."

"We went to the Cape once."

"Yeah?"

"Yeah. We stayed at a motel. I was eight and my brother was five. We were supposed to stay three days, but on day two, my dad got antsy and said we should go back and check on the farm. It was the first time we ever put our toes in a swimming pool, and we actually sang Peter, Paul, and Mary songs in the car on the way home. Mom did. Dad's not a singer."

She laughed. "I have no idea who Peter, Paul, and Mary are."

"I love that memory."

"That's what's amazing about you. Do you know about vulnerability?"

I automatically crossed my arms over my chest. "Um, what?"

"I've been doing some reading. This woman talks about vulnerability, and she says that it's basically the key to everything. Vulnerability is allowing people to see you exactly as you are, which is really hard, because when you're vulnerable you can get hurt. Most people armor up with bravado or something, but those people are missing out, because without allowing yourself to be vulnerable, it's tough to have, like, any emotional experience at all. Letting people in is really vulnerable, and most people—especially introverts—have trouble. But you just let me in."

I didn't know what to say. What she was saying felt a little weird and New Agey to me, but I didn't want to hurt her feelings.

"Guys especially struggle with it. You're all taught that men don't show weakness. But the thing is, this woman says, vulnerability is not a choice. Either you do vulnerability, or it does you."

"It does you?"

"Yeah. Like, you hold in all your feelings, and then you drink, or you do drugs, or whatever it is, instead of feeling stuff."

I thought about that. It was like how I'd gone directly to my plastic screwdriver when I was feeling pissed at Rafe. Was that what she meant? I really couldn't ask.

"Interesting," I said.

She laughed. "You're just saying that."

I wasn't sure, actually. It *was* kind of interesting, and it kind of made me want to run away and drink orange Gatorade and vodka. Instead, I leaned in and kissed her gently on the lips, and she put her arms around me and pulled me toward her, and my stomach wrenched up against the middle console but I didn't mind because being pulled toward Hannah was a feeling I wanted to, needed to, have more of, immediately.

16

I read the sentence four straight times: *Instead of moving horizontally and vertically from the origin to get to the point in two-dimensional space, we could instead go straight out of the origin until we hit that point, and then determine the angle this line makes with the positive x-axis.*

My eyes went over it again and again. Shit. Why was this stuff so boring to me, and why was it just slightly beyond my grasp? I'd diligently taken notes. I'd studied those notes. I had tried, with varying levels of success, to memorize formulas without understanding what they really meant. We'd have our first calc test in the morning, and I felt totally unprepared.

Earlier that day, I'd gone to Ms. Dyson after class. She'd given back our pop quiz from the week before. I'd gotten an eighty-three, and I asked her if other students were having the same problems with the subject or if it was just me.

"It's all in your mind," she said, arranging homework in a pile and putting the papers in her briefcase. "You did well, didn't you?"

"Yeah, but the night before I was up 'til three studying."

She clicked her briefcase closed. "That's what high school is about.

You study hard. You'll need to get used to it for college. There you study harder."

"It's not the studying hard that I'm concerned about. It's my lack of understanding. I feel like the beginning of calculus made logical sense to me, but ever since we moved into three variables and some of the other stuff, it's been like nothing I've ever seen before. Maybe I should transfer into an easier math class."

She looked up at me as if she was annoyed with me.

"Ben, aren't you the Pappas Award winner?"

"Yeah, but—"

"I think you should push harder. Students who are far less talented than you get through this class. You don't want to have a lesser math class on your transcript. It won't read well to the top colleges. Maybe you're not applying yourself fully."

"Maybe," I said. I didn't want to whine about it, but I wasn't sure it was supposed to be this hard.

When I didn't walk away, she closed the book in front of her. "Look. Why don't you try the math lab? Get a tutor? A lot of students use tutors. If you want to work something out, I do some tutoring."

I looked down at her desk and sucked in my lips. Carvers didn't need extra help. It just wasn't done. And we couldn't afford tutoring. I knew if I asked my dad, he'd tell me to buck up and work harder.

"Just put everything away this evening, take out your book, and start from the beginning. It makes sense, Ben. You just have to see where you lost your way, and build from there. It's not beyond you. I promise."

I hadn't thought of that. I wasn't going to let laziness get the best of me. If my award and scholarship counted on it, I'd prevail.

"Thanks," I said. "I can do that."

She smiled at me, and as I left, I imagined that "Let's Get Ready to Rumble" song playing, and a montage of me successfully kicking calculus's butt. I laughed. It would not make for scintillating viewing.

Now it was night, and I sat and read and re-read the text until my eyes blurred. Finally, I slammed the book shut and went into the hallway, looking for a break.

I knocked on Rafe's door. Albie opened it. He was wearing pajama bottoms with various tropical fruits on them. I wasn't sure if this was some ironic hipster thing or not.

"Benjamin," he said, staring at the ground. Rafe wasn't there.

"Hey," I said, also staring down. We had really never spent time alone together before. I was pretty sure that even if he liked me, he considered me a jock, and Albie didn't trust jocks. "Where's Rafe?"

"Study group. Philosophy."

"Ah. What are you, um, up to?"

"Oh, uh. You know. Studying hard."

I looked at his desk. On it, next to his police scanner, was what appeared to be a bunch of Matchbox cars.

"Sure," I said. I looked over at him and I could tell he'd seen me see the cars, but something told me not to push the matter.

We just stood there, and I was trying to figure out a nonawkward exit strategy when he said, "Okay. Maybe I'm not studying. I'm—you're going to make fun of me."

"I won't, Albie. I promise."

He stepped aside, and the floor behind him was littered with pieces of notebook paper that had drawings on them.

"I'm making a town," he said.

"Oh," I said, rubbing my bottom lip.

"It's this thing I've done, like, all my life. I create a town and then these cars . . ." He points at his desk. "These cars are like the people, I guess."

I walked inside. "Huh," I said. One of the pieces of paper said, "Rosita's Fruit Stand," and on it was a crude pencil drawing of a table with lots of pieces of fruit on it.

"You think I'm a dork."

"We all have weird things." I was racking my brain for something similar about me, but beyond liking to go to World War II museums by myself, there wasn't that much to compare to this.

"I guess," he said. "I think I like creating the world, and then—why am I telling you this?"

I smiled at him. "Because we're friends, I hope."

He averted his eyes from mine, but I could sense that he was glad I'd said it. "I guess I like the stories that I make up about the people-cars."

"So the cars are people. Got it."

"Yeah. It's weird. But I like to make up stories in my head, I guess."

"I think that's cool," I said.

He laughed. "Yes. Ben Carver, king of the baseball team, thinks my nerdy car-town thing is cool."

"Captain," I corrected. "And, well. What kind of stories?"

He went over to his desk and picked up a purple car that looked like maybe an old Chevy with those exaggerated fins. "So this is Martin. He's, like, me, I guess. He's a detective. And sometimes he'll just watch. He might see two car-people at the bank, and then those cars speed off and it's a robbery. He has to, like, figure out who did it."

"Have you ever written these stories down?"

He shook his head.

"You should."

He seemed to contemplate this. "Maybe I will."

"Cool. I'm just looking for a study break. Have this horrible calc test coming and I'm not ready."

"You?" he said. "You're always ready for everything."

I rolled my eyes. "Not exactly."

"Do you know about the keys?"

"The keys?"

"Shit. Well, you're not a narc, right?"

"No, not a narc."

"Tommy Mendenhall has all the answer keys to quizzes and tests in most courses. Not Mr. Bisbee in earth science; he changes things up. Also Ms. Patrick in history, I hear."

"Oh," I said, folding my arms in front of my chest. I'd heard about this. It was a tradition at Natick. Every year, a senior inherited the answer keys that had been assembled by students over the years. It had never meant much to me; if other people wanted to cheat, it was none of my business.

Albie studied me. "You're cool with it, right?"

"Yeah," I said. "Not my thing, but I don't care." Even if I wanted to cheat, I wasn't sure how a person would do it in calculus. Ms. Dyson would probably ask us to show our work, so just knowing the correct multiple-choice answer would mean nothing.

"You don't need the help, clearly," he said.

"Actually, BC calc is killing me. Literally, it's reaching around my neck and strangling me."

"Ms. Dyson?"

I nodded.

"I'm pretty sure Ms. Dyson does the same tests and quizzes every year. Ask Tommy."

I shook my head. "Nah," I said. "Not for me."

"Sure," Albie said. "Well. My town beckons."

I saluted him and headed back to my room, my heart pounding in my chest. The cheating didn't sit right with me, but as usual I was too much of a wimp to voice my opinion.

Out in the hallway, I ran into Mendenhall.

"Hey, I was hoping to catch you," he said.

"Oh." I leaned against the wall, and he leaned in toward me in a way that made me want a buffer of about a foot. Maybe two.

"Listen," he said. "I've been thinking about the whole captain thing. I think you're in over your head. You look back at the captains the last few years, and it's always someone outgoing who is in the center of things. That's not you."

I crossed my arms over my chest.

"I think you should try to be more social, maybe. You're too quiet, and the thing is, at the end of the day, this is my senior year. I want to win. And for us to do that, we need a captain who can do the job, get us united and fired up. You hear me?"

I nodded.

He laughed. "You really are reserved, aren't you?"

"Yes," I said. "I don't say everything that comes to mind." *And you should be glad I don't.*

"And that's cool. I mean, there are definitely good things about being the strong, silent type. You're not annoying, and that's good. And you're a good player. You can probably teach the others some stuff."

"Thanks."

He raised his chin like a king who had deigned to compliment a peasant.

"The crap about no initiation stuff is dumb, in my opinion. If that's what you want, fine. But you still probably need me if you want to motivate the guys. You don't have their ear yet. What if I help you there?"

"Sure," I said. "That would be good."

He smiled. "You're a good guy, Carver. Let's try to make this work, okay?"

"Okay."

Back in my room, I tried to shake off the feeling that I was about to get bulldozed by Mendenhall. I looked in the mirror, and I focused on my arms. They were big and thick. I was no wilting flower. Yet I'd just allowed him to talk down to me with no pushback. Would I stand up to him if he really tried to take my role away from me?

One time I'd stood up for myself with the other athletes. It was during soccer in the fall. Some kids were making homophobic comments aimed at Rafe before he came out, and I shut that down in a hurry. It had felt good. Where was the line? How far would I be pushed before I pressed back?

I sat down at my desk, opened my calculus book, and stared at the symbols. Every time I found my eyes glazing over, I powered through, reminding myself that I was a Pappas Award winner and a Carver, and doing poorly in BC calculus wasn't an option for either role. I started pounding Gatorade around 2:30 so I could keep my eyes open, and at 5 A.M., when I finally figured out how to use the fundamental theorem to evaluate definite integrals, I collapsed in my bed, setting my alarm for 7 A.M. so that I wouldn't sleep through breakfast or my test.

Lying there in a half coma, I wondered how I was going to keep this up. How many more sleepless nights would calculus cause me? I was pretty sure I'd do well on the test, but my nerves were shot.

17

I drove home to Alton the final weekend in January because it was my mom's birthday. When I got there Friday night, my mom and dad welcomed me in their typical understated-but-loving way. Mom's first words were, "I made cookies," and then, once I'd taken my jacket off, set my bag down, and taken one, she came over and gave me a big kiss. Dad said, "You look taller."

Luke was in our bedroom, lying on top of the comforter in gym shorts, despite the fact that it was below freezing out and my dad doesn't believe in using heating oil. He was playing his Game Boy per usual.

"What up?" he said, and I could swear his voice had gotten lower in the six weeks I'd been away.

"Yo," I responded.

"You missed Mom getting into trouble," he said.

I sat down on my bed and took off my boots. "What?"

He looked up and turned off his game. "This hippie-dippy woman talked her into selling all sorts of crap at the store. Dad said no way. Said the lady is banned from the store. Mom started crying."

113

"What?" I asked. In all my life, I'd never seen my mom cry. I'd never heard of it either. In the Carver family, tears are relegated to the *something fell on me* category.

"It was wicked crazy," he said.

"Did you talk to her?"

He shrugged. "And say what?"

He had a point. Luke was probably not the most comforting person in the county.

As I unpacked my bag, he updated me on some things.

"I got people to stop calling her Bulldozer," he said, and I remembered the girl he'd told me about when we went for our swimming lesson over winter break.

"That's cool. Do you guys talk?"

He shrugged and picked up his game again.

"What was her name again?"

"Julie."

"Oh, okay," I said, and I knew that was probably the end of the conversation. And it was. I pulled out a book and Luke kept playing his video game. No one spoke again until Luke said, "G'night, brother," after I'd turned off the lights, and I said back, "G'night."

I dreamt that Mendenhall was cornering me in my dad's barn and telling me how to do farm work. Even as I was in the dream, I realized that my father and Mendenhall had merged into one extremely judgmental person, and I wondered if I'd ever make either of them happy.

The next morning, I woke to a sharp chill in my forearms, and I quickly pulled them under the flannel blanket to warm them up. I could hear the wind hissing and whipping through the bare trees outside. Negative ten at the most. Windchill probably around minus forty. Luke was sleeping with two bare legs exposed on top of his down blanket, and I shook my head and smiled to myself. Doesn't matter if it's fifty degrees or twenty below—Luke's never chilly.

I lay there in the comfort of my own warm cocoon thinking about hypothermia. I've read accounts of people trying to scale Mount Kilimanjaro, where it's so cold at the top that their body temperature drops several degrees, and as it does so, a strange calm comes over them, like the total absence of heat is actually warm. In reality it's their organs shutting down, but it doesn't feel like that.

Bryce told me once that Tibetan monks practice a type of meditation that allows them to raise their core temperature. They do it by envisioning flames at the base of their spine. I wondered if I could do that, so I tried it. It was tough to imagine the flames and not allow other thoughts to get in the way. *Perhaps,* I thought, *Tibetan monks practice this, and don't just try it once on a frigid New Hampshire day for five seconds, fail miserably, and then drop it.*

I watched out the window as my dad, in just a sweater and a hat, walked his lanky body over to the barn, with our goat, Becky, following close behind. *Cows don't care it's winter, and neither do I,* he used to say. I swear there's some truth to the fact that heredity makes some people immune to cold, because nothing seems to chill my dad. He comes from generations of Czech farmers who don't bitch about the weather; they may talk about it endlessly, but they never complain.

While Luke stayed in bed, I bundled up to go out to the barn. Farm work was not my forte, but I could help clean the barn stalls and spend some time with my dad.

The morning air Popsicled my teeth. I stuck my gloved hands deep into the pockets of my ratty old brown down jacket. "Hey," I said, entering the barn, my breath a white mist that barely traveled six inches before freezing. My lungs ached.

"Benny," my dad said. He was on his knees in the stall with one of the cows, milking away. Clamp base, squeeze down, alternate hands.

I grabbed the pitchfork and shovel and went into another stall, where Becky lay on a bed of hay. The floor was littered with chicken shit, hay, and what looked like a half-eaten cantaloupe. The ceiling was just six feet high, so I had to bend over as I shoveled up the debris. The sharp smell of frozen manure assaulted my nostrils.

There was an utter absence of sound on our farm in the winter. Because my dad didn't believe in using anything other than wood for heat, there was no buzz of electricity, or hiss of oil or coal. I let the silence envelop us for a while, and I kept up my shoveling, feeling warmer by the second.

And then it gets too quiet, sometimes.

"Cold today," I said, when it got there for me. About six minutes, maybe seven.

"Yup," said Dad. The cow he was milking moaned a bit.

Silence again beyond the sound of milk squirting into the red bucket.

"You got enough warm clothes down there at school?"

"Yes. Thanks." I swept the debris into a small pile, and we worked some more in silence.

"It was actually pretty warm in Natick before I left," I said.

"How warm?" my dad said.

"Forties. Maybe forty-five?"

"You don't say," he said.

"Yep. It was pretty warm."

No more words. I stepped into the stall where my dad was, carefully navigating the frozen mud, to sweep up some manure.

"Doing better with the schoolwork," I said, and it was like he didn't hear me. He just kept milking. "I also met a girl," I added. He didn't say anything to that either, so I concentrated on sweeping, and we worked like that until the cows were milked and the barn was as clean as it was going to get.

I loved my dad, but why did I even bother trying to squeeze conversation out of him? It was like squeezing warmth out of an ice cube. I'd come to a frozen barn to get warm. That never works. Even if you get so close to freezing that it feels warm, it's just a mirage; it's hypothermia. And then you die.

While Dad sized up the job I did on the barn and did a little additional sweeping in Becky's stall, I walked toward our farm store, my eyes so dry I figured I might never be able to blink again. Inside, I was hit with the warm smell of chocolate and mint.

"Mmm," I said.

My mother was at the stove in the store's small kitchen area, pouring boiling water into a cup of cocoa. She smiled at me. "Want one?"

"Happy birthday! And sure. That'd be perfect," I said.

The store was connected to the front of our house, but it had a separate entrance for customers. Mom spent most of her time running the store, selling jams and produce, and during the summers, when I wasn't in the fields with Dad, I'd help her too. Dad tended to count on me for tasks that used muscle, and Luke for things that involved farm skills; mine were, as my dad loved to tease me, not exactly Future Farmers of America level.

I sat on a stool next to Mom's. She reached over and put a gentle hand on my bicep and squeezed.

"You okay?" I asked.

She nodded. "Sure."

"Luke said something."

She cringed. "He shouldn't of done that. Don't matter."

"Mom," I said. "Tell me. What happened?"

"Your father said his piece. Don't matter to get into it now."

"Who was this person? C'mon. Tell me."

It wasn't like me to push her. Maybe it was things at school, the way I was beginning to realize that unlike my family, I liked conversation. Sometimes I could be in a humdrum mood and talk to Hannah on the phone, and when I was done, I'd feel like a different person. Or with Rafe, I'd buzz for hours after we talked, playing back different parts of the conversation. I didn't need constant talking like some people, but some, I was beginning to learn, I really liked.

Mom took a deep breath. "Her name is Hazel."

"Okay. Who is Hazel?"

Mom's eyes lit up. Her eyes never did that.

"Unusual-looking woman. Hair down to her behind." She laughed a bit and shook her head. "Figured she was one of the summer people. Came to the store one day and . . . So friendly. You know I don't like to get involved with that type. The ones who spend summers at the lake and have fancy leather pocketbooks. They change everything."

"You sound like Dad."

She shot me a parental look that said to me, *He's your father. Don't talk about your father that way.* As long as I could remember, I'd get that look anytime I brought up anything negative about Dad, like it was a reflex. I knew Mom felt most of the same things I did about Dad from the *Your father thinks* comments she would make about various things that bugged her but she went along with anyway.

Your father thinks we should stop processing chickens for summer folks until they pay. I told him we can't treat 'em different than the others, but you know your father.

Your father thinks I ought to keep the store open 'til after the fire-works in case someone wants a lemonade. That would mean 5 A.M. to midnight, but you know your father.

"She kept coming, every day. One day I had a cold. Must have been mid-September? I was blowing my nose all over heckfire, and she said she had something would fix me right up. Ran out to her truck and came back with a bottle of cough syrup, it looked like. Helped herself to the kitchen and came back with a tablespoon. She said, 'Two spoonfuls of this and you'll be good as new.' It was purple and sweet. 'What is it?' I asked.

"She said elderberry syrup. Explained she was an herbalist, and that she could cure Ebola if she had to. Told me that the body knows how to heal itself and we just need the cures that are already in nature. You know me, Benny. I thought it was all a bunch of hooey. But darned if I didn't feel better the next day! And she came in that next day and she didn't even ask; she knew I'd be better! We really became friends. When's the last time I had a friend?"

The last part she asked herself, and I studied her, thinking the same thing. It was almost like I'd never thought of my mom as a real person. She had never seemed to need a friend. She had Dad, and while they didn't talk much, they didn't seem to need much either. He ran the fields and the business; she ran the store. If she needed a couple chickens, she'd tell him to process them. If a beef order came in, she'd say so. Words didn't log or hay or feed or milk.

"Hazel would visit and we'd just gab away. One day your father came in and I introduced them. I don't know what I was thinking. Of course he thought she was weird. She *is* weird, Benny, I have to say. But I liked her. And she taught me so much about herbs! A couple times she took me to her place and showed me the tinctures she was making for this friend or that. Not a business, but she said she was thinking it could be. And I thought: What if we sold them at the store?"

She was talking now almost like I wasn't there. Passionate in a way I'd never heard before from my mom.

"I knew the answer. But also, it's not like the store is so busy that I couldn't dry some burdock root and wild sarsaparilla. And I put some yellow dock root in vinegar in a bottle, and I left it for six weeks, and every day Hazel would tell me what it could do for people when it was ready, and I tell you, Benny, I got excited! I couldn't wait to try it.

"I knew what your father would say. Asked me was I crazy. Told me herbs was hippie-dippy stuff, and did we want to lose all our customers. Folks don't like new stuff like that, he said. And Benny, I thought, 'Some folks don't, some folks do.' But I didn't say nothing, of course.

"So I did try the yellow dock root." She smiled at the memory. "I harvested it in early December. Cooked it up and it tasted as bitter as tonic water and citrus peels combined. But darned if my stomach trouble didn't clear up just like that! Got a little more in the back. Don't tell your father. Just for me. Not selling it or nothin'."

"Wow," I said. "So yesterday, Dad said no selling?"

She clasped her hands in front of her.

I asked, "Did he say you couldn't, like, see her anymore?"

A glimmer of something overcame my mother's face. Regret? Her eyebrows twitched just a bit.

"Just weren't worth the trouble," she said.

And as we sat there, sipping cocoa, saying nothing, I wondered: If I had hypothermia, what did my mom have after all these years? Did my mom ever say what she really thought to my dad, or was she always playing the role of the perfect wife? And then that thought felt a little close to home, so I stopped thinking about it.

Before I left to go back to school on Sunday, I went and talked to my dad in the barn again. He was cleaning and re-filling the water buckets.

"You got enough money for things you need? Books?" he asked, not looking my way.

"I'm fine," I said. "Hey, there is one thing. The baseball team. They're going to Fort Lauderdale, Florida. We're going. Spring break. The school is actually paying my way."

Dad frowned. "We don't need their help."

I shrugged but didn't say anything, because actually we did. No way did we have a thousand dollars or whatever it would cost. And there was nowhere good this conversation could go if it became about my dad and his ability to provide for me.

"I know," I said. "But. Can I go?" I knew I'd need to get his permission.

The water got close to the top of the bucket, and he turned off the flow. "Your grades better now?"

I nodded.

"We'll see, then. Keep 'em up and we'll figure it out."

I stood there, a tightness in my throat, my head buzzing a bit. There was so much more to say. About Mom. About us. Everything. And I knew I would never say it.

18

The Wednesday after my visit home, Coach Donnelly turned over infield practice to me while he went to the other side of the gym to work with the outfielders. It was the first time I'd run any part of practice by myself, and my whole body felt jittery. The seven other guys milled around, waiting for me to get things started. I jumped in before my brain could tell me stuff about how I had no business acting as coach.

"Okay, gloves down," I said, my voice sounding deeper than normal, and I glanced over at Mendenhall, half expecting him to roll his eyes. He didn't. He just dropped his glove like everyone else.

"Pair up, and everyone grab a ball." All the guys partnered up, leaving me with Clement, the freshman. I got everyone to do the drill Coach taught us, where we roll a ball to our partner, who ranges over, his glove hand on the floor, to field it before rolling it back. The right way to field is to stay low and move with the hop, in case the ball decides not to come up to you, so the drill got us comfortable remaining in fielding position.

"Do it like you mean it!" I yelled not to anyone in particular, trying to sound captain-like. I rolled a ball toward Clement. He seemed jarred by my yelling, and he fumbled the hop.

I jogged over. His back was arched, but his legs were straight.

"Legs," I said. "Watch me." I showed him the correct fielding position, and he imitated it.

"There ya go," I said. "You'll find it easier now."

Clement said a quiet, "Thanks," and I jogged back to my spot. He did better on the next few rolls, and then I started to challenge him by rolling to his right and left, and he was up to the challenge and seemed to be really energized every time I said, "Attaboy."

After about twenty minutes of various drills, I clapped my hands loudly and called everyone over. I'd seen previous captains do psych-up speeches, and they seemed to mean a lot to the other guys. They always left me cold.

The guys circled up around me, and I jumped in.

"What's the goal this year?" I said.

No one said much of anything, so I barked it again. "What's the goal?"

"Win," Mendenhall said, nodding.

"That's it! Let me hear you say it, guys. C'mon."

"Win!" the guys said, looking around at one another like they were surprised this was coming from me.

"Again!"

"Win!"

"Again!"

"Win!" I glanced over again, and Mendenhall was shouting just as loud as the rest of the guys.

"That's what I'm talkin' about!" I said, sounding like another person entirely. "We're here to kick some ass, and I want you to put that kind of energy into everything we do, because it matters. Preparation is everything. Attitude is everything. Are we winners, or are we losers?"

"Winners!" they shouted.

I couldn't help but smile. We *were* winners. "Now let's get back out there and do those drills again, the same, in order, but, like, twice as serious. Got me?"

"Yeah!"

And I felt it in my head, this buzzing, wild sensation that came from being up to the challenge. That came from being the guy the team needed me to be.

19

Rafe and I were studying in my room on Thursday night. I had a psych test the next day as well as enough calculus concerns to keep my nose buried in a book for the next decade. Well, I was studying and Rafe was kneeling at the foot of the second bed in the room, going through a pile of my books. There was something totally annoying about how Rafe took frequent breaks while I couldn't afford to do that, and also something totally Rafe about it. In a good way. He didn't get all intense about things like I did.

I guess he didn't really need to. His family had plenty of money, so he'd be able to pay for college wherever he got in. Privilege.

"What the hell is the Museum of World War II?" he asked, picking up a pamphlet that had gotten stuck in among my books.

"Are you struggling with context clues?" I asked.

He laughed. "I mean, like, where is it, and all that?"

"It's in Natick. Before I had a car down here, like back in ninth and tenth grades, I used to take the bus around to places. The Natick Historical Society, or the World War II museum. I was a member there, actually. Honorary. Came back a couple times, and they gave me a free member card."

He sat down on the other bed, the one that used to be his. It was still a little weird to see him on it. "Which gave you one free Luftwaffe for every ten you bought?"

I laughed. "There's actually a fair amount of history in Natick. Harriet Beecher Stowe lived here for a while. Henry Wilson was from here. He was vice president under Ulysses S. Grant."

He threw the pamphlet down onto the floor. "You know so many facts! I think one of the differences between us is you are interested in things and I'm interested in people."

"Most historians agree that Ulysses S. Grant was, in fact, a person."

"I mean, like, a person now. Someone we could meet and get to know."

"Yeah, I guess that's true. I'm not, in general, a huge fan of people."

"Present company excluded, I'm sure you mean."

I shrugged in an exaggerated way and he blew a raspberry at me.

"So anyway, Wilson," I said. "He was a radical Republican and a staunch abolitionist."

"I guess Republican meant something else back then?"

"Uh. Yeah."

"I guess I knew that. I wonder how a political party could change so much. It was like Democrats and Republicans switched teams."

"I'm not entirely sure."

"Are your folks Republicans?" he asked.

I shook my head. "We're staunch Democrats."

"I didn't know that. I figured they were superconservative."

"They are, Rafe. They're old-school Democrats, like the southern Democrats who got Jimmy Carter elected. Socially conservative. At least, my dad is."

"Oh," Rafe said, and I knew he didn't know what I was talking about.

"Yeah. My dad basically banished my uncle when he came out as bi. Wouldn't accept him. My uncle went to China to teach English because he needed to get away from our family. He came back and pushed his way back in, but my dad never accepted him. My dad thinks my mother is hippie-dippy because she wants to sell herbal remedies at our farm store."

Rafe whistled. "That's . . . Wow."

"Yeah. And I love my dad. But. That's where I'm from."

"How is that possible? You're so smart and inquisitive and open-minded."

I shrugged. "I'm not my dad, I guess."

"I didn't mean that. I meant—"

"No, I get it. I wonder that sometimes too."

Rafe sprawled out on his stomach and opened his history book. He was studying the Russian Revolution, which I would have been happy to talk to him about if he wanted to, but he seemed utterly disinterested in doing anything beyond memorizing dates.

His head snapped toward me. "Oh! Did I even tell you? I walked into my closet last night just before lights out and Toby was standing in there. I was like, um—"

"He did that to me!" I said, putting my calc book down. "My first night back. Tried to subliminalize me."

"That's what he was saying to me. Said he was going to help me with history using subliminal suggestions."

"He has so many issues," I said, and Rafe laughed.

We studied and neither of us spoke for maybe thirty minutes, at which time Rafe dramatically shut his book and sat up.

"We need to get Toby," he said.

"Must we?"

"I mean revenge, not fetch."

"As I said: Must we?"

"I think we need to subliminalize him."

"Huh," I said. I closed my calculus book and looked at him.

"You don't love the idea."

"Well, I guess I just think, what will that do? If we're successful in not waking him up, we'll, what, spend all night in his closet talking softly?"

He chuckled a little. "I may not be the greatest prankster of all time."

"We'll think on it," I said. "Maybe we can make it better."

Rafe nodded, and a few minutes later, he stood up and went to the bathroom.

While he was gone, I went into my closet, where I kept my mini refrigerator, and grabbed two orange Gatorades. No vodka this time. Ever since I got sick the last time I drank, I'd been off the stuff.

He came back and sat down on the other bed. I threw him a Gatorade.

"Holy bright lights, Batman!" he said, catching it.

"Huh?"

He pointed at my closet, where I'd left the light on.

"Oh, that," I said. "I couldn't see my clothes, so I went and got a seventy-five-watt LED bulb at Home Depot." I admit it took me a while to get used to the glow, but there was something nice about it, especially in the winter, when the natural light wasn't as plentiful.

"It's so bright white! Is that where we go when we die? I think I see my dead relatives in there."

"Har har."

"NASA just called, Ben. They say the only things they can see from space are Las Vegas and your closet."

"You get one more."

"I think some douchebag just opened a Hard Rock Café by your button-down shirts."

"Weak."

He kept chuckling to himself as he re-opened his English textbook. I admit the jokes bothered me a little — I'd spent birthday money on the bulb — but they also kind of settled him back in to the space a bit. And I was glad for that.

We studied and talked and gabbed and worked until it was one thirty in the morning, and then Rafe said, "So are you ready?"

"Um, what?"

"Are you ready? To get Toby? Back, I mean. For the subliminalizing."

"Do I have a choice?"

He shook his head no, and I shrugged. He explained that we were going to wait until Toby was asleep, sneak into his room, make a little noise to wake him up, and then jump out of his closet and scare the shit out of him.

Normally I would not do such a thing, especially because I didn't want to get into trouble. As the Pappas Award winner, I had to be careful. But it sounded tame enough, and if I did get into trouble, it would be with Coach Donnelly, who thought I walked on water. Anyway, I was dead tired of being the good kid. The *killer of fun*. I simply said yes.

Rafe suggested we both bring our cell phones so we could text each other while we waited, but I had to remind him — my phone plan didn't include texting.

"Nineteen ninety-seven wants its phone back," he said, and I thought about explaining that whereas his birthday present was an iPhone, mine was a lightbulb I bought myself. Instead, we brought a

129

pad and a pen so we could write back and forth as humans once did, and Rafe brought his phone for the flashlight app.

We cracked my door open and looked both ways. No light, no sound. I led us down the corridor all the way to the end, to Toby's single room.

He was sound asleep and snoring when we crept in. His window overlooked the other side of the dorm from mine—the street rather than the quad—and the streetlights illuminated his skinny face and now-pink hair. We tiptoed to his closet, opened it in slow motion so as to not make a sound, and crept in and closed the door at the same speed. Toby's breathing never changed; he was still asleep and had no idea that he was about to find out what happens when you try to sub-liminalize the wrong people.

We had not prepared, of course, for just how weird it would be in Toby's closet. Here is a partial inventory of what we found strewn about on the floor when Rafe turned on the flashlight app:

- Angel's wings

- A half-eaten Hershey's white chocolate bar

- A pair of roller skates, the right foot seemingly larger than the left by a good two sizes

- A turquoise kimono with a floral pattern

- Condoms organized in four neat piles of exactly the same height

- A bow and arrow, the quill of which was painted lavender

- A pair of women's Spanx

- A flyer for two-for-one pregnant yoga at the Natick community center.

We looked at each other. Rafe opened his mouth to say something, but I thrust my finger in front of my lips and handed him the pad. He took it and scribbled.

> Do you think he's killed?
> *Oh yes, definitely.*
> Do you think he'll kill again?

I grabbed the angel's wings and pantomimed devil's horns, and for some reason that made Rafe almost laugh out loud.

We settled in, me sitting up with my knees against my chest and him leaning up against the far wall. His feet were inches from my butt, and I could feel the warmth of his skin radiating off his toes.

There was a huge farting sound from the other side of the door, and then snores, loud. I put my fist over my mouth to stop myself from laughing, but Rafe wasn't quite as lucky. Giggles exploded past his lips, and I had to give him another look. He gathered himself, closed his eyes, and made sure he was composed. We waited. No sound. Constant snoring.

Well, he's asleep, Rafe wrote.

> *Sounds that way.*
> How long do we wait?

I shrugged. I had no idea. I shifted my seat, rubbing up against a black overcoat. I hoped the noise couldn't be heard outside the closet.

"You're too literal, Albie," we heard Toby say in a conversational voice that sounded as if it was part of his dream, followed by some words I couldn't make out.

He's out cold. Let's do this, I wrote.

Okay.

We stood up, careful not to make any noise.

"I AM THE MUFFIN MAN!" Toby's voice was like a monster's now, and Rafe and I, startled, grabbed each other. My heart was pulsing as I wished I'd brought a baseball bat or something. I'd heard about sleeping people who get woken up and do crazy things. What if Toby—and then I realized: I was staring into Rafe's eyes, my hands around his shoulders.

"I AM THE MUFFIN MAN! I AM THE MUFFIN MAN! AAAAHHH!" He really sounded like a monster, and aside from the intense staring with Rafe jarring every part of me, heating up my skin from the inside, I wondered whether I might die in Toby's closet.

Rafe pulled away from me and scribbled on the pad.

On a scale of one to "I may never sleep again," how scared are you?

I motioned with my hand to show that I was closer to the extreme side of that scale.

"I DID NOT KILL THAT MAN. HE DESERVED TO DIE. DIE, SCUM, DIE!"

There was a thump outside the door. I pulled Rafe close to protect him.

The closet door opened.

"Really?" Toby said, hands on his hips. "Really? Truly?"

"Shit," I exhaled, and then I realized I was still holding Rafe.

"Well, this part makes it all worth it," Toby said. "Thank fucking God."

I let go of Rafe, and then, realizing how Rafe might take that, I patted him on the back. He seemed entirely neutral to all this, and I didn't know what to make of that.

"You mess with the king, you better kill him," Toby said, shaking his head.

"Don't you mean queen?" I said, and both Rafe and Toby looked shocked.

"Oh no he didn't," Toby said to Rafe.

"He did, though. He did," Rafe said back.

"So all of that? All the talking in your sleep, including the thing about Albie?"

"All a ruse. I heard you guys way before that."

"The farting thing too?" I asked.

Toby's face turned a shade darker than his hair. "Uh, yeah," he said, eyes averted. "Yes. Total ruse."

We were nestled in my bed. I was pressed against her, spooning her soft, maple syrup skin, the heat of our bodies combining into something a little like heaven.

I ran my fingers against the nape of a long, feminine, swan-like neck. I looked down at the smooth back, milky white.

Rafe rotated his neck so I could see his profile. Not Hannah. Rafe.

No, I said, but the words wouldn't sound as I said them. *Please no.*

"Yes," he said back, smiling. "Yes."

"Yes," I repeated, and warmth encapsulated my entire body. I whispered, "You're home" in his ear, and he giggled, and he said, "More like second base," and I laughed too, and I held him close, my chest pressing into his back, and I smiled. He smelled ever-so-lightly of vanilla.

Then my eyes opened to reality and I looked up at the ceiling, assailed by all the physical feelings running through my chest, my legs, my hips. My body was a maze of electrical impulses, and they were all lit.

Rafe. Jesus. Rafe.

I felt this guilty feeling twisting in my gut as I thought about

Hannah, whom I really, really liked. I felt like I'd cheated on her, in a way, even if it was just a dream. But I couldn't stop thinking about Rafe.

I thought about the first time we kissed, out in Boulder over Thanksgiving, and how Rafe had exploded upon lip contact. And I'd thought in that moment, *I can do this. This can happen.* Then we slept apart, and as I'd tried to fall asleep, other, more worldly thoughts had entered my brain. About my dad. About what I heard in the hallway when I was twelve, what he said to my uncle, who had come over for the first time in five years.

"Rejected you? You rejected us. We didn't move to China. You did."

"I moved there because you and Dad said I was no longer family."

"I don't know what you want from me. Only straight bones in this family. You're the one who's choosing men instead of women."

"Men as well as women. And not choosing. This is who I am."

"Talk normal. You want to be family? Be normal."

I heard that and I knew what they were talking about but I didn't. Like, all I really heard was the *be normal* part, and I made a pact with myself, then and there, to always be normal, no matter what.

Or else I'd lose my family.

So that night in Boulder, I stopped thinking, *I can do this. This can happen.* Because it couldn't. And anyway, I still thought about girls when I wanked, so.

I rolled over.

How the hell had that dream happened? Is Rafe a wizard?

The closet was intimate, I guess. It had brought back memories of that night back at Natick, just after Thanksgiving. Stuff I still didn't really know how to handle.

I had been tossing and turning and writhing in bed. We weren't talking and I was dying inside and I needed him but I couldn't have him because pride and fear had created a toxic jelly that floated in my bloodstream, stopping up my jaw, making it impossible to say words, any words, to him. Still, it was like I could taste him, and all I'd ever done was kiss him but now I needed to know what the rest was like.

And then those footsteps. It was the cadence, a touch faster than walking and a step slower than running, like he was yearning to be somewhere else, faster, sooner. If I had to guess, his cadence would be twice mine.

I heard them, and I jumped up. I opened the door.

The kiss happened right away, and it was wet and juicy and unbelievable. Our bodies pressed together felt different than it had felt with my first girlfriend, Cindy. Like hard against hard, with no soft relief, and that felt alien. I explored more because I could, I guess. I pressed my lips against his neck and there it was, Rafe's skin. I flicked my tongue. He had an aftertaste, like burning wood and chocolate, like the air around a campfire the morning after, where you know there's been a fire but it's out now.

I thought when I took him in my mouth that it would make me feel like a girl. It didn't. Truth be told, that part was less exciting to me than tasting the skin of his neck. I needed — wanted, maybe — to be near his face.

When he used his mouth on me? Well. Describing the way sex feels is like saying how steak tastes. It tastes good. It felt good. Great. But it still didn't surpass that first moment, the kiss, our heads connecting and neither of us pulling away.

I opened my eyes and looked at the ceiling again. That was then, this was now, and he didn't belong in my dreams anymore. Hannah was in my dreams, and she belonged there, and we were working toward something great. With Rafe, I was very okay with a close friendship, but beyond that, it got . . . complicated. And my life did better simple.

At breakfast the next morning, Rafe waved ecstatically from the entrance to the dining hall while I was in the omelet line. I wanted to run away, but our friendship had just come back, and it was tentative, and I didn't want to ruin that.

"Sleep well?" he asked.

I shrugged. "Fine, I guess. Not long enough."

We went through the line. I ordered an omelet with bell peppers. Rafe ordered one with ham, which is weird since he's Jewish. Then we went to the fixin's station and I loaded up on ketchup and Rafe walked away.

I didn't pick up on the vibe until I got to his table.

He didn't look up at me. "You're doing it again."

"I'm not."

He pursed his lips. "Yeah, but you kinda are. The closet thing last night freaked you out. Sorry. Why do I even?" He shook his head.

"No — not at all. No. I'm just. I'm tired, bud." I tried to casually punch him in the shoulder to show I was cool with a little contact.

Rafe looked at me and I saw the hurt in his eyes, and I realized I wasn't the only one out on a ledge.

"Really," I said, softer. "I'm really okay. I promise."

This finally got him to smile. "We should have a chaperone."

I laughed. "Definitely. That would definitely be normal. 'Excuse me, but we're going into a gay guy's closet to scare him. Will you accompany us?'"

Things got better and we joked about Donnelly, who apparently came into Albie and Rafe's room this morning and told them a parable about a ship that arrived at a port late. It was pretty clear this was in reference to a complaint about a missing lab report from Albie's science teacher, but somewhere in the story, Donnelly got lost in his metaphors.

"The point is—the point is, you gotta ride a lot of boats, Albie," Donnelly said, and Albie assured him that he would, in fact, take a lot of boat rides.

"What are you up to tonight?" Rafe asked. "We're thinking about a little scanner pong." Scanner pong was this absurd game Albie and Toby had made up that involved listening to a police scanner Albie had in his room, and drinking when certain words were said.

"I can't," I said. I was going to see Hannah. "Another time."

"Uh-oh! Big date?" He said it like he was totally okay with it, but there was something so not okay about having this conversation that I couldn't look at him. I speared a loose piece of bell pepper with my fork. When I didn't answer right away, I heard him exhale.

"Sorry," I said. "I don't know what the right thing is. I don't want to lie."

He violently speared a piece of omelet on his plate, then stuffed it into his mouth. He chewed, slowly, not looking at me. When he finished chewing, he looked down at his plate. "We can't keep doing this to each other."

I was so glad we were alone at a table, and that no one was nearby. I lowered my voice. "You brought it up."

"Well, I shouldn't have."

"Yeah, probably not."

He shook his head. "I just don't think I can do it anymore," he said.

I couldn't look at him. "Wait. Are you breaking up with me as a friend? I really don't think—"

"Why can't you love me?" Rafe blurted.

The words settled on the table in front of us, little specks of something toxic, spoiled. I clenched my jaw so hard I was afraid my teeth would crumble.

"We've been over this," I said.

"I know. I just. I get that I brought it up, but. Please don't talk about Hannah in front of me. I know it's wrong, but you have to get that you're magenta and I really, really, really like magenta."

I blushed, and I felt my body heat up, remembering the dream I'd had. It was all off-limits. And that sucked.

"Use your words," Rafe said. "Seriously. You cannot not say something here."

"Eh," I said, struggling to get the words out. I took a deep breath. "I don't know what to say."

"Say anything. Please."

I closed my eyes. My heart was pulsing. Aware that I couldn't sit there not speaking forever, I finally forced myself to talk.

"Look. I'm magenta and you're actually—well, you're lavender, I guess." I lowered my voice. "And I *like* lavender."

Rafe's eyes widened slightly. My heart sped up.

"Lavender is kinda becoming my best friend again, to mix metaphors even further. So just, I don't know. I'm sorry. I won't mention Hannah. I get that it's messed up, so you will not hear that name again."

Rafe put his head down and picked up his fork and seemed like he was consciously trying to not react as he ate some of his omelet, but I could see in his face a glimmer that told me that I'd said the right thing.

21

Classes, baseball, Model Congress, and studying had been enough to keep me occupied most hours of the day, and now there was Hannah, and my renewed friendship with Rafe, and calls home to check in on Mom, who still seemed sad, and Luke, who rarely said anything of note but got pissed if I didn't call at least three times a week. Everybody wanted something from me, and some days it felt like I was being pulled in thirty different directions, and I wondered how anyone figured out how to be all things to all people without going insane.

The next Friday night, Hannah and I were at Bryce's favorite diner in Natick, sitting at a table in the back. Hannah had a pumpkin spice decaf latte, and I was working on a cup of green tea, thinking about how most of my teammates were probably knee-deep in beer right now at some shindig or other. Hannah was wearing her hair up and tied in a ponytail, and her skin looked particularly soft and lustrous. I couldn't look away, and I didn't want to say anything, but I was definitely thinking about spending a little time in Gretchen with her.

"There's a girl—person—at Lonna who is thinking about transitioning," Hannah said, sipping her latte. "Becoming a boy."

"Wow," I said.

She cocked her head. "I haven't quite figured you out in terms of, like, politics yet," she said.

"Huh? Why does that matter?"

She narrowed her eyes at me. "Um, it matters," she said. "I know you're a nice guy, and I know you're thoughtful, but are you, like, okay with people of various genders and such?"

I shrugged. "Well, I'm actually doing an argument in Model Congress about how religious freedoms are under attack by gay rights advocates."

Her mouth was a perfect O.

I waited a couple extra seconds, as long as I could, before I cracked up.

"I'm kidding," I said, smiling. "Well, not about the argument, but I was assigned that. I don't believe that kind of thing. Not at all."

She exaggeratedly wiped her shiny forehead with the back of her hand. "Phew," she said. "That was scary for a second."

"So if I were a — transphobe — that would be, like, a deal breaker?"

"It wouldn't be a good thing," she said.

"Well, I definitely believe that there are more things under the sun than we understand, and people are just people. Live and let live and all that."

"Phew," she said again, smiling.

I sipped my drink, which was getting a little cold, and something occurred to me. It was something she'd said to me, and it was the kind of thing that typically, if someone said it to me, I'd ignore. But this was Hannah. And more and more, I was learning to trust her. And more than that, she was melting me a bit on the inside. My throat always felt jittery when I was around her, because part of me couldn't believe a girl this beautiful would want anything to do with a huge goober like me.

So I took a huge leap.

"You remember when you said we should be the kind of friends who say things to each other?" I asked.

This got her attention, and she put down her latte. "Sure."

"So I don't know if what I'm going to tell you is a deal breaker. But. I will say I hope it isn't a deal breaker, because. I really like you, Hannah."

She smiled the sweetest, juiciest smile. Even without lipstick, her lips were so soft and red.

"I really like you too, Ben. Tell me things. What's up?"

"So, I've actually never told anyone this. It's something that happened last year, and it's quite a story and I won't bore you with the whole thing. But. So."

"Tell me," she said.

I gulped. "Last semester, I had this thing with my best friend at the time. He's gay and, well, I'm straight. But, like, I felt, you know, really close to him. We connected on such a deep level, and I just wanted to be with him, which was weird because—I can't believe I'm telling you this."

Nothing about her expression made me feel like she was about to judge me, and she nodded as if to say, *Go on.*

"It was weird because I'm definitely, definitely, like, NOT into boys, and not like one of those guys who lies to themselves and then dreams about Justin Bieber. He's a person, right?"

She laughed. "I think so."

"I mean not gay like actually not gay. Other than this one guy, I haven't ever thought of guys that way. And girls, I do—" I stopped, embarrassed at how forward I could be when I let myself. It was like she was bringing it out in me.

"You're hilarious," she said. "I love this *you tell me things* thing."

I averted my eyes, well aware that I was way past the point of no return by now. "So we were together once. Twice, I guess, if I'm being completely honest. And I am."

"Wow. Did you like it?"

I shrugged. I didn't think this was the time to lie, but it also probably wasn't the time to go nuts with the whole *I fooled around with a guy and I really liked it* angle either.

She took a sip of her drink and rolled her shoulders back, like she was worried about her posture. "I actually think it's awesome that you're open enough to explore that with a guy. So many guys, you know they think about it, but they act like the thought never crossed their minds."

"Could you with a girl?"

She seemed to ponder that, and she made a face. "Not with my best friend, but that's just because she had a boob job. I prefer my ladies au naturel."

I laughed. "Me too." How lucky was I? I had this hot, thoughtful girl who was into me. Who was beginning to actually know who I was, and she liked me anyway.

"Just so it's said and it's not hanging out there—"

"Yes. I've noticed you leave so many things unsaid."

She stuck her hands out toward me, and I took them in mine.

"Just so it's said, you doing that is, like, the opposite of a roadblock for me. I think it's awesome that you have that side of you. I sometimes think I could be pansexual, but I'm probably more pansexual in my brain than in reality, you know?"

I nodded.

"Where are things with the friend now?" she asked.

"We kind of went through a weird thing. Long story, but we're friends again. Friends with boundaries."

"Good," she said. "Because I'm a liberal gal, but I'm not sharing you with a boy."

We did go back to my car, and I started the engine but didn't leave the spot. I took her head in my hands and pulled her face toward me. The kiss was breathless and deep, and I could feel myself needing to feel her skin against my skin, and I must have made a noise without meaning to that expressed some of that, because then she made a noise too. I could see people walking by along the streets of downtown Natick, but I was drunk on this girl and I didn't care.

"I'm ready for more," she said.

I nodded and nodded. "Yeah," I said.

The back door to the theater at Lonna Grace had a broken lock, Hannah told me. I was afraid we'd get caught and I'd get in trouble for being there, but she said it was really her ass on the line. That didn't make me feel all that much less nervous, but just seeing her without a coat at the diner had lit something in my chest, and I had driven all the way to Lonna Grace in what felt like an epic haze.

We crept behind the theater in silence and anticipation. Hannah pushed the door open and there we were, backstage, black curtains draped everywhere and various wooden cutouts blocking my path in all directions. My heart pulsed like crazy. She turned on the lights, and the buzz of electricity was so loud that she immediately turned them off.

"If we have to hide, it's easier if it's dark," she whispered.

She took my hand and led me around the corner to the front of the stage. On it was a real live car from the fifties, bloodred with lightning strikes painted across the sides.

"*Grease*," she said, doing a cute arm dance with both her index fingers pointing outward. "Go greased lightning."

I chuckled. "Do girls have to play the boy parts?"

"I think our schools used to do shows together, like a couple decades back, but no more, so yeah," she said.

"You ever do a show?"

"My freshman year I was Dr. Gibbs in *Our Town*."

"Ah." I'd heard of the play but hadn't ever seen it.

"That's the main guy's dad. So yeah, I was very believable in that role. Typecasting, really, seeing as I had such a terrific role model of a father."

"Of course."

"Actually, George Gibbs, the main guy, is basically you. A baseball star whose goal is to go to college. Well, agriculture school."

I winced. "So he's really like the inverse of me, since I come from a farm, and have no interest in going back to one, ever."

"Right, I guess," she said, but I could tell she was distracted.

"What's up?" I said.

She sat down on the stage and I sat next to her. Her scent was like cold air and wintergreen Tic Tacs.

"Nothing. Just a little nervous."

"I know. Me too."

She ran her hand through her hair. "It's just, you know. There's always been a barrier between us, and now there's, like, no barrier."

"We don't have to do anything," I said.

She smiled. "You're literally perfect," she said.

"Yeah. Perfect," I said, thinking about my remedial calculus studying. "That's me."

"Why do you do that?"

"Do what?"

"That thing where you treat yourself like a piece of crap."

"It doesn't matter," I said.

"It does matter. Ben, you're one of the good ones. Do you know how different you are from Cliff?" Cliff was the *highly regrettable person* from Natick she'd dated before me.

I shrugged.

"How fast of a runner are you?"

"Non sequitur alert. Pretty fast."

"Good. Because if someone comes in here, I need you to jet. I can be in here, that's not a problem. You in here with me would be the end of my academic career, I think. And as much as rebelling against Daddy sounds like a good plan, being expelled would seriously suck."

"We don't have to do this," I said.

"I want to."

"Okay. I promise. The moment we hear something, I'm gone. Do you think that's gonna happen?"

"I don't know. Here's to hopefully not getting expelled for bringing my boyfriend into the theater," she said.

I felt heat throughout my body. She'd never used that word before.

"Hear, hear," I replied.

"And to us," she said. "I really like us. Is that weird to say? I just feel like we fit together, somehow."

"Yeah," I said, and the blood went to my face. This. This was happening. I took hold of her hand and traced her palm with my index finger. "So will you be my date to the Valentine's Day dance?"

146

The dance was one of two formals held during the year. The one in the fall was held at Lonna Grace, and this one was a week away, next Saturday night at Natick. I had mixed feelings about the dances, because I did love to dress up formally and see everyone in their suits and all the girls in pretty dresses, but I owned just one ratty suit, which I'd inherited from my dad in ninth grade. It was a little small for me now, and there wasn't much I could do about it.

"Mmm," she said. "Really?"

"What, you don't want to go?"

She took her hand back and put it in her lap.

"I don't want to broadcast our relationship," she said. "As soon as I do, you know what's going to happen? Rhonda and all her minions will figure out how to get your number, and they'll start texting you." Rhonda was the girl who had written, "Hannah munches rugs" on Hannah's door.

"I don't text," I reminded her, and she laughed a little.

"Well, then, we should be all set."

"Come on," I said. "It'll be fun. I want to slow dance with you."

She sighed and rolled her head back. "I must really like you, because I swore I'd never give them more ammunition. Fine."

"Good," I said. "Excellent."

She jumped up. "Come with me," she said.

I stood up too. "Where are we going?"

"Backstage. I think we're too exposed here."

That sounded pretty good to me.

Backstage, we took our jackets off and lay them down on the cold, black floor. She sat and then reclined on her jacket, and then she patted mine. I tentatively stretched out next to her. It felt so good, feeling the heat of her body next to mine. I sighed.

"This is nice," I said.

"Yeah?"

"Yeah."

She turned to face me, and she rested the side of her head on her hand. "Cliff broke up with me via text message."

"Oh, man," I said.

"Yeah. He did it after we had sex for the first time."

"That sucks."

"It wasn't great, no. I thought he was better than that. So, you know. I am trying to figure out if you're better than that."

I took her small hand in mine. "What do you think?"

"I think you are."

"That's the mystery of life. Not finding out that someone isn't all that great, but. You get to know someone and over time you figure out that they aren't exactly like the fantasy you've created in your mind about them."

"That's deep," she said.

"I like this part. I like both parts, I guess. I like the fantasy, and I can't wait to find out exactly who you are too."

Her eyes lit up, and this time I kissed her, and she put her hands on my chest, and I put my free arm around her and pulled her into me.

"I'm ready to go further," she said, and I moaned as my body reacted to her words.

"I don't have protection."

Her sweet expression, the way the skin around her eyes slightly creased when she smiled, was unforgettable to me. "I do," she said.

Driving back to school in my car, I laughed most of the way. Joy is such an amazing feeling, like you can't get enough oxygen in your head, or you just want more and more and more of the moment, and the car ride home, it could have taken forever because I was feeling so much joy traveling through my spent body.

Hannah. My girlfriend, Hannah. The first girlfriend I'd ever had who felt . . . right. I felt like I could talk to her, maybe not exactly like I could talk to Rafe or Bryce, but close. And I couldn't wait to talk to her on the phone the next day and share this laughter with her, because somehow I knew that at that very second she was laughing too.

After Wednesday's practice, Mendenhall caught up to me walking across the quad back to the dorms.

"You're doing good," he said. "Really."

I didn't reply.

"The only thing is this. Talk more, Carver. You eat meals with us, but you barely say anything. That's not captain-like. You don't have to be center of everything. You just need to—contribute, you know? I mean, you're never gonna be the funny one or the cool one. But you could be part of things. People like you."

"Thanks," I said as we got to the dorm. "I'll try."

Mendenhall charged upstairs ahead of me, and as I climbed the stairs, I thought about what he'd said. I'd never be the funny one? No, maybe I would never be the greatest joke teller, but I definitely loved to laugh. I just had different ideas than Mendenhall about what was funny. Bryce, for example. Albie and Toby. Those guys made me laugh. The mainstream stuff that made Mendenhall cackle was usually really crude. And mean. But Bryce's stuff could be mean too, just mean in a different way. Albie and Toby too. I'd have to figure that puzzle out someday.

I was just — quiet. I didn't feel the need to tell people every little thing about me. Like, I'm sure if Mendenhall had been in my shoes the previous Friday night, he'd have been bragging about what happened backstage in the Lonna Grace auditorium. I hadn't told anyone. That was just who I was, and I was fine with it.

After changing, I went to the library and raced through my other work, intent on saving the evening for calculus. I wrote an essay for history about Manifest Destiny. I wrote a dry page about Freud's theory of displacement for psychology, ignoring the niggling fact that displacement sounded like a bunch of bullshit to me. I did some chemistry homework and my English reading, and I was done in plenty of time to devote a night to math. Joy.

Then I thought about Model Congress, and remembered that we had to go through the historical folder of arguments and refute one. The school kept copies of every Model Congress argument since the program began in 1965. I had one week before it was due, but I decided to pick an argument to refute. I got the folder from the librarian and began to page through it, year by year.

When I got to 1967, I got shivers up and down my arms when I saw Peter Pappas's name listed on the roster.

I was going to find a Pappas argument, and I was going to refute it.

His first argument, typewritten on thin, yellowing paper, was in favor of passing the Equal Rights Amendment for women. I read through it, and he did a good job of using conditions of rebuttal and making an impassioned plea for gender equality. I couldn't imagine arguing against him there, since obviously I agreed.

His second one caught my attention.

It was a fervent diatribe against escalation in the Vietnam War.

Against.

Shivers.

In the argument, Pappas gave the data about how the number of American troops in Vietnam had escalated from 189,000 in 1965 to 385,000 in 1966, and how approximately seventeen Americans were dying there every day. Then he went into the root causes of the conflict, going all the way back to 1945, when the United States refused to do what it normally did and sympathize with revolutionaries against colonial powers—France, in this case. He argued that by backing France, and by paying heed to the idea of a domino theory by which we might lose control of Southeast Asia to communism, we started down an incorrect path.

He concluded with a humanitarian plea, writing that the human cost of this war was greater than the ideological need to fight communism. He used the example of a family in Boston that had already lost two sons, and ended by saying, "How many more families must lose their children over a struggle that has nothing to do with them? Defending democracy in our homeland would be one thing; defending it around the globe with the blood of our own soldiers is reprehensible and must be stopped."

I put the yellowing pages down gently. The irony. A man who had died in a war, arguing against that war. The Model Congress teacher must have pulled a Mr. Sacks and had students argue against their own beliefs. But Pappas had done it so much better than I could, and again I found myself wondering if I deserved this award. There was no way I'd be able to argue so passionately against my own beliefs about a topic such as war.

I chose a random argument from the 1980s about Reaganomics. I wasn't taking on Peter Pappas. No chance in the world.

I went to dinner and made sure to be part of the conversation. It was about the Red Sox, which I actually knew something about, so I said a few things about the team's prospects for the upcoming year, and Mendenhall smiled at me like he was a proud father, which was weird.

Back in my room after dinner, I couldn't stop thinking about Pappas. He clearly had it all figured out. Not only could he write amazing, impassioned arguments against his own beliefs, but he'd probably fit in with his teammates better than I ever would. I imagined him laughing with his buddies fifty years ago, at the same table we'd just sat at, and a chill went down my spine.

By the time I picked up my calculus book at around 7:30 P.M. and started to study, I was feeling pretty damned inferior. They gave this award to straight-A student-athletes who were popular. I was zero for two. And how would it feel if I had to tell my dad that they'd taken the award away from me when they figured out I wasn't good enough?

My brain got going pretty good on that subject, and as I stared at page after page of calculus equations, my stomach felt queasy. The numbers blurred together. I began to wonder why they chose dy and dx, and why you couldn't just get rid of the d's, since they should cancel themselves out, and then that felt like a moronic idea.

You're stupid. You'll never understand this. You've reached your math limit. They'll laugh at you when the award is taken away from you and given to someone more deserving.

I slammed my book shut and threw it at the wall above the other bed. It smacked the wall hard and fell onto the mattress, with the cover hyperextending open. I put my head in my hands. *Shit shit shit.* Then I stared out the window and tried to come up with a solution.

There was none.

I took a break and wandered down the hall until I heard some noise. It was coming from Steve and Zack's room, and it sounded like laughter. I paused before knocking. I wanted diversion, but was this the diversion I wanted? More laughter streamed out of the room. Screw it, why not? I knocked.

"Carver!" Steve whispered when he opened the door. "Get the hell in here. We're messing with Mendenhall."

Mendenhall's room was next door, so I automatically looked at the adjoining wall. Steve and Zack were hovering over a computer. "Uh-oh," I said. "What are you doing to him?"

Steve said, "We created an imaginary girlfriend for him. Her name is Brandi Lovelace. She goes to Lonna Dyke."

I tried to make sure my wince at the slur wasn't visible. "Brandi Lovelace sounds made up. How long have you been doing this?"

"Like three hours," Steve said, and I moved closer so I could see what they'd done. Some social media site was open, and the profile picture showed a pretty blond girl in a bikini. She looked a little bit like a female version of Standish, complete with a surfboard at her side.

"You guys are going to hell," I said, laughing. "Have they met yet?"

"Mendenhall is online, and we just chatted him. We had to make sure her profile was filled out completely, and we even got her some other friends so she doesn't look made up."

"I admire your stick-to-it-ive-ness."

"He answered!" Steve said, slithering into the seat in front of the computer. "He said, 'What up?'"

I watched the screen. Steve typed, **I'm good. Go to Lonna Grace. U Natick?**

Mendenhall typed back. **Yup.**

Brandi: Ur cute

Tommy: U2

Brandi: What r u doing

Tommy: Studying

Brandi: U

Brandi: R

Brandi: Crazy!

Tommy: lolz

Brandi: Wanna hangout sometime

Tommy: Hells yah

"'Hells yah'?" I asked. "Is that what the kids are saying these days?"
"Dude is a mess, yo," Zack said. "Ask him if he has condoms."

Brandi: U have protection

Tommy: Yup got it all taken care of. U know how to get here? I cn sneak u up

"No shit!" Zack said. "Boy has game."
"Gotta up the ante," Steve said, typing.

Brandi: Sure cutey can I cum now

"Hey now," Zack said. I laughed.

Tommy: U got it

"You just gonna stand him up?" I asked.
Steve shrugged. "I'll keep him on the hook all night if I gotta. Dude's gonna be tired and pissed tomorrow."

Brandi: Tell me where to go. Be there in 20.

Tommy: I'll text u directions

"Shit," Steve said. "He has all our numbers. Unless . . ." He looked at me. "Mendenhall have your number?"

I shook my head. "I don't use texting."

Steve scowled at me. "You don't text? What the fuck?"

I shrugged.

Zack jumped up. "I have an emergency phone," he said. "My dad thinks I need to have a backup."

I resisted rolling my eyes as Zack rummaged through some drawers. "I got an idea," I said. "I need some supplies, though."

This got Steve's attention. "What's the plan?" he asked.

I shook my head. "Do you trust me?"

"This better be good," Steve said.

"Better than keeping him up all night, I promise," I said, thinking about what Mendenhall had said to me earlier. *You're never gonna be the funny one.* Hmm.

So when Zack found the phone, and while Mendenhall exchanged numbers with Brandi, I got going. I collected three pillows—one each from me, Steve, and Zack—some duct tape, and some magic markers. While Mendenhall and Brandi went back and forth with their plan, which utilized the broken bathroom window on the first floor, I worked on my art project. I taped the pillows together, convinced Steve to part with a blue pillowcase, which I fashioned into a skirt, drew a face and blond hair on the top pillow, and then added boobs for good measure.

When Steve saw what I was creating, he cracked up.

"Okay," he said. "Not bad."

I didn't even have to explain what I was doing. When I finished a few minutes later, Brandi was a pretty primitive-looking topless girl in a blue skirt with an idiotic grin on her face. We stood and admired the spooky piece of art.

"You're twisted," Steve said to me, and I smiled, proud of my handiwork.

When we heard Mendenhall sneak down the hallway a few minutes later, we sprung into action. I carried our pillow girl to Mendenhall's room while Zack stood watch. His door was unlocked, thankfully. Once in his room, I tucked Brandi into Mendenhall's bed, and I got the hell out of there.

When we were safely re-assembled in Steve's room, Zack texted Mendenhall.

> **Brandi:** I came and you weren't there. I left. Sorry. Goodnight.
> **Tommy: I was there! Wtf?**

Brandi didn't answer. We sat quietly and waited. Finally we heard him walking back to his room down the hallway. We heard him open his door.

"What the fuck!" we heard him yell through the wall, and we collapsed onto the floor and writhed in silent hysterics.

> **Brandi: I WAS IN YOUR ROOM.**

"Who the fuck did this?" he yelled, and Zack jumped up and turned off the light and closed the computer. Steve jumped onto his bed and hid under the covers. Zack burrowed down under the comforter on his bed, and I hid under Steve's. We braced for Mendenhall's entrance.

The door cracked open. Light streamed into the room. Steve fake snored, and I held my breath. The light stayed for a few moments, and then, quietly, the door closed again. We all stayed very still as we heard Mendenhall walk farther down the hall, looking for the guilty party.

"Epic," Steve whispered. "Nice work, Carver."

"I aim to please," I whispered back, a huge smile on my face.

"Give me a tour of your room," Hannah said to me via Skype on Thursday night, two days before the dance. Part of me was already plotting a way to bring her up here, even though Headmaster Taylor had made it very clear that anyone found bringing a girl into the dorms would be suspended, no questions asked.

"We've Skyped, like, five times," I said.

"Yes, but I've never gotten the full tour."

I slowly spun the computer. "There's a door, there's a closet, there's a bed, there's a desk, there's another bed."

"You'd be, like, the worst real estate agent ever. More detail. I want to experience the place."

I sighed dramatically and brought the computer back to my face so she could see my look of mock annoyance. "Fine. There's my bed. It's a standard dorm mattress, probably made of whatever it is they make mattresses with, or whatever they made mattresses with in nineteen sixty-five. The bedding includes a red wool blanket, which my mother knitted for me. It's very warm and a little scratchy."

"Stuffed animals?" she asked.

"Seriously? You think I'm harboring stuffed animals in here? You haven't spent much time at an all-boys school, have you?"

"I didn't know you were so concerned about what the other boys thought of you."

"There's a difference between being concerned about what others think of you, and having a flock of plush teddy bears," I said.

She giggled. "Fair enough. Do you want to see my stuffed animals?"

"I would like nothing better in the entire world."

She moved her computer to face her bed. I hadn't taken her for a girl who would have a flowery comforter and three stuffed animals perched on it, but there they were: a pink bear, a light blue elephant, and a yellow bird of some sort.

"This is Teddy," she said, in a cute voice I hadn't heard her use before.

"No. You haven't named your teddy bear Teddy."

She focused the camera on her face and turned down her lower lip. "I know you're not making fun of Teddy."

"No. Far be it from me to do something like that," I said. "I love Teddy."

"Good. Teddy loves you too, though Ellie is not yet sold on you."

"And Ellie is, I am guessing, the elephant?"

"I got her when I was six from my dad. I was crying because I wanted a stuffed animal, and he promised to go get me one, and instead of going to Walmart or Target or something normal like that, he went to Pottery Barn. I'm serious. He got me this extremely scratchy brown giraffe that wasn't soft or cuddly at all. I started screaming, apparently, and my mom went out to Walmart at like ten at night and got me Ellie. She and I have been inseparable ever since."

"That's really sweet," I said. "How do I get on Ellie's good side?"

"You'll have to meet her," she said.

I felt my face heating up. "Tell Ellie I'm excited to make her acquaintance."

We were quiet for a while, just staring into each other's eyes on the computer screen. I finally shook my head.

"What?" she asked.

"I can't wait to dance with you," I said. "I can't wait."

"You're the only boy in the world who could convince me to go to a formal at Natick. I hope you know that!"

I blew her a kiss. "I'll make it worth your while," I said.

An hour later, Rafe and I were studying in my room. I was working on calculus with a side of SAT words, because that was coming up too. I had just taken a math test and had no idea how I'd done, even after I'd re-studied the entire textbook two nights earlier. There was another test coming up the next week, and I figured with another all-nighter the night before, I'd be in reasonably good shape. I could do this. I was also still thinking about "meeting Ellie," as it were.

"Well, you're in a good mood," Rafe said, watching me, and I smiled and put my book away.

"I am, I am," I said. "You too, huh?"

He gave me this shit-eating grin, and I gave him one back, and I started to laugh.

"Okay, are we gonna talk about the obvious elephant in the room?" he asked.

I immediately thought of Ellie, and then remembered Rafe had no idea who Ellie was. I closed my textbook and put it down on the bed next to me. "And what elephant, pray tell, would that be?"

"You know how I said I couldn't handle it if you were hanging out with Hannah and I didn't want to hear about it? I think I'm changing my mind. Because, I mean, look at you! You're all happy and everything."

I couldn't avoid smiling. "Guilty."

"It's Hannah, isn't it?"

"I don't know."

He stared at me, and under the weight of his scrutiny, I rolled my eyes. He smiled in a way that I wasn't sure was happy or not. "I kinda thought so."

"Is that okay to say?"

He flopped down on the bed. "You know what? Sure. If you and I can't — you know — be like that. Sure. I mean, Jeff isn't you, and he'll never be you, and he's shallow and he's afraid of his own gay shadow and all that. But we have fun. And I guess you're — having fun too?"

I nodded and nodded and nodded and nodded, and Rafe broke out in giggles. "It's funny because it's awkward," he said.

"I know. I'm sorry. Can we just get past the awkward?"

He came over and sat next to me, and I froze up a little. He put his hand on my shoulder, and then he put his chin on his other hand. "I'll always love you, Ben. Magenta. But, yeah. I can deal. I'll be, like, the best man at your wedding."

I couldn't quite look at him with his face so close. "And I'll officiate your wedding. You and Jeff. Yay."

"Oh, please. No wedding is forthcoming, I promise. We do *not* talk well."

I kept staring straight ahead, my heart pulsing, and Rafe seemed to get the message and stood up, stretching. Then he lunged back toward the other bed and grabbed his Norton Anthology. "Yay, *Beowulf*! It's great that the teachers here are finding work that really resonates with the youth of today."

"Truly," I said. "Truly."

"I'm proud of you," Ms. Dyson said as I gathered up my books after calculus class the next day. "You obviously took what I said to heart. Look what you can do when you put your mind to it!"

"It was only an eighty-six," I said.

She put her hands on her hips. "Did you study hard?"

"I studied all night."

"Well, then. Looks like you're a B student in calculus. There are worse things to be. I'm really proud of you. You're putting in the effort and you're getting good results."

I'm a B student?

I wasn't used to working that hard and getting a B. Was that acceptable? I wondered what my dad would say if I told him. Would he tell me to study harder? Was that possible? I was juggling so many things, and I wasn't sure what else I could do. At least a B was good enough for me to keep the award and scholarship. That was worth something, I guess.

"I'm very proud of you," she repeated.

"Yes, ma'am," I said.

She laughed. "Ben Carver, you're the only student in all of Natick who calls me ma'am. It's partially insulting, and partially wonderful."

I shrugged and laughed a little. "I guess I was raised to call people ma'am and sir," I said.

"Well, you're a throwback. You work hard, you're polite, you're an athlete and a scholar. No wonder they gave you the award. You really deserve it, Ben."

"Thanks, ma'am," I said. But I was thinking about limits. In basic calculus, we learned to find the limit of a particular function. I'd never thought that it had meaning out in the real world. Had I found my own limit? And what if your limit is unacceptable to you?

In baseball practice later on Friday, I took aside some of the freshmen while Coach Donnelly was doing base-running drills. I wanted to try something I'd never seen a captain do before, but I'd always thought would have been good when I was a younger player.

"So I wanted to give you a chance to ask questions," I said to the group. "When I was in my first year playing, nobody told us anything, and I think we were supposed to just stay quiet and not worry about the things we didn't know. I hated that. Anything I can do to make you feel more confident out there, I want to do. Any questions?"

The guys looked at one another, almost like they thought this was a trap. I couldn't blame them. Just a month ago, they were being asked to crawl around a cold and wet locker room floor. This was . . . different.

"Um," said Peterson. "When do we find out what team we made?"

I laughed. "Sorry. I'm laughing because I remember having the same question and wondering why no one let us know the answer. Coach Donnelly usually creates the freshman and JV rosters right after spring break."

Peterson nodded, relieved that I hadn't barked at him for asking a question, I guess.

"What if we want to try out for a position that he didn't put us at?" Clement asked.

"Let me know," I said. "Coach is pretty rigid once he puts you somewhere, but if you really want to switch things up, maybe I can put in a word."

This kid Martin raised his hand meekly. "Any chance a freshman can make varsity?"

"It's happened, but it's really rare. I made it sophomore year, but not freshman."

They all were just standing there, so I said, "Anything else?"

They shook their heads no, so I motioned for everyone to go back to base-running drills.

"Thanks," Clement said to me, quietly, as we broke up. "That helped."

"Don't worry about it," I said, feeling warm inside. "Not a problem."

24

I showed up at the dance five minutes early, in case Hannah got there early too. The gym was nearly empty still, so I lingered at the door for as long as I could before it felt even more awkward to be standing there than to be inside. So I wandered over to the punch bowl and ladled myself a glass. It was pure colored sugar water, not even fruit flavored.

"Carver! Wassup?" Steve yelled over to me as the baseball guys arrived in a pack. They skulked to the back, which was generally how things went at parties. The guys talked a big game with girls, but at parties and dances they'd start out shy and aloof, and then, at some point, someone would break the ice and they'd act like it hadn't been awkward ten minutes earlier.

"Hey," I said, tossing my punch and walking over to them. I high-fived a few guys. Everyone was wearing a jacket and tie, and the girls were beginning to arrive in dresses. I felt kind of embarrassed about my suit, though Rafe had helped me out by lending me a sharp black-and-white tie.

"I didn't think you'd be coming," Mendenhall said, looking at my suit jacket like you might look at a pile of horse manure. I still couldn't quite look him in the eye after the pillow incident.

"Never one to miss a part—" I paused, because I'd been about to say "partay," the irony of which only Rafe would get, since it was an inside joke. "Party," I said.

The guys from the team milled around, establishing their dominance by putting each other in headlocks. It was obvious they were showboating for the girls on the other side of the auditorium, and the girls pretended they were oblivious to this fact.

I felt a hand tap me on my back. I turned and it was Rafe.

"Yo, what up, Blood?" he said, and I stifled a laugh. He was parodying the way my teammates talked to one another.

"Hey," I said. Under his dapper black jacket, he had eschewed a shirt and tie and was instead wearing a form-fitting turquoise T-shirt that I'd never seen before. I knew Rafe wasn't exactly a fashion magnate, so I figured this was his friend Claire Olivia's work, via FaceTime, probably.

"Well, this is exciting," I said, referring to the dance.

"Yup." Behind him, Jeff approached us. His wavy blond hair was just perfect, like a Ken doll's.

"Hey," I said, making sure to sound friendly. I stuck out my hand. We knew each other only tangentially.

"Hey," he said, and I could swear he lowered his voice. I looked at Rafe, wondering what he'd told Jeff about me, if anything.

Rafe clapped his hands together as if to break the awkwardness of the moment. "Well," he said. "As soon as those girls get wind of who the gay guys are, my dance card is gonna be filled for a million years."

I had no idea what that meant, but I laughed anyway.

"Girls love to dance with gay guys," Rafe said, translating.

"Ah."

Jeff shook his head like he was embarrassed, and he walked away. Rafe looked at me and shrugged. I shrugged back.

"Is the famous Hannah here yet?" he asked.

"The famous Hannah is not here yet, no." I worried that maybe she'd changed her mind.

Toby and Albie appeared. Toby was wearing a powder-blue jacket with a sequined rose brooch. His pink hair was spiked taller and slicker than usual, and again he was wearing eyeliner. Albie was wearing a black T-shirt under a black blazer. He looked like a bouncer at a comics convention.

"And then there are gay guys who girls don't particularly want to dance with," Rafe said, hugging Toby.

Toby made a big show of checking out Rafe. "Is that a roll of quarters in your pocket, or are you just happy to see me?"

I looked around, hoping no one was hearing this.

"Neither," Rafe said, deadpan.

Toby said, "Ha" really loud, and then made a big show of pretending to see someone across the room, waving ecstatically and then walking away. Albie skulked after him.

"Anyway, gonna see what's up with Jeff," Rafe said, and I told him I'd catch him later and watched him walk away.

As I scanned the crowd for Hannah, Mendenhall approached me.

"What's up with you and the gay kids?" he said.

"Two gay kids and one straight kid," I corrected him. "Rafe is my best friend."

"He doesn't hit on you?"

"Nah. I'm not his type," I said.

"What is?"

I looked at Mendenhall and took a calculated risk.

"Sort of the antithesis of you," I said. "Handsome. Smart."

"Cool. I give you a lot of shit, but I think it's cool you're so open-minded. Junior year there was this gay college football player—"

"I was here," I interrupted. "I was a sophomore."

"Right. Well, that was—different. I mean, he definitely wasn't like a stereotypical fag or something." My eyes got big, but Mendenhall was oblivious. "I guess nowadays all kinds of dudes are that way. I mean, I wouldn't. But whatever, I mean."

"Sure."

"Anyways, I think it's cool, but I probably wouldn't be friends with a kid like that."

"Sure," I said. "You have a reputation to uphold with the ladies."

"Check that," he said. "You grew up on a farm, right?"

I nodded. "Uh-huh."

He shook his head. "Lucky."

"Why?"

He shook his head harder and laughed. His gaze was distant. "You have no idea. The pressure. My dad expects me to follow in his footsteps. I don't give a shit about finance. If I could, I'd just work on cars. Not good enough for my dad."

"That's rough," I said, and I meant it. Maybe our families were from different worlds, but our dads certainly had some things in common. Mine thought I was interested in a lot of foolishness too.

Mendenhall nodded and nodded, and I glanced around again for Hannah, and thankfully, there she was.

"Excuse me," I said, and I hurried over to her.

She was wearing a pale green, low-cut dress that showed off her beautiful legs. Her hair was done up in a bun, and I couldn't stop smiling.

"Well, you're a sight for sore eyes," I said.

"Sorry. Took me a second to get up the courage to come in," she said.

"Really?"

She was acting weird, standing really still. "Are they looking at us?"

I glanced around. A couple tall, skinny girls were, in fact, sizing me up.

"I don't know. Does it matter?"

She sighed. "It shouldn't, I know. I just get nervous, is all."

"You look so beautiful," I said. I took her hand in mine, and I leaned in and kissed her.

That seemed to do the trick. Hannah smiled and looked at the ground, only a little flustered. Her face was red.

"Come on," I said. "You haven't lived until you've had a sip of red-colored sugar water, and you really haven't lived until you've seen me dance." I pantomimed a little arm dance to the beat of the music.

"Look who's coming out of his shell!" she said.

"What can I say? I'm happy."

"Me too," she said.

We danced to a bunch of songs I didn't know, and Hannah was about as bad at dancing as I was, from the looks of it. She kept her feet in the same place and just sort of bopped and swayed. It was adorable, and I didn't give a shit if people thought we were the world's worst dancing couple.

Hannah excused herself to go to the bathroom, and of course Steve and Zack ran up to me as soon as she was gone.

"Carver!" they said. "Score!"

"She's nice," I said.

"Yeah? You been hanging out? How come you didn't tell us?"

I shrugged. "I'm a private person."

"I get that, dude. Good stuff. She's kinda hot," Steve said.

They walked off, and then one of the blond girls who had been sizing me up walked over.

"You're dating Hannah Stroud?"

"Yup." I didn't look at her.

"You can do better."

"I doubt it," I said, and the girl shook her vapid head and walked away.

Hannah came back from the bathroom and I resisted the urge to tell her about her blond friend, who may or may not have been Rhonda Peterson. I pulled her to me just as a slow song began.

"C'mon," I said, and she tentatively walked out to the dance floor with me.

I put my arms around her and held her close. We rocked side to side to the music.

"I don't know any of the steps, so this will have to suffice," I said.

She put her cheek on my chest. "It so much more than suffices," she said.

As we danced, I knew everyone was watching us, and I felt an odd sense of — pride? I had spent my life afraid to do the wrong thing, and suddenly, these past few days, that part of me was disappearing, and I was feeling confident.

Out of the corner of my eye, I saw Rafe sitting in the bleachers, alone. His posture was bad, and I knew what had happened. My heart sunk a bit.

"Shit," I said.

171

"What?"

"My buddy Rafe. I think his boyfriend just dumped him."

I resisted the urge to spin so that she could see him. Rafe and Hannah meeting was something I'd thought about leading up to the dance, but I wasn't sure how that would go, and moreover, I wasn't sure I wanted them to meet yet.

"That sucks," she said. The slow song ended, replaced by something a little peppier.

I pulled back. "Would you mind terribly . . . ?"

"Oh," she said, and she looked down at the floor for a moment. Then she looked back up at me and smiled, crossing her arms over her chest. "Not at all. You want me to come too? I'm good at cheering people up."

"I think I'd better—"

"Sure," she said. "He's your best friend. I wouldn't mind going back to school early."

"You don't have to—"

"No. I made an appearance here. That's good enough."

"You sure? If you want, I could try to find a place—"

She smiled more. "It's okay, Ben. Do what you have to do. I'm okay, really. A little bit of a formal dance goes a long way with me."

"Me too." I pulled her close and kissed her softly on the lips. "Sleep tight," I said. "You got a ride home?"

She nodded. "Sleep tight," she said.

When she left, I walked over to Rafe. He looked more deflated than I'd ever seen him look before.

"Hey," I said, sitting down next to him.

"Hey." His voice lacked its usual color.

"What happened?"

"I told him to fuck off. He wasn't willing to dance with me. Shit. I'm not hanging out with a guy who's afraid to be seen with me. Fuck that."

I put my arm around him. "I'm sorry," I said.

"Yeah, well."

"No, really."

"Thanks. She's really pretty, by the way."

"Thanks. She's heading back to Lonna. You wanna get out of here? Go for a drive?"

. "You'd do that for me?"

I laughed. "No. I wanna stay and hang with my new buddy Tommy Mendenhall. Let's go."

We didn't change into anything more casual. Instead, we just got into Gretchen and went. The sky was vivid and bright for a winter's night, with stars so crisp I felt like I could taste them.

"You didn't have to do this," Rafe said. "You could've hung with your girlfriend."

"It's fine," I said. "She understood."

"She understood you choosing a friend over her? At a dance?"

"She understood me choosing to comfort my best friend, yes."

I turned right onto the street that leads to I-90 from school.

"Where are we going?"

"No idea," I said.

We were quiet for a bit, and I put on a little music. Jazz. It fit with the night, somehow—soft and gentle and easy.

"I just feel like, why do I keep on dating not the right guy?"

I shrugged and slowed down to let a Chevy merge into my lane.

"I mean, I don't mean you. Well, I guess I sort of do. I mean, I met Jeff and I knew what kind of guy he was, and that probably meant that on some level I knew, up front, that he wasn't *the one*. So why would I waste my time?"

"Maybe you're experimenting?"

"I don't know. Are you experimenting?"

I tensed up. "I don't know. Maybe," I said. If Hannah was more than an experiment, Rafe didn't need to hear that right now.

"Huh," he said, and we were quiet some more.

"What do you like about her?" he asked.

"She's beautiful, and she's nice to talk to, and she's—it's hard to explain. She's a little messed up but in a good way, like she's maybe too self-aware, almost?"

"Interesting. How is it different? Being with a girl as compared to a guy?"

I took a deep breath and kept my eyes on the road. "Girls are softer."

"And you like that?"

"Yeah."

And that ended that conversation. I saw a sign for I-90 East, and I pulled onto the highway. We listened to the music, and Rafe tapped his hands on his legs to the beat. As we passed the sign for West Newton, he cranked down his window. The wind whipped through the car, chilling the air and drowning out the music.

I tried to look over at him to say something, but the wind blasted me in the eyes and I had to turn back forward.

"You want me to close it?" he yelled.

I smiled. "Nah. I like it."

We let the wind run through our hair and freeze our foreheads and ears. I couldn't help but laugh, because it felt awesome. Freeing. I opened my window too, and we stared forward as we allowed the wind to beat us into submission.

We let it ice us for a good fifteen minutes, and soon I could feel it in my molars. I glanced over at Rafe and saw his teeth chattering, so

I rolled up my side. He closed his. We looked at each other as I turned up the heat and the jazz hit our ears again.

"You ever feel like just saying, 'Fuck it'?"

I laughed. "Basically every day of my life."

"Really? I think of you as so comfortable and reserved."

I thought about that for a good minute.

"Is that really what you think?" I said.

Now it was his turn to sit quietly. It was like I could hear his brain working.

"Yes. No. I don't know. I guess I think you're one of those people who wants everyone to think everything is fine with him all the time, and I genuinely don't know half the time if you're freaking out or totally cool."

I went around a slow-moving SUV. No one had ever said that to me before. That maybe I wasn't completely okay. I felt horrified, exposed, like he'd seen something I'd been trying to hide all my life. It was out there for people to see. I pictured my father's stern face, and I remembered the time with the pineapple.

I was five. It was one of the summer family reunions before Uncle Max came back from China, and we were at Grandpa Mirek's, outside in the backyard. All the relatives I saw once a year had told me how much I'd grown, and I was standing there by the buffet table in silence. Dad had told me to mind my behavior, not to do anything that would embarrass him. Luke was still a baby, so Mom was carrying him around.

There was pineapple carved on a platter. I'd never seen pineapple before. It looked exotic, with the scaly exterior of the top of one on display, the sharp, green leaves pointing at me. I took a piece and tasted it. The juiciness shocked me. It was like a festival of flavors in my mouth, and I remember smiling wide, and I remember my great-aunt Sylvia smiling back at me from across the buffet table. I took another chunk. Then another. It was so good. It was the best, most special thing I'd ever tasted.

I may have eaten most of it. I don't remember. I guess I probably did.

Dad saw me finishing off the tray, and he grabbed my left arm and pulled me across the lawn and inside the house. "I told you not to embarrass me. Why do you always have to embarrass me?"

He bumped me on the side of the head with his palm.

After, I went and sat in the backyard on the grass and pulled up sunflowers.

I felt Rafe's eyes on me. Maybe a minute had passed, and I hadn't said anything.

"Bleep. Bloop. Bloop," he said, pantomiming pressing buttons in front of him.

"What the hell is that?"

"I'm turning back time to before we got all awkward because I said too much."

I grinned. "Bleep. Bloop. Bloop," I said back, pretending to press the same buttons.

We enjoyed some more quiet as this Ella Fitzgerald song came on that I especially liked. Rafe pulled out his phone.

"Do you know I'm seventeen, and I have never, ever felt the wind through my hair like we did earlier?" I said. "And it's not like anyone is stopping me. I just have never done that."

"I love that feeling," Rafe said.

I looked over at him and smiled.

"Take Exit 18. Toward Cambridge," he said, playing with his phone.

"Where are we going?"

He didn't answer. "We're jointly saying, 'Fuck it.' Me to Jeff, and you to the world."

I smiled again. "Okay."

He used his phone to navigate us north and then east, and soon it was like I could smell the beach air, even though the car windows were rolled up and the heat was on.

We parked in an abandoned parking lot. The sign read, REVERE BEACH.

"The British are coming," I said.

I could feel Rafe smirk as I turned the car off. "I thought this would appeal to your history-geek side."

The brittle night air greeted us as we stepped out of the car. It was probably about thirty-five, not so cold for a February evening. I could see my breath, but it dissipated quickly. In my suit and tie, the air permeated my bones right away. Rafe, in his suit jacket and T-shirt, looked positively frigid.

Rafe took off running toward the sand. I ran after him. The sand was hard, nearly frozen. There were no lights illuminating the beach, but the bright moon sat over the water, giving us just enough light that we could see the small waves lapping toward seaweed and smooth sand.

He came to a halt about ten feet from the waves.

"Low tide," I said, my teeth chattering.

Rafe curved his hands around his mouth, looked up at the night sky, and howled. The howl then turned into a scream. It juggled my insides a bit, nestling into my chest cavity.

"What was that for?" I asked, once he was done.

"My mom believes in shouting out emotions."

"Of course she does," I said, smiling. Rafe's mom had shocking red hair she wore in a ponytail, and she wore overalls.

"You should try it."

"No, thanks."

"Come on! You know you want to."

"You know what? I kind of do."

"Fuck it. Fuck it. Fuck it," he chanted softly.

"Aaaahhh!" I said, just a bit louder than my speaking voice.

"Oh my God, that was pathetic," he said, and he showed me how a howl/scream is done again. "Let it go, Ben Carver. Let it all go."

I looked down at the sand. I wasn't used to all this. Emoting. And yet, his scream was still nestled in my chest cavity, and it felt a lot like fuel and energy, like something that I was supposed to use in a way. So I clasped my hands around my mouth, arched my back skyward, and let it go.

The howl felt like it could go on forever. It was filled with ice and fire, mixed together, and frustration, and giddiness, and hopelessness, and all sorts of stuff we don't talk about in my family. I howled and howled and howled, and when I was done, I turned toward a radiant Rafe, who was looking at me like a proud dad, kind of, and I couldn't take that sort of response, so I said the first word that came to my mind.

"Tackle," I said.

His eyes got big. "You've heard about Tacklers Anonymous?"

I nodded and deadpanned, "It's the next big thing, don't you know?"

He backed up a few steps, and then he turned around and sprinted, his suit jacket flailing in the wind behind him, the back of his turquoise shirt helping me see him as he booked it away from me. I charged after him, every part of my body feeling alive and engaged. He was fast, no doubt about it, but so was I, and soon I was gaining on him, and then—fuck it, fuck it, fuck it—I leapt at him from behind.

My weight pushed him forward, and we thudded together on the hard sand. My heart was pulsing wildly. He turned his head, stunned at the hard tackle, shocked, like me, that I'd done it. He pushed back, struggling to get free, but there was no way against my weight, so I let him get up.

His eyes were flashing like crazy. He reached down and pushed me into the sand.

"Jerk," he yelled.

I grabbed on to his arm, and I pulled him down again and rolled on top of him.

"You're the jerk."

He struggled free, and then he rolled on top of me, and he cracked up laughing, so I did too. And we rolled like that a bit, our breathing loud, grunting like animals on Animal Planet. Finally, I was on top of him and our eyes met.

"Victory!" I yelled as I jumped up. I felt like a different person.

Rafe got up too. He swatted sand off himself, and I did the same.

There was so much to say. There was so little to say. We caught our breath together.

"How cold do you think it is in the water?" he finally asked.

"Like maybe just above freezing?"

"Would we die if we just took everything off and walked in?"

I looked at him. I threw my jacket off. The wind pierced my shirt like it wasn't even there, freezing my arms and chest and especially nipples.

He did the same, and then crossed his arms over his scrawny chest.

We burst out laughing.

"Bad idea?" I asked.

"Way bad." He reached down, grabbed his jacket, shook it off, and said, "Brr."

I nodded. He took off for the car, so in one movement I grabbed my ratty jacket and slung it over my shoulder as we ran back to the car as fast as we could.

We were quiet as we drove back. For me, I was playing back the tackle and the wrestling on the sand. There was something sexual there, obviously. But I had a girlfriend, and maybe friends did that, I don't know. I knew that I was glad to have a friend whom I could tackle, and get maybe a bit rough with because it was the right thing in the moment.

"I didn't mean the jerk thing," Rafe said. "I'm sorry I said that. Heat of the moment."

"Yeah, you did," I said, surprising myself.

"Maybe. Maybe a little. I'm not used to rough play."

"Me neither. I didn't hurt you, did I?"

"No. You just shocked me, is all."

"Good. I shocked me too."

He laughed, so I did too, and I turned up the tunes, and we zoned out on jazz for a bit.

"Did you know goldfish have five-second memories?" Rafe asked as I turned onto the highway back to campus.

"Nice segue. No, I did not know that," I said. "How could they ascertain that?"

"I don't know. Research?"

"But what kind of research? It would be pretty hard to ask goldfish what they can and can't recall, wouldn't it?"

The highway was surprisingly empty for a Saturday night. Then I realized: It might not even be Saturday night anymore. I'd totally lost track of the time.

Rafe said, "Maybe they set up a maze for the goldfish, and they let them go through it, and they found that after five seconds they keep bumping into the walls?"

"Maybe," I said. "What would that be like, to have a five-second memory?"

Rafe laughed. "Hey, it's food! Chomp chomp chomp chomp chomp. Oh, hey! It's food!"

I said, "My name is Goldie, what's your name? Hi, Thomas, nice to meet you. . . . My name is Goldie, what's your name?"

"Stupid goldfish. They don't remember anything," Rafe said.

I told him about the fact that I was being asked to argue against gay marriage. He told me his mom had called Mr. Sacks a fascist when they'd met on Parents' Weekend last fall. That cracked me up. I could imagine her saying it.

I got off at the Natick exit and asked Rafe the time. He told me it was 12:15. Past curfew.

"Oops," I said.

"Oops. You think we'll get in trouble?"

"Donnelly loves me, so probably not," I said.

"Everyone loves you," he said.

"Yeah." I rolled my eyes.

We parked and let the car go quiet for a bit.

I smiled in the silence. Despite all the bad stuff that had happened between us, we'd gotten through it. It was, at the moment, crystal clear. Maybe I loved Hannah, but in a way I loved Rafe even more. It was agape. Higher love. There was just something about him that set me free. Made me light. Got me weightless.

Even if once in a while I had a dream that I probably ought to keep to myself.

As I opened the car door and stepped back into the chilly night, I was thinking that maybe the key to life is to have goldfish memories. So you can't remember the time a friend hurt you. So you can give second and third and even fourth chances. To yourself too. Because sometimes it takes multiple chances to get things fully right, to put your universe in order.

The next night, I called Hannah.

"What's up?" I asked when she picked up.

"Not much."

"Did the girls give you shit about me?"

"I don't know. Some."

"Are you okay?"

"I don't know."

"What's going on?"

She sighed but didn't say anything.

"Wait. Are you upset with me?" My brain was spinning with possibilities. Did she decide overnight that she didn't like me anymore? Had I done something wrong?

"I don't know, Ben. I don't know."

"You don't know if you're upset with me?" What had I done—oh. Shit. "Is this about comforting Rafe?"

She didn't say anything.

"But you said it was okay."

She sighed, deeper this time. "I know what I said. But I guess I don't feel like I should have to tell you what's normal behavior.

It's not normal to invite your girlfriend to a dance, convince her to come, and then, halfway through, send her home so you can tend to your male friend with whom you once had sex."

"Whoa," I said.

"Yeah. Not my favorite evening of all time."

"You should have told me! I would have stayed with you."

"Well, obviously you wanted to be with Rafe. Or else you would have stayed with me. And I don't want to have to convince you to stay with me. I already told you about my dad. I don't need any more disappearing guys in my life, okay?"

"Shit," I said. "I didn't even . . . God, I'm sorry."

She didn't say anything.

"I'm really, really sorry, Hannah. I get what you're saying."

"Well, thanks, I guess. If you decide you actually want to spend time with me, like more than you want to spend it with your best friend, let me know, okay?"

And then she hung up on me.

I lay down in my bed and curled into a ball under the sheets. I had hours of studying I should do, including a lab report that sat unfinished on my laptop that was due tomorrow. But all I could do was replay the conversation I'd just had.

I'd chosen Rafe over my girlfriend. I mean, but. He needed me. What kind of best friend would I have been to ignore him when he was upset?

But of course he would have understood. How could I have been so stupid?

I sat up. I didn't have time for this. I rubbed my eyes and shook my head, trying to jiggle the bad thoughts out of my mind. I closed my eyes tight.

This is stupid. I don't need to go here. I didn't choose Rafe over Hannah. I chose a friend in need over a friend who I thought knew how I felt about her, since we'd just slow danced in front of everyone.

And of course I wouldn't pick a boy over a girl I really liked, because choosing a boy over a girl, even just a friend who is a boy, carried with it all sorts of icky feelings I'd come to know last semester. Then I would be considered, well, I don't know what. Gay? Bi? Which I wasn't. And if I was, that meant I was something my dad thought was bad. Unlovable.

Had I actually chosen Rafe over Hannah? What if there was a desert island, and I was only allowed one companion? I'd choose Hannah, right?

I mean, it was hard to say at the moment, as she'd just yelled at me. But in general, you picked the girl who you could have hot desert-island sex with over the boy with whom you'd discuss goldfish and their memories, especially if she was someone you genuinely liked talking to and being with, which I did. Hannah and I wanted the same things. We were truly compatible.

And Rafe was just a friend. But he was also my best friend, maybe ever. Last night in the car, I felt so at ease. How many times in my life had I felt like that? But both of them made me feel like that. And now I had to choose between them?

No, I didn't have to choose. I mean, people were allowed girlfriends and best friends. Maybe I just had to prioritize better.

I went to my desk and opened my science notebook. I'd focus on my work, let Hannah blow off some steam, and the next time we talked I'd make sure I let her know that she was the girl for me.

Mr. Sacks rounded out the applause for Jimmy Ross, who had just made a compelling argument in favor of wind energy.

"Let's hear from Mr. Carver, who is—let's see—arguing that religious folks are facing persecution because of gay rights advances. Okay!"

It was Tuesday afternoon, and for the first time I wished I was in baseball practice and not Model Congress. I stood up and ambled to the front of the room, my index cards in hand. As much as I liked the research part of Model Congress, I always felt pretty stupid standing at the front of the classroom, pretending to be a congressman. It just felt so . . . artificial.

Not to mention that I was arguing something I didn't believe. But while practicing the night before, I reminded myself that Peter Pappas himself had done this, and done it really well. He'd argued passionately against the Vietnam War, and then, less than a year later, he'd voluntarily enlisted to go there. I cleared my throat and rested my hands on the podium in front of me.

"Rosalie Sanchez is out of a job. She used to be a florist in Nashville,

Tennessee, but then gay marriage became the law of the land. And despite her strong, lifelong religious beliefs, she was told that she couldn't deny service to anyone, including a gay couple that wanted to get married.

"Imagine. You're a person who believes with all your heart that something is wrong. The book you live your life by tells you that it's wrong. And then a gay couple walks into your store, arm in arm, and asks you to provide flowers for their special day.

"To you, their special day takes something you consider sacred — God's law — and spits on it.

"So anyway, these people who live in a way you consider sinful ask you to be part of their special day. This goes against everything you believe in.

"Your conscience, your gut, tells you that you must say no. After all, it doesn't make sense that you should be compelled to take part in an event that goes against your beliefs and way of life. In the same way that a person who doesn't believe in witchcraft should not be forced to participate in a Wiccan ceremony, you should not have to be involved.

"But when you refuse, you are sued. And the law of the land comes into play, and you are told to provide the flowers, or lose your business.

"This could happen. This is wrong.

"Now, some people might say that these religious beliefs are mean-spirited and discriminate against gay people. That may be true, but we have freedom of religion in this country. It is granted by the First Amendment. Freedom of religion means that people retain, as James Madison wrote, 'equal title to the free exercise of Religion according to the dictates of conscience.' It doesn't mean people get special rights, but it does mean a religious person has the right to follow their beliefs, and not be compelled to behave in ways that go against their religion.

"So we have two groups, and both claim certain rights by law. When two laws contradict each other, which should we listen to? The one granted in the Constitution, or the one that was just granted a few years ago by a deeply split Supreme Court?

"I believe that it is a grave injustice that Rosalie Sanchez is out of a job. She should be given a religious exemption that allows her to honor her strongly held religious beliefs, whether or not those beliefs are deemed politically 'correct.' She should be allowed to politely decline to provide flowers for a gay wedding.

"Thank you."

The class clapped. So did Mr. Sacks.

"Good job, Ben Carver. Excellent. Notice Ben's use of conditions of rebuttal. Anyone?"

This kid Peter raised his hand. "He anticipated an opposing argument and neutralized it."

"Exactly," Mr. Sacks said. "He might have given us one more, but one is acceptable."

I reddened. I hadn't thought of adding additional conditions of rebuttal. Next time I'd have to do that.

Mr. Sacks said. "I happen to agree with your argument, Ben. Is there anyone here who disagrees?"

No one raised their hand at first, and I felt my throat tighten. I disagreed. Should I say something? It was my job to argue something, not be true to my own beliefs. Finally, Mitchell Pomerantz raised his hand.

"I've always disagreed with the whole religious freedoms thing. But

I have to admit that was pretty solid. Not sure how to argue against it," he said.

Mr. Sacks nodded. "To me, the argument against religious freedoms is a perfect example of political correctness. Why not allow the free market to dictate these things? If a person wishes not to provide flowers for a gay ceremony, they should be allowed to decline. And then people who find that action wrong should have the choice to take their business elsewhere."

A conversation ensued about the pros and cons of allowing the free market to settle all things. I wanted to ask: What about when the same argument—religious freedoms—was used against those entering into mixed-race marriages? I'd done my research, and people had argued that. Was that okay to everyone? Would it have been okay to send away a black person who wanted flowers for their marriage to a white person?

But I kept quiet. My opinion didn't matter. Showing my ability to advance any side of an argument was the main goal here. Not being right for the sake of being right.

Maybe I really was an appropriate recipient of the Pappas Award. Maybe I had some flaws, some limitations, but like him, I could make a compelling argument against my own beliefs. That had to count for something.

In my call home, my dad brought up grades for the first time since our talk over winter break.

"How's the schoolwork?" he asked.

"Good," I said.

"How good is good?"

"Pretty darn good," I said. It was true; a B on a calculus test was good. I just wasn't sure he would understand that.

"Attaboy," he said, and reflexively I felt warmth from his praise. Even though I knew he didn't really know what he was praising. When I hung up the phone, a heaviness descended upon my shoulders.

I thought about calling Hannah. I owed her a call, as I hadn't called in the forty-eight hours since our fight. But what would I say? She might give me an ultimatum about hanging out with Rafe, and I definitely wasn't giving that up. I scrolled through my phone for her name and stared at it. And then I put the phone down.

Wednesday was a warm day, and after fifth period I decided to take a walk in the woods to clear my head. On the way across the quad, I ran into Steve.

"A, baby, A," he said, holding out what appeared to be a test of some sort.

"Good job," I said. I was having trouble figuring out if Steve and I were real friends now. I definitely liked him more than I liked some of the others.

"Got this thanks to Mendenhall. I don't give two shits about chemistry and I never will. Nice to be able to skate through and never pick up a book."

And then there were limits to our burgeoning friendship. Here I was, working my ass off, and this rich kid was cheating, and he'd never be caught. But I wasn't going to say that.

"Cool," I said.

The wooded area just to the north of the quad used to be where kids lit up, got high, whatever. I didn't think it was like that anymore, but who knows.

I took the trail along Dug Pond, just inside the tree line. There's something about being under foliage that really changes a walk for me, makes it more solitary, lets me bask in my thoughts a little bit more. I put my gloved hands in my pockets.

"Hey, stranger, want a doobie?"

I turned toward the voice, and there, sitting on a flat rock, was Toby.

"Hey," I said.

"Hey." He didn't seem like the typical happy-go-lucky Toby I was used to seeing.

I walked over, frozen leaves crunching under my feet. "What's up?" I asked.

"Eh," he said. "I'm being a little Debbie Downer today."

"You wanna talk about it?"

He sighed. "Yes, but I'm pretty sure as soon as I tell you what's up, you're gonna go running."

"I won't run," I said.

"That's funny, because that's pretty much your thing, sounds like."

"Ouch," I said. "I guess I deserved that."

"Not really," he said. "I'm just kind of having a day."

I motioned for him to scoot over, and he cleared a place on the rock for me. I sat down. The rock felt icy and hard under my butt.

"So if I tell you something, will you promise to, like, not tell anyone? If you tell, I could possibly be kicked out of school, so."

"I promise," I said. "I consider you a friend, Toby."

He half smiled. "Thanks. I'm kind of—figuring shit out right now."

"Okay."

He took a deep breath. "I'm—I think I'm—I'm gender fluid."

He looked away, and I looked down at the ground. "Okay," I said.

We sat in silence for a bit.

"You don't actually know what that is, do you?" he asked.

I shook my head. "I mean, I guess I have an idea. Does that mean you like to dress up like a girl?"

"Um. No, not really. I mean, yes, there are times that appeals to me, but it's more like, some days I feel more like a guy, and other days I feel more like a girl. Inside, I mean."

"Okay," I said. "What do you mean, feel like a girl? Like, feminine?"

He shook his head. "No, not exactly. Like, female. Like if a teacher calls me 'Mr. Rylander,' I think they're talking about someone else, because I'm definitely not a mister. And then there are other days when I'm fine with it, because it feels like I am male."

I put my hand on Toby's shoulder. "That's got to be really hard."

He laughed and shook his head. "You have no idea. And my stepdad is really not going to get this one. He was, like, so confused that a boy who likes to shoot guns sometimes could be gay, and now it'll be even worse because —"

"Do you have to tell him?"

Toby looked at me. "Well, yeah. I mean, he's important to me."

"What about your mom?"

"She'll be totally cool, as usual."

"Why do you feel like you need to tell him, if you know it will just upset him?"

Toby jumped down from the rock and paced in front of it, kicking leaves up.

"You ever hear of left-handed paths?" he asked.

I shook my head no. This was the first serious conversation I'd ever had with Toby.

"Okay, you see, most people in the world take paths that are expected. They go to school, get a job, get married, have kids. Then there are the rest of us. We're on left-handed paths. It's not what's expected. The world would like it better if we didn't take these paths, because the world doesn't know what to do with people who buck the system, or explore things that are new. I'm on a left-handed path. So is Rafe. Albie too, even, because I'm pretty sure he's asexual, and that's definitely left-handed. You, I'm not so sure about. You had the thing with Rafe, but having a girlfriend and, like, being baseball captain of the universe is pretty right-handed."

"Huh," I said.

"Anyway, my whole thing is, whatever path I'm on, I'm on. I'm not going to avoid it because it's harder for the world, or even harder for me. I'm, like, I gotta be me, you know?"

I couldn't answer. Looking at Toby, I realized he was everything I wasn't. If you were to ask one hundred Natick students to pick the brave one between me and Toby, they'd all probably pick me. But they were wrong. Toby. He was the brave one.

"I—get that," I said.

"I just, honestly? I'm scared. Like, I'm not sure I'm fully ready to do it, but what if I dressed female one day? Would they allow me to stay here? I really, truly don't know. And I like it here, you know?"

"Wow," I said.

"Do you think—never mind."

"What?"

"Do you think Albie will think it's weird?"

I turned to him, surprised. He knew Albie way better than I did. But here Toby was, looking all vulnerable. So I guess he really needed me to answer.

"No," I said. "I really think he'll be cool with it. He's your best friend. He loves you for you."

Toby smiled. "Thanks. I needed to hear that."

"No problem," I said.

Walking back to the dorm, I felt like I had one too many things in my brain now. Cataloging them, I got confused:

Hannah
Rafe
Pappas speech
Toby
Baseball
Calculus
Dad/Mom/Luke
Rafe

Wait. Did I list him already? My brain was tired.

I set up at my desk for an evening of studying. I started by trying to work on the introduction to my Pappas speech. I'd tried it twice before, but nothing good had come of it.

Students, faculty, and friends of the Natick School.

Friends of a school? What the hell did that mean? How was I supposed to make it feel formal without sounding completely weird?

Thank you. I am honored to be here.

Duh. This was hopeless.

Then I glanced at my computer and thought, *I should Skype Hannah.* And then I thought, *Oh, right. She's pissed. If I call, it's gonna be a real conversation.*

The Hannah situation weighed heavy on my mind. I knew I had to call her and let her know I was still interested. Because I definitely was. Maybe I loved Rafe more, in a way, but in the way of a girlfriend, Hannah was *it.*

Yet the craziest thought came to me as I sat there, staring at my computer. My jumbled mind was playing my conversation with Toby back, and I thought: *What if my left-handed path isn't just choosing my best friend over my girlfriend? What if the true path for me is choosing my best friend as a boyfriend?*

I laughed. Because I'd been down that road before. And it hadn't ended well. And if I thought about it even just a little, being with Rafe didn't exactly get me all the things I wanted. How would that work as baseball captain? If the other guys found out? Would Dad go nuts if he found out and take me out of school? Probably not, but that would definitely be a possibility.

I went over to my bed, realizing I was way too tired to study. I needed a night off. And a night off wasn't going to help me stay on top of my calculus, but sometimes the whole *We're Carver men. We work. We work hard* thing gets old.

I fell asleep thinking about Hannah and Rafe and Rafe and Hannah, imagining them both on separate private islands, beckoning. Hannah, naked, her maple syrup skin calling out to mine. Rafe, my home, in a way. I smiled. Being with Rafe was easy. And not like drinking alcohol was easy. I thought about the alcohol simile again, and a new thought came to me: Alcohol impaired my judgment. I became someone else when I drank. With Rafe, my judgment became more mine; I became more authentically me.

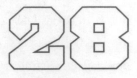

I spent that Friday afternoon at the Bacon Free, speeding through my homework. Rafe had mentioned going to Walden Pond on Sunday with Toby and Albie if the weather was nice, and I wanted to have one day without the pressure to excel pounding at my gut.

I still hadn't called Hannah. I didn't know what to say. It was like I was two different people. One wanted to be with Hannah all the time. The other was petrified she'd bring up Rafe and ask about my feelings about him. I wasn't going to lie to her. I'd been lied to in a relationship of sorts, and it hadn't felt good. Better to just give things time to play out so I knew exactly how I felt before I called her.

I did a lab report for chemistry. After I finished, I got an idea. I descended from the cozy loft and got on a computer to search the library website for "Pappas, Peter."

Up came two articles from the *Boston Globe*. The first was an obituary. I pulled it up, and it was a re-hashing of what the *Natick Newsman* had in its write-up. The second was more of a surprise. The headline was, "Students Turn Out for Massive Anti-War Demonstration." I figured Peter Pappas would probably be quoted as a counterargument. Like, these students were against the war, but here's one local student who isn't.

That wasn't the case.

Peter Pappas, a strapping 16-year-old from Dorchester who attends the prestigious Natick School, chained himself to a fence post in front of the State House.

"The current administration has blood on its hands," Pappas said. "We are allied with a corrupt regime, blindly battling an enemy based solely on ideology. The powers that be are too old to fight, so it's my generation that will die, and for what?"

A tingle crawled up my spine. This was more like the Peter Pappas from Model Congress. How could this be the same Peter Pappas who went to fight in the very war he was lambasting here?

I scanned the article more, and I saw that his sister's name was Lolita.

What was the real story of the guy for whom this award was named? How could an anti-war guy wind up fighting in that war? And how many Lolita Pappases could there be in the greater Boston area?

I typed her name in Google. A Facebook page came up for a gray-haired woman with high cheekbones and a scarf around her head. It mentioned Dorchester as her hometown. I checked whitepages.com and found her phone number. I scribbled it down and hurried out of the library.

Back in my dorm room, I called the number.

"Hello?" a woman's voice said.

"Is this Lolita Pappas?"

"Who wants to know?"

"My name is Ben Carver. I'm this year's recipient of the Peter Pappas Award at the Natick School."

"Eh," she said. "Whattaya want?"

"Sorry," I said. "I didn't mean to bother you. I'm confused about something I read, and I wondered if you could help me out."

"It's a long time ago. Not sure what I could tell you. That award still happenin'?"

She pronounced "sure" as *show-ah* and "award" as *awahd*, and her Boston accent put me at ease a little. I was used to the way people talked at home, though my dad especially worked hard not to speak in New Hampshire vernacular, because he thought it sounded common and he didn't want people to think he was poor. When I came to Natick, I expected everyone would talk like, *Pahk yaw cah in Hahvahd Yahd*. Turns out it's a class thing. Rich kids generally don't speak that way.

"The award is not a family thing?"

"The award is some big foundation. Our father was involved before he passed. Bunch of corporate chuckleheads from Boston, nothin' to do with us."

"Oh," I said.

"So whattaya want me to tell ya?"

"I was researching your brother for my speech, and I read this old article in the *Boston Globe*. It was about an anti-war demonstration, and it said you guys both went. I thought, *Wait. Peter enlisted. How could it be that a year before he was all anti-war?*"

The other end of the line was quiet.

"Ms. Pappas?"

"I'm here," she said, pronouncing it *he-ah*. "Just thinkin'."

"Sure," I said.

I gave her a minute. As I sat there on the line, I thought about what she might be about to tell me. I couldn't quite imagine. Did something happen to change Peter's mind? It would have had to be really important to make him go from protesting the war to sacrificing his life for it.

"How do you feel about war? What did you say your name was?"

"Ben. And I'm generally anti-war. Why?"

She exhaled. "I just don't have the time to waste with chuckleheads. The war people. Took too much from me, and nowadays I'm too tired to argue with someone who thinks we had any business in Vietnam."

I didn't really have a strong opinion on Vietnam. I knew more about World War I and II, and they were more clear-cut to me. But I agreed with Peter's argument against the war in his Model Congress speech, and I didn't think the United States needed to intervene every time a country decided to go in another direction.

"No. Definitely not a warmonger here. When I read the article in the *Natick Newsman* about your brother, um, I guess I couldn't really fathom why someone would give their own life for a concept."

She laughed a little. "Good kid," she said. "Stay that way. You wanna know the truth?"

"Yeah, of course."

"You sure? Because, this award? It ain't right, to my way of thinkin'. I think my brother would go nuts if he knew about how he's been remembered these last forty years."

"I'm sure. I want to understand who he is."

"You got a car?"

"Yes."

"Can you get to Dorchester?" *Dawchestah.*

"Sure."

"You want to take me out for coffee? There's the Flat Black over on

Washington. I know traffic is the shits on a Friday afternoon. Could ya come tomorrow?"

"I can, but," I said. I wasn't sure how to explain that I had a debit card for gas, and otherwise had seventy-two dollars to last me until June. What the hell. This would be worth it. "Sure. What time?"

We made a plan to meet in the early afternoon, and I hung up with my mind racing. The last thing I needed was more stuff on my brain, but sometimes it was hard to resist.

Dorchester was a forty-minute drive from Natick, just south of Boston. I'd never been there, but I wrote down the directions and kept them on the seat next to me. I almost asked Rafe if he wanted to come along and make a day of it, but in the end I decided to take the trip alone.

My phone rang while I was heading east on the 93. I glanced down. It was Hannah. My heart pulsed.

I picked up and put it on speaker. "Hey," I said, almost like an apology.

"Are you dead? What the hell, Ben?"

I laughed, uneasy. "No, not dead. Just insanely busy. Right now I'm driving to Dorchester to—"

"I don't give a fuck," she said. "I am just, like, incensed with you. We were doing great and then you act like an asshole at the dance and I give you an easy task—just tell me that I matter more to you than your boyfriend or whatever he is. And what do you do? Absolutely nothing!"

"I'm sorry," I said. "Really."

"Well, yes, that makes sense, for starters. What the fuck is taking you so long?"

I was quiet for a few seconds. "It's complicated."

"You're gay. You're bi. Is that what I'm hearing here?"

"No. I'm. I'm — I just don't want to lie to you. You asked me a really important question when we last talked. You asked if I wanted to spend time with you more than I do with Rafe. I want to make sure. I know how I feel about you. What I don't know is how I feel about — him. Okay?"

She took a deep breath. "No. Not okay. I mean, I get what you're saying, but no. Not okay. The way I feel right now is definitely not okay."

"I'm so sorry," I said. "I promise I'll call you within a few days. I absolutely promise. I'm a man of my word."

"Knock yourself out. I'll be waiting restlessly by the phone, obviously," she said, deadpan, and then she hung up.

Shit. I'm so stupid. Of course I should have called. Just said anything. Even if it wasn't entirely, totally true, just said something to reassure her, because she's amazing, and I really like her, and she could be, like, a great girlfriend. Stupid, stupid, stupid.

I parked at the coffee shop and carefully navigated the black ice on the sidewalk. Inside, the stench of burnt coffee invaded my nostrils.

I saw Lolita right away. She looked exactly like her photo on Facebook. She didn't smile at me, exactly, but she waved me over to her table in the back. She had a purple folder in front of her.

"Hey," I said.

"Price of admission is a large regular," she said. *Lahge regulah.*

I nodded and went to the front to get it for her. A few minutes later, I returned with her drink and a cup of water for me, and I sat down across from her.

She laughed. "You don't like coffee?"

"It's okay," I said. In fact, I loved coffee. I was hoping to use birthday money to get a coffeemaker for my room next year. But I only had enough cash for one cup.

Her eyes got wide. "Oh, shit," she said. "I figured . . ."

"What?"

"You're a scholarship kid, ain't ya?"

I looked down at my outfit. Was I that obvious? I was wearing Dad's hand-me-down jacket, and I realized that of course, in the world of Natick, the way I dressed was pretty much a dead giveaway about my family's lack of money. I said nothing.

"Where ya from, Ben? You a Southie too? Don't sound Southie."

I shook my head. "New Hampshire."

She smiled. "Up north! Shit, look at me, stereotyping boarding school kids. We grew up in Dorchester. Our father worked in a flour mill. Ever since Petey went to that school, I've been a little pissed. Of course, it didn't help when he died and a bunch of fat cats named an award after him that made him sound like some war hawk." *Wah hock.* "I get so mad. Still." She held her hands out at me, fingers wide.

I gave her a smile. "I definitely get it."

She stood up. "What kind of coffee?"

"It's okay—"

"What kind," she repeated.

"Just regular."

"Milk? Sugar?"

"Milk," I said. "Thanks."

She came back to the table with my coffee, and we got along a lot better after that. Like Hannah, Lolita was a bit of a firecracker, saying whatever crossed her mind. And like Hannah, she seemed to immediately accept that I didn't speak quite as openly as she did. She cracked a few jokes about "the establishment," which I laughed at even though I only thought they were a little funny, and then she told me her brother's story.

"Petey and me, we grew up here. Dad worked at the factory, Mom was at home. This is not—how do I even say—an intellectual place. But Petey." She shook her head. "Man oh man. What a brain on that kid. I like to think I'm pretty smart, but jeez. He was reading Tolstoy in sixth grade. I remember when JFK was shot. Petey must've been in eighth grade, because I was in tenth. He created this huge project about the president's unknown accomplishments. We all thought it was a school project, but it wasn't. He just did it and brought it in to show his teacher.

"That's when Dad figured out he was special, I guess. Applied to Natick and got a nice scholarship, so that's where he went for high school. Petey was just so excited because of all the stuff he could learn at a fancy private school."

I shook my head. It was uncanny, the similarities. I'd never done extra-credit projects at school back in Alton, but I'd go to the library back home and be the only kid there. The only person under fifty, usually.

"Why you shakin' your head?"

I smiled. "His story is a lot like mine. I mean, I don't think I'm as special, probably. But the same—trajectory."

Now it was her turn to smile. "'Trajectory,' eh? Yeah. You sound kind of similar." *Similah.*

"Going to Natick was interesting, because it changed my brother. Or maybe it was more like, away from Dad, he wasn't so afraid of his smarts. He spread his wings some. Growing up, I could always count on being the rebel, and Petey toeing the line for Dad. And suddenly around ninth grade, Petey had all these political ideas. Liberal ones. They weren't in line with Dad's way of thinking, that's for sure. Petey told me stuff, because we were always close. And suddenly Petey was anti-war, and I was just glad to have an ally.

"But he wouldn't say nothin' around Dad. Never could do it. And we started to go to rallies. He'd drive back east from Natick, and I'd meet him in Boston. After I graduated high school, so maybe that was eleventh grade for him. When Dad saw that anti-war demonstration article in the *Globe*, he flipped. Threatened to pull Petey from Natick. He said it was brainwashing him."

"Wow," I said.

She nodded. "Petey was torn. Dad was his idol, and suddenly Dad is talking down to Petey, treating him like he always treated me, I guess. Everything I ever did was wrong. And boy, was Dad good at spreading that around. Man. I'd hear him on the phone with Petey, and see them at Sunday dinners, and Dad really let him have it. The brave kids were going and fighting for our country's freedom while a bunch of un-American hippies like who Petey had become sat on their asses and whined. Education was for sissies. And Petey . . . It just broke him. I remember getting a call from him at Natick. My brother, in tears. Saying he couldn't do it anymore. I don't know if he ever knew what *it* was, but I did. Out of the spotlight of Dad's admiration, he felt like he was nothing. I always wondered why Dad's approval mattered to him so much. Three months later, he shipped out. Skipped his senior year to do it. I was so wicked pissed at him. Felt like he'd abandoned me. And then, of course, he was gone." She wiped her forehead, and instinctively I did the same.

206

"And Petey, the idealist, the anti-war demonstrator, my brother, he disappeared. Like he never existed outside of being a so-called war hero.

"I'm amazed you're the first one to have seen the article. Don't you boys do your research?"

"I guess not," I said.

"Well, good for you for doing it. It turns my stomach that Petey is honored by some foundation as something he most certainly wasn't. Before he let our father's disapproval change him, he would have been so pissed to think that one day he'd be thought of as a symbol of that stupid war. He was so much more than that, Ben. So much more. He loved Russian literature. The Red Sox. Carl Yastrzemski. He could throw a ball from the wall in right field to home plate on a line. He sang like an angel and he loved the Beatles. None of that mattered after he was gone. Just that he was a war hero, whatever that means."

"Wow," I said. "Thank you. Thanks for telling me."

She pushed the purple folder over to me. "This is for you."

I opened it. Inside were several photocopied, handwritten letters. I flipped through. They were all dated from the late 1960s.

"Read these," she said. "It's more complicated than they make it seem."

"How?" I asked, looking up at her.

"Read," she said, smiling. "I can tell you're a good kid, Ben. I trust you with my brother's story. You do what you think should be done, okay?"

"Thanks," I said. "Really. Thanks."

Back in my dorm room, I started reading Pappas's letters randomly, choosing one from the middle of the small pile.

December 25, 1967

Hi Lo,

A merry merry to you, Sis!

Christmas in Vietnam is oddly festive. The guys put up a tree outside our barracks. It's called a "thingan," and it's not quite an evergreen but it will have to do. The guys hung empty beer cans from the branches, and last night we did a white elephant gift exchange. I got Ring Dings, which was perfect, as you well know.

I have one buddy here, Clete, from South Carolina. He's the only one who understands me when I talk books. Everyone else just says, "Pappas is getting heavy again" and walks away.

You always got me. You never walked away. Even when suddenly we were at different sides politically. Thank you for that.

We got to watch LBJ's speech, and you know what? When he says the entire free world is at stake here in Southeast Asia, it makes me feel like I'm doing something, you know? I know. You're still dead set against it. You'll come around soon.

Did you watch the speech with Dad? Did he say anything about me?

I'm picking up some language from the locals. "Chào" means "hi"; I say it every time I go to the store now. I've also learned "Tôi mong quý hòa bình," which means "I wish you peace," and "Tôi có thể giúp thực hiện bất cứ điều gì cho bạn?" That means "Can I help carry anything for you?" Chivalry is not dead.

I love you.

Bye,
Your Petey

January 21, 1968

Hi Lo,

Thanks for the books. Just getting a package at all reminded me that there's a world back there, and I kind of need that reminder right now. Good choices. I started with The Sun Also Rises. I like the crisp prose; I'd always intended to read it, but you know me and my summer reading pile. The book transports me to Paris, and it's almost jarring when I look away and find myself in our hooches. You ever smell week-old coleslaw? I can't get any closer than that to describing the peculiar stench.

There's a lot of waiting in war. When there's contact with the enemy, it tends to be violent and sudden and then over *before you can really register what is happening. I have not fired my weapon yet. I hope I never do.*

Please don't ever tell Dad this, but these last few months I'm all over the place on this damn war. You look into these people's eyes — the Vietnamese peasants — and you see the fear. I do think the Vietcong are evil, and perhaps we will succeed and push them back, but at what cost? Until you see a frantic mom carrying a bloodied infant with half its leg hanging off, it's hard to really explain why I may never actually fire my weapon. Maybe it was enemy mortar fire; perhaps it was one of us who did it. Who knows? We are just doing our jobs, and if our job can result in that atrocity, it makes no sense.

Dad would scoff at me if he knew that I'm petrified to pull the trigger. He'd call me a sissy. And maybe I am a sissy, because it just doesn't seem right to me. I think maybe I'm broken. How else does a guy go from war protester to soldier to whatever the hell I am becoming now?

Are you still angry at me for volunteering? Some days I am.

I don't care what you think about God. I don't give a crap what I think of Him. Pray for me, Lo. Pray for all of us.

Love,
Your Petey

March 6, 1968

Lo,

Clete is dead. He was sleeping in the bed next to me. We were sound asleep. All I heard was a jarring explosion like it was

inside my eardrum, and I swear to you I looked to my right
and the bottom half of Clete was all that remained.
It happened so damn fast I still can't believe it.
You don't really cry here. It's like you make these connections
that are closer than intimate, and then your friend is gone and
you just — suck it up. Be a man.
I am not cut out for this. I know Dad will never forgive
me, but if I could walk out of here tomorrow and not be
captured and tortured, I absolutely would. It's not human.
It's not right.
If I ever get out of here, I'll go down to North Charleston
and visit with Clete's mother. She sounded like a real nice lady.

> *Love forever and always,*
> *Your Peter*

I looked for the next letter. There was none. I shuffled through to the beginning ones I'd missed. All from 1967.

I'd just read Peter Pappas's final words to his sister, and my heart plummeted into my stomach.

Peter. Who would have been a friend and an ally, had we lived at the same time. Who liked Hemingway and deep conversations and Ring Dings.

Who was no war hero. Not because he was *a sissy*, but because he objected to it. Who died for his dad's love and approval.

How the hell was I going to accept an award that was a lie about the person after whom it was named?

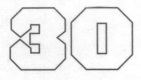

"They call this Pakistani spring," Toby said as we got out of Albie's car at Walden Pond. The parking area was mostly empty despite the warmish temperatures, as it was the last Sunday in February.

"What the hell are you talking about? It's a pond, not a spring, you idiot," Albie said.

"No, the weather. When it gets warm like this before it's actually spring, the racist powers that be decided to name it Pakistani spring. Like Indian summer, sort of."

"You have so many issues," Albie said.

"You have no idea," Toby said, glancing over at me.

The sun was out and yet the sky was still a wintery gray hue, as if the atmosphere itself was trying to decide whether it was spring yet. Toby was celebrating the premature fifty-degree day by wearing a yellow tank top. He twirled, arms in the air, as we stood in the empty parking lot. I hadn't been here since we took a field trip freshman year. All I remembered was the guys sneaking away to smoke a joint while Bryce and I sat by the lake and tried to write a poem about nature, which was the exercise Mrs. Crowley gave us. The poems the lake inspired that day were memorable only for their awfulness, if I recall correctly.

"They named this place after the poet, right?" Rafe said.

"I think so," said Toby.

"It's called Walden Pond," I said.

"Right. Walden."

"The poet's name was actually Henry David Thoreau," I said. "He wrote a book called *Walden*, based on living simply in nature, here at Walden Pond."

No one said anything for a while, and I felt my teeth clench. I hate being that guy, but people being wrong about American literature is like nails on a chalkboard to me.

"Are you sure?" Rafe said. "I swear there was a poet named Walden."

"Not that I know of," I said.

"Huh," he said.

"Let's go to the phones," Toby said, grabbing his phone out of his pocket like a gun from a holster. He typed feverishly as we walked. "Walden . . . Yep. Henry David Thoreau. Ben for the win. . . . Ooh. Not a handsome chap, this Henry David. Transcendentalist — that means he transcends," he explained, looking up at us. "Naturalist — that means nudist."

I laughed. "Yes. Thoreau, the famous author, was a transcendent nudist. Good job, Toby."

"I would NOT want to be at that nude beach," he said, shaking his head and putting away his phone.

We stopped to check out a wooden sign staked in front of a ramped footpath toward the pond. It read,

THESE PARKING AREAS ARE PAVED WITH
POROUS PAVEMENT
PAVEMENT THAT LEAKS
SINCE 1977, IT HAS RAISED THE LOCAL
WATER TABLE WHILE REDUCING EROSION,
POLLUTION, AND THE NEED FOR STORM
DRAINS OR ROAD SALT.
A BROCHURE IS AVAILABLE.
A DEMONSTRATION PROJECT BY
MASS. DEP & MASS. DEM.

"Man, even the signs here are poems," Albie said.

I burst out laughing. "A really bad poem. Especially the end."

"'Pollution, and the need for storm.' I may write a poem with that title," Toby said.

"Write it. Now," Albie demanded.

As we approached the sand, Toby put his arms out in front of him, as if he were a great orator. "'Pollution, and the Need for Storm,' by Toby Rylander. Hmm . . . One sec, gotta take this." He picked up his phone. "What? Oh, sure. Of course. Thank you. God bless." He put his phone down. "My agent just called. She said she didn't think it was the right time for me to undertake a project like this."

We stood at the foot of the water, which tentatively lapped toward our feet like it wasn't sure of its own power. The gurgling sound of the tiny ripples made me feel truly calm, and I imagined being here in the nineteenth century, alone, like Henry David Thoreau, noted author and nudist. I glanced to my left and right at my friends. Rafe, who was probably thinking about something else, per usual. Ditto Toby. Albie, who wasn't much for literature unless it was written by someone with a fondness for postapocalyptic dystopia. But they were here with me, and I could be me with them. And that was a lot.

"So peaceful," I said.

"Yup," said Rafe.

"C'mon," Albie said, pulling at Toby. "Let's give the boys a moment sans Toby."

"No fair," Toby said. "I want a moment sans Toby too."

"Tell me about it," Albie said, and he started walking down the beach.

"Wait up," Toby said, not moving.

Toby looked at me, and in a millisecond I realized what was about to happen.

"Albie, Rafe?" he said.

Both boys nodded.

"What if I told you I was gender fluid?"

Neither Albie nor Rafe said anything for a moment. Then Albie said, "I guess I'd wonder what's new with that? I mean, you've always been a little bit that way, right?"

Toby nodded, and then shook his head. "No, yes, I don't know. It's kinda new. It's like, I've been thinking recently more and more about it. The fact that some days I think I'm like, female. And other days, male. And then sometimes, both or neither, I guess."

Rafe smiled, walked over to Toby, and gave him a big hug. "I know about that stuff," he said. "My mom was asking me leading questions about my gender orientation all last summer. I was like, 'I'll, um, let you know, 'kay?'"

Toby kissed Rafe on the cheek. "Thanks."

"What's your preferred pronoun?" Rafe asked.

Toby looked over at Albie. "I'm okay with he or she, depending on how I feel. Or they, I guess. Although 'they' makes me feel like I'm more than one person."

"And one Toby is plenty," Albie said.

Toby cracked up. "Right?" He and Albie looked at each other. "We okay?" Toby asked.

"Of course," Albie said. "I don't give a crap what gender you are. You're Toby until I hear otherwise. Are you, like, going to transition?"

Toby shook his head fast. "I don't feel certain enough about anything to, you know, do that kind of thing. I'm just me, and me is confusing."

Rafe looked over at me. "You okay with all this, Ben?"

Relishing the spotlight for once, I went over and picked Toby up. He whooped and clasped his legs around my waist. "Toby's my buddy," I said.

"I thought you'd be confused," Rafe said, studying me.

"Actually, I already knew. So put that in your pipe and smoke it."

Rafe actually looked a little impressed, glancing over at Toby, who confirmed this fact with a nod. "'Put that in your pipe and smoke it,'" Rafe repeated. "Jesus. What century are you from?"

"Nineteenth," I said.

"C'mon," Albie said to Toby. "Let's take that walk." They tromped off down the beach.

"That was interesting," Rafe said.

"I love how Toby is just—Toby," I said. "I admire that."

"Yup," Rafe said.

We stood there for a while, and my thoughts drifted back to the letters I'd read yesterday. I turned my head to him. "So what if I told you that Peter Pappas wasn't necessarily a fan of the Vietnam War?" I asked.

He picked up a pebble and chucked into the water, creating a ring of small waves. "I'd tell you that Peter Pappas is dead and has been for many, many years, and his opinions are not so important to me."

I reached down and grabbed a smooth, round pebble. "Well, they matter to me, a little," I said, throwing my pebble high and deep. "I have to write a speech about the guy, and yesterday I met with his sister and she gave me these letters he sent from Vietnam."

"That's intense," Rafe said.

"Yeah, a little. And he's totally not who the school makes him out to be. He was basically just a kid who wanted to make his father proud, and he went to fight a war he didn't believe in, and then he died."

"Well, if you want my opinion, which, why wouldn't you, I'd say give the people what they want. Who the hell cares as long as they're happy, and you get your scholarship? Is it your job to set the record straight?"

I shrugged and knelt down to find more stones. *Had he heard what I said?* When I didn't respond, he knelt as well.

"I think you're amazing, Ben. Porcelain. Oops. Magenta. Whatever. Only you would be stressed because your acceptance speech for a hugely valuable scholarship might not reflect the utter truth of the guy you're talking about. That's just part of what makes you magenta. Okay?"

I smiled a bit. He was basically right. Why was it my job to right all the wrongs of the world? "Okay."

We stood back up and stared out at the water for a bit, and then I glanced over and there was Rafe, and my body just sort of sighed in contentment.

"Quarter for your thoughts?" Rafe asked.

I shrugged. "Not worth it. . . . Keats."

"Keats? Like the British guy?"

I laughed. "You're such a scholar. Yes, the British guy. I was just thinking of 'Ode on a Grecian Urn.' 'Heard melodies are sweet, but those unheard are sweeter.'"

"Um. So would it be better if I pretended to understand, or do you want to translate for those of us who watch too many celebrity gossip shows in our free time?"

I focused on the way the sunlight bounced off the placid lake water. "Keats is looking at this beautiful urn, which shows these young people celebrating, and he's marveling at how, in that frozen moment that is captured on the urn, everything is — eternal. Nothing gets old. The feelings of expectation and . . . excitement . . . don't ever go away."

I could feel Rafe smile a bit. He turned toward the water. "Wow," he said.

We stood there, side by side, staring at a placid lake. Then I reached down and grabbed his hand.

It wasn't like I planned it. I just did it because it was right.

We turned back toward each other. His hazel eyes held a question in them, and they danced around, glancing left and right as if afraid that the moment might not stick. I wanted to assure him of the un-assureable.

"I wanted to hold your hand. I kinda wanted to in the car the night of the dance too. But now I did it."

"Yes," he said, gulping. "You did it."

"Yes."

He looked down at the sand underneath our feet. "Are you sure?"

I laughed. "I wouldn't have done it if I wasn't sure."

"Wow. Should we talk about what this means?"

I shook my head.

"Okay . . ."

The fireworks pinballed inside my chest. It felt so . . . perfect. I felt alive. Vibrant. Light.

"So Hannah?"

I shook my head. "The heart wants what it wants,"

"Your heart wants . . . me?"

I squeezed his hand, and he squeezed mine back, tightly.

"Standing where Thoreau once possibly stood reminds me of a famous quote of his," I said. "I may mess this up. It's like, 'In any weather, I have been looking to improve the nick of time. To stand on the meeting of two eternities, the past and the future, which is precisely the present moment; to toe that line.'"

"You really lean on the classics, don't you?"

"It's all been said so well already," I said, staring out at the horizon. "'To stand on the meeting of two eternities, the past and the future, which is precisely the present moment; to toe that line.'"

Neither of us said anything for a while.

"It's like we're there," Rafe finally said. "We're in this historical place, which is your place, and we're talking about the future, which is kind of more my place, because it freaks you out."

"It doesn't freak me—"

Rafe interrupted me. "It's okay. The point is that we're here now. My dad always says this thing, that when you have a foot in tomorrow and a foot in yesterday, you're pissing all over the present."

I laughed, and then I laughed some more, thinking about Mr. Goldberg saying that. "I guess that's true," I said.

"Yeah," Rafe said. "It's like we're more comfortable living in the past or the future because the present moment is too uncertain and scary. Do you think that's what Thoreau meant?"

I kicked at the sand in front of me. "I think that must be the nick of time. Like this sliver of a moment that is now, that's where the past and future meet, and once you're there and you recognize it, it's gone. You can't think it. You just have to live in it."

"Wow," Rafe said. "Wow."

Time just stood still, like the pond was an urn, and I felt like I could fly. I wanted to look over at Rafe, my best buddy, my—who knew what? My person. The guy who made me feel like me. But I didn't need to. He was there, and that was plenty.

I said, "This present moment is particularly pleasant."

"And now it's gone," he said, and I could tell by the sound that he was smiling.

31

I don't know exactly what I expected when I called Hannah, but I hoped for some closure. The idea that she was out there, waiting for me to call, was painful to me. I put it off as long as I could, finding various things to keep myself busy. On Monday night, I studied for the math SATs and conjugated a ton of Spanish verbs. On Tuesday night, I studied Taylor polynomials and then read Pappas's letters to his sister over and over. I took a couple tries at starting my Pappas Award speech. Then, when I could find no other excuses and my mind went to how, two days earlier, I'd held Rafe's hand at Walden Pond, I called Hannah.

"Hey," she said.

"Hey. How are you?"

"Meh," she said. "What do you want, Ben?"

I laughed, because it was awkward. That was the question, and I knew the answer, and I felt like I was about to know what it felt like to tell someone that they'd been rejected from a school they'd applied to.

"I think you're perfect," I said. "I've never met a girl like you, and you're just right for me. But. My heart is, well, there are two people in my heart, and I think, I guess, that can happen. But Rafe is in my heart first, and, even though I'm straight, I think I need to see where that goes, because if I don't, I'll never know where it could have gone. I think you're the right choice, but Rafe is the choice I'm going to make, because my heart is there. Okay?"

She laughed. Like, an incredulous laugh. She just kept laughing.

"What?" I said.

"Oh my God," she said. "This just clinches it. I thought when my father cheated on us with a Marnie that I'd hit bottom, but I hadn't yet been dumped by a straight boy for another boy."

"Come on—" I said.

She interrupted. "Ben. You chose a boy over me. You're a straight guy who chose another guy. Over me. How did you think that would make me feel?"

"I know," I said. "I'm so sorry."

"Are you, like, hooking up with him?"

"No. I wouldn't do that without talking to you first. I'm not like that."

She laughed again. "Wow. I've never actually wanted to punch a boy more than I want to punch you right now."

"You want to punch me?"

"You're so virtuous. And it's like, a person can't be mad at you. You say all the right things, but. You chose a boy over me. That's what just happened here."

"I just thought I should tell you."

"Yes, well. You told me. Thanks for that. And fuck you, by the way, and when you get finished discovering yourself and decide you like girls again, please don't call me. Bye."

I put my phone down and opened my history textbook to a painting of a battle scene at the Alamo, and I studied it, focusing on a bronze

222

cannon facing an entire army of Mexican troops. I took a deep breath and felt my throat constrict. I read a page about how James Polk beat Henry Clay for the presidency because Clay was too wishy-washy about Texas.

Had I been too wishy-washy? What if I'd just said, "Listen. You said to call you when I was ready to choose you over Rafe. I'm calling because I'm not ready to do that. I thought you should know."

Would that have been better? Better than all that equivocating and trying to be her friend when obviously she wasn't going to be happy with me no matter what?

I slammed the book shut. Damn it. That heavy, underwater feeling was back, and there was no air in my room.

I knocked on Rafe's door, and for once he was there and Albie wasn't.

"You look like someone who just found out Coach Donnelly is his history teacher," he said.

"Har har."

"What's wrong?"

I sat down on his bed, and he sat next to me, which made my head buzz.

"Hannah just went off on me."

"Oh," he said. "Sorry. You okay?"

"I have no idea. I just hurt a girl I really like because—"

He looked down at his lap. "Do you want to call her back and say you made a huge mistake? And have things go back to the way they were, like, a week ago? Because that's fine with me."

I looked over at him like he'd pulled a rug out from under my feet. "Are you serious?"

Rafe shook his head slightly. "I don't want to be."

"Good. Because I don't want that. Okay?"

"Me neither," he said. "And if you had said yes, things would have gotten even more real than they got with Hannah."

I laughed a little and took a deep breath. "I just want to be happy."

"Me too. I mean, I want you to be happy too. I wouldn't mind being happy either."

"Are you?" I asked.

He ran his hands through his hair. "Yeah," he said. "I mean, magenta is sitting on my bed with me, so, um. Yeah."

"So here's the question. Could you imagine us going out on a proper date?"

Rafe giggled. "You're so twentieth-century."

I ignored him. "Thursday night. Will you go on a boy-boy date with me?"

"Um," Rafe said. "Nothing would make me happier in the world."

During my free period the next day, I went over to the administration building to talk to Headmaster Taylor. I had to sit in the waiting room for about fifteen minutes, so I took out my calculus book and tried to get through a chapter about Heron's area formula. I couldn't wait for the day I could test out of math and focus my studies on things that made sense.

I also couldn't wait for tomorrow. My first official date with Rafe. Was this really happening? What did it mean?

My thoughts were interrupted by Headmaster Taylor's assistant, who told me I could see him now.

"What can I help you with?" Taylor asked when I entered his office. He was eating a tuna fish sandwich.

"I wanted to talk to you about my speech for the Pappas Award."

"If you want some examples, you can check the library. I understand we have a folder of all the speeches printed out by year."

I hadn't known that, and I made a mental note to make sure my speech was proofread for grammar when I was done.

"Well, I've been doing some research on Peter Pappas."

"Good," he said. "We have an archive."

I nodded, even though I knew that the so-called archive was basically two articles. "Yes, sir. I also did some research at the Bacon Free Library."

He smiled. "Why does that not surprise me? Good man."

I nodded again. "Thank you, sir. It's just. I was just wondering whether anyone knew about Pappas's conflicted feelings about the Vietnam War."

He raised an eyebrow. "News to me."

"He gave a Model Congress speech against it, and he went to an anti-war demonstration a year before he enlisted." I didn't mention talking to his sister. I wasn't sure Headmaster Taylor would want to know that I bothered her.

He shrugged. "I wouldn't spend too much time worrying about it. The fact is that he's a war hero, and he's remembered that way. The award and scholarship are given by a foundation that wants him remembered that way. If I were you, I'd gloss over his objections. Just write about bravery, Ben. Surely a boy who volunteered to go to war and then died for the cause can be seen as brave, correct?"

"Well, yeah. I just thought—"

"Don't overthink it. As a recipient of the award, your job is to pay homage. No more, no less. Whatever drama surrounded the facts would be inappropriate to bring up in a speech. You don't want to give the foundation any reason to re-think their award choice."

"Yes, sir." I bowed my head.

"Is there anything else? I need to finish lunch before a meeting in fifteen minutes."

I crossed my arms over my chest. "One thing: Where am I, GPA-wise?"

He tapped the desk with his fist. "You're fine, Ben. Ms. Dyson has told me you've improved on your C plus in calculus. So long as you keep at least a straight B in that class, you'll be great. Just keep doing what you're doing. Anything else?"

Our next calc test was a biggie. It was on Tuesday, or three days before my speech. To keep up a B average in the class, I'd probably have to get at least a B minus on the test, and that was going to mean a few all-nighters, and even then it wasn't certain. But that wasn't something you said to the headmaster.

"No, sir. Thank you."

"Anytime," he said. "And check out that folder. Just do like the other boys did, and you'll be in great shape."

Mendenhall was holding court in the locker room when I arrived for practice that afternoon. "How do you make a blond's eyes twinkle?" he asked.

"How?" a guy yelled out.

"Shine a flashlight in her ear. What do blonds say after sex?"

"What?"

"Do you guys all play for the Patriots?"

I cringed, thinking about Hannah and what she'd said. *What does it say about guys that they act like they hate the very thing to which they're most attracted?* A shiver went through me. I didn't want to start thinking about the whole Hannah debacle.

Out in the gym, the jokes continued while Coach Donnelly hit grounders to the infield. Mendenhall, at shortstop, had an endless supply.

"What does a Lonna Dyke girl say when she wants to have sex with you?"

"What?" someone yelled.

"No," he said.

Some kids started laughing, but I felt my face redden. And for once, I didn't hide it.

"You do realize your mother is female, right?" I said to Mendenhall.

There was an "ooh" chorus that embarrassed me. I hadn't said what I'd said to get attention, or show him up; I'd said it because of what I'd been thinking: Misogyny sucks.

Mendenhall stood there with his arms crossed, rigid. "Don't you ever say another word about my mother," he said.

"I said your mom is female," I said. "She is, right?"

More oohs.

"I just told you. Not another word about my mom."

I faced him. "Then stop with the rape jokes. Are you that stupid, that you think rape is funny?"

Mendenhall took a step toward me, and instinctively I took a step toward him. I was done with being his little lapdog and playing along with his stilted view of the world. Even if a lot of the guys thought that way, I was done being part of that.

"Boys," Coach Donnelly said. "Enough. Minds on the drills, please."

I got back into fielding position, and Coach hit one my way. I could hear the sizzle of the ball off the bat. It was a hard grounder, two bounces, just to my left. I got in front of it, but somehow I misjudged the hop off the gym floor. It got me right in the shin, and I muttered, "Damn," and hopped around.

"More concentration, less mouth," Mendenhall yelled over from short.

"You too," I said back.

Then it was batting practice. Clement, who was probably going to wind up on the freshman team even though he was pretty good, was

228

up and struggling. He was a lefty, and he was hitting every ball down the third-base line. I knew that meant he was swinging late. Donnelly was tossing batting practice, and I put my hand up to ask him to hold up a moment.

"Clement," I said, approaching him. "Your step is too long, I think. You're having trouble catching up with the ball. Do this." I took the bat from him, and even though I'm normally a righty, I stood in from the left side and spread my legs wide. "Until your bat speed picks up, why don't you forget the leg kick and just swing? That leg kick isn't doing you any favors."

I handed the bat back to him, and he took a wide stance and pulled the bat back. The pitch came in, and while it was a bit awkward for him to swing without stepping, he hit the ball back to the pitcher. He did it again, this time a bit harder, and he looped one into shallow right field.

"There ya go," I said. "Get your timing down, and little by little, you can see about shortening your stance and adding some leg to it."

Coach gave me a thumbs-up, and when I ran back out to third, Mendenhall gave me a thumbs-up too.

I nodded to him, and he nodded back, and I realized that I might not fully understand the rules of team camaraderie. Just a moment earlier I thought we were going to fight, and now here we were, on the same side again.

The next batter smashed a ball down the third-base line. I didn't have time to think; I dove sideways, my outstretched glove leading the way and my body fully airborne. It was all instinct, the kind of thing that happens when you play a lot. You do what you have to do to stop the ball. I felt the ball pull my glove upward just as I was sinking to the hard gym floor. Oof. The landing jarred my rib cage, but somehow I closed my glove around the ball. I leapt up and fired a bullet to the first baseman, and then, as the guys started to whoop and holler, I put my head down, afraid I'd been showing off a little.

"There he is," Mendenhall said. "Dude's an asshole, but he can pick 'em."

"Screw you," I said, stretching out my bruised ribs but unable to hold in a little laugh. He laughed too, and I thought, *Yeah. No idea how this works.*

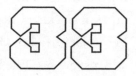

That night, the night before my first real date with Rafe, I barely slept. So many thoughts ricocheted through my addled brain.

I pictured a Play-Doh man, his arms being pulled until they snapped off.

I thought of a Ralph Waldo Emerson quote that I liked. "To be yourself in a world that is constantly trying to make you something else is the greatest accomplishment."

That quote had always resonated with me, ever since we read it freshman year. But now it was different somehow, like Emerson had reached inside my brain and knew exactly what it felt like to be me.

Was I becoming more me, or less? Was I someone who went on dates with a boy and it was no big deal? When it came to the baseball stuff, the whole "having words with Mendenhall but everything was fine" thing had felt good but foreign. Would the new me constantly fight with people and then shake it off like it hadn't even happened?

And then there was the whole thing with my family. A chill ran through me as I imagined my dad's face if he heard about the date tomorrow. He wouldn't be okay with me dating Rafe, not at all. Was there something wrong with me, that I was doing this? Had there been something wrong with Uncle Max, when he'd done things like this? Would my mom be okay? The chill seeped into my bones as I imagined my mom's face, and I wondered whether she'd turn her back on me if she knew. Because that wasn't something I'd be able to handle. What about Luke? He thought I was a good older brother. Would he still respect me if he knew I was dating another boy?

A thought came to me. *What do I think about the date with Rafe? Here I am thinking about what everyone else would think, and I haven't taken even a second to have my own reaction. Weird.*

If I put all that stuff away, I was looking forward to it. Rafe and me, hanging out together. I grinned. Yeah. That could work.

Rafe chose the spot for our Thursday night date. He picked a coffee-house in Lowell, and while I wasn't thrilled about the traffic or that I needed to spend gas money on a sixty-mile round-trip, I wasn't about to say that to Rafe.

"I love the trees here," Rafe said as we sped up 95 toward northern Massachusetts. I nodded, aware that he was as nervous as I was. And that was very. I was having a lot of trouble looking to my right. How was this happening? What if it went well? Would we go on more dates? Was there any way to just hang out and not call it a date? Because it was the word that I was uncomfortable with, mostly. It was so hard to get my head around this. I had always thought of dates as something that boys and girls did together. Boys and boys hung out as buddies, and that had been the case for me always, and now I was broken open and all this new stuff was seeping in, and my head was so noisy.

What if I was gay? What if I'd only been interested in Hannah and other girls as a defense against the truth? In psychology class we talked about the ego and defense mechanisms, like denial. Was I in denial?

232

How did you know when you were denying something? I wasn't gay. I couldn't be. Hannah had definitely not felt like a defense mechanism.

Was I bi? *Hi, I'm Ben Carver, I'm bisexual.* It just sounded so . . . foreign. Yes, my uncle was bi, and obviously a lot of people were. But to me, bi meant equally attracted to boys and girls. I wasn't that. I was basically attracted to girls and one specific guy.

There had to be a term for that.

"You probably ought to go back and get that," Rafe said, and stunned out of my thinking fit, I glanced over at him.

"What?"

"I think I just saw a bit of your gray matter on the side of the road. The explosion was nasty."

I laughed tentatively.

"Earth to Ben, earth to Ben," he said, and as an answer, I cracked a smile. The tall trees whizzed by as we roared down the highway. The sun was setting to my left, sending quick blips of brightness through the foliage.

"Did you know that the original word for the National Socialist Party was Nasos?" I asked. "It was an abbreviation. The word 'Nazi' was first used as a term of derision by a journalist, and it caught on. It was derived from a Bavarian word that meant 'simpleminded.'"

"Good date talk," Rafe said.

"You never know when you'll be involved in a little drive-by *Jeopardy*-ing."

We were quiet for a bit. "Why did you bring that up? That was really weird," he said.

I thought for a moment. "I was thinking about how this was complicated. I don't think I'm gay, but I'm on a date with my best friend, who is male. But on the other hand, complicated is often good. It's when things get narrowed to the lowest common denominator — hate, fear — that society gets into trouble. The Nazis were the opposite of complicated."

"You are so going to a better college than me," Rafe said.

"But don't you think that labels are exceedingly narrow? Not complicated enough?"

Rafe looked out the window. "That's where I was last semester. I was, like, labels can't describe a person. I still think they can't, but also, it's complicated. Because as crappy as labels are, I think we get lost pretty quick if we try to do away with them.

"How do you point someone out in a restaurant without labeling them? Like, tall, or male, or even, like, black or Latino. Those are just descriptions. They don't embody a person, I don't think, but that doesn't mean they aren't useful."

I'd have to think about that one for a while, I realized.

The venue, it turned out, was a coffeehouse called Brewed Awakenings. I thought a coffee shop was actually a really nice place to go on a date, and I was looking forward to a good talk. But when we got there, I realized that there might be some good talk, but it would be by slam poets, not me.

"What the heck is this?" I muttered when we brought our coffees to a free table. College guys with beards and girls with multicolored hair milled around us.

"Are you kidding me? You never watched slam poetry?" I shook my head. "It's a real mix. Some of it is amazing, and some of it is, like, hipster hell."

Could we go somewhere else? Anywhere else? I almost said. I didn't give a crap about slam poetry, and this wasn't even Boston, where I felt like we could be on a date without any trouble. I didn't know much about Lowell, and these people looked perfectly nice, but this was on the route to my parents' farm. A little uncomfortable. Instead I smiled and said, "Yay, slam poetry."

Rafe smirked, rolled his eyes, and said, "Open mind."

That became difficult immediately. The first act was a bearded, bespectacled guy who looked like a college student or maybe a little older. He had set up a boom box, a mic, and a couple small speakers on the makeshift stage. The fifteen or so people watching waited in anticipation and, in my case, a small amount of fear. Especially when the guy turned toward the audience and I saw he had a beard on one half of his face only.

And then the music started, and even I recognized it as an old song, the one where the guy is bringing sexy back. Then Half-Bearded Guy approached the mic and opened his mouth and we learned of his plan.

"I'm bringing Chaucer back. Yeah! Those other poets don't know how to write. Yeah!" he sang.

Rafe and I looked at each other with wide eyes as the performer scurried back and turned off his boom box and then rushed back to the mic.

"Yo yo yo yo! Geoffrey Chaucer was off the hook, yo!" He punched the air in front of him. "Homeboy forgotten these days, yo. But Chaucer—dude brought it!" His mouth was too close to the microphone, and feedback ruffled my ears. He scanned us in a way that made it clear he'd practiced having an intimate moment with his audience.

"Rap gets a bad rap, right? But you know what? And this isn't said enough. Rap is poetry! No, I'm serious. Rap is poetry. It's flow. It's words, flowing together, meaning tripping over meaning. It's stories, told by the teller. That's what rap is.

"So I want to share with you today some slam poetry I wrote that is heavily influenced by *The Canterbury Tales*, which to me is the first-ever rap, which to me is the story of people, and people are the thing, yo, that I write about, that I live for."

I leaned over and surreptitiously poked Rafe in the side, not once taking my eyes off the performer, whose eyes were now closed as he swayed back and forth, mentally preparing his slam poem.

"What did you do to me?" I whispered.

"Beautiful train wreck," Rafe whispered back. "I think I'm in love with another man, Ben."

This earned him a harder poke in the ribs, and I realized that I was actually having fun. Out of my comfort zone.

The man began to rap his slam poem with what sounded like a Scottish accent.

> *E sleh-pen al the nicht with open ay-yuh*
> *Me gehrl-a-frind hath faned anow-ther mane-uh*
> *The ahn-ger thot I fale is oopen-ended*
> *It feeles like on tha Fass-a-book De-frinded*

The rap had an actual smell. Like rotten citrus. I tried to look as if I was carefully listening to this beautiful story of being de-friended on Facebook, but mostly I was trying not to laugh, because we were pretty close-up and I didn't want to hurt the hipster's feelings.

When he was finally done, Rafe and I shared a look, glanced around to make sure Half-Bearded Guy had left, and burst out laughing.

Laughing with Rafe made me feel as if it was just like old times, and I was so damn grateful to be back there.

The next speaker was a Latino guy wearing wire-framed glasses and a Red Sox cap. He didn't have a boom box, or anything, really. He just grabbed the mic and started talking.

"I've been thinking a lot lately about how I live my life. Do I live it out LOUD? Or do I live it *soft*? What do I do when I see a friend, or a stranger, on the street? Do I ignore them because I'm too busy, or do I engage them, because they are me and I am they. Because we are, people. We are one. We are people.

"And I think what it all comes down to is a simple question, people. Are you in, or are you out? Do you accept that we are all in this together, and do you greet your fellow person with the dignity they deserve? Or do you spurn them?

"And when they put themselves out there, do you go there with them? Or do you stay isolated and laugh at them because you think they're a fool?"

The guy walked out into the audience. He focused on the table next to mine, where four college-aged people sat. I glanced over. Two had cell phones out and were busy texting.

He leaned in, resting his hands on their table. "Are you in, or are you out?" he asked, his voice booming, his eyes boring directly into the eyes of one of the girls at the table.

She just stared at him and said nothing.

The speaker then asked the same question of one of the guys at the table.

"I'm out," he said.

The speaker gently tapped the table and moved on. "You are out. And that is your choice. Continue to live in two places at once. Continue to ignore those standing in front of you while you chat with those far away. That is your choice, to be out."

Now he came to our table, and, perhaps sensing that Rafe was the extrovert and I the introvert, he chose me. His dark eyes stared into my own, and he smiled. I held his stare, my mouth trembling into what felt a bit like a smile. I wasn't sure.

"You, my friend. You are sitting in a coffee shop, listening to me, as I put myself out there, in the world. Are you, my friend, in or out?"

I realized I wasn't breathing. "In," I mumbled.

"What? I did not hear you. Are you in or are you out?"

I looked at Rafe. He was smiling at me, his cheeks reddened.

"I'm in!" I yelled.

The speaker's eyes lit up, and he grabbed my arm and raised it. "Yes! This man is in! This man is part of the human race, ladies and gentlemen, and I am grateful for it. Give him a hand!"

And people clapped. Seriously. They clapped. And then a really crazy thing started to happen. My eyes started to water a bit, and I wasn't sure why. But I knew I loved it.

I was in. And when the slam poetry event ended, I'd forgotten what time it was, and what day it was. I'd actually listened to strangers for however long, and while some of it was more interesting to me than other parts, I'd loved it all.

Rafe and I drove back holding hands, talking intermittently and also sharing some nice silences. It was nice that we could be quiet together and feel comfortable. To me, that was just as important as good conversation.

"Thanks for that," I said. "I wasn't sure about the slam poetry when we got there, but that turned out to be epic."

The sky looked purple to me, with the lights on the highway illuminating everything just right. I wanted to remember it for always.

"All that stuff about in and out made me think about the GSA," Rafe said.

I tensed up a bit, and Rafe noticed.

"I felt that way at first too. Like, why do I need to align myself with people just based on sexual orientation? But then I went, and I'm telling you it's been awesome for me. The guys in it aren't, like, my best friends—well, Toby is one of them, I guess—but they are people who understand what I've been through, and we go through it together."

I took a deep breath and tried to really focus on what he was saying, but the noises in my head were very loud. I sat in the driver's seat, thinking that maybe I wasn't so much in the driver's seat in life. I mean, if Rafe was out, and if I was dating Rafe, would I have to come out? And as what?

I took another breath and let the thoughts go. This was a first date. So I squeezed his hand and he squeezed mine back.

When we got back to Natick, he walked me to my room, and then he asked if he could use my laptop. Was this some excuse? Was he making a move? The idea was so exciting I could barely nod. He did some searching around online and then looked up at me.

"May I have this dance?" he asked.

I laughed, and then I stopped laughing because he was serious, and not only that. I was glad he was serious. And yes, I totally wanted to dance with Rafe.

The song was sung by a woman with a beautiful voice. I'd never heard it before, but then again, I'd never slow danced with a guy before either. Rafe let me lead, which was good because at least that position came naturally to me. The best thing was the way it felt to put my right arm around him, and to rest my hand on his low back, and close my eyes, and feel the heat of his face next to mine. And as she sang about being caught up in the rapture of love, I felt myself getting caught up in it too.

34

It was nearly impossible to get through classes on Friday. Every moment I wasn't with Rafe, I felt it, like a void in my chest. I wanted to watch his mouth as I made him laugh. I wanted to see his face light up with the spark of whatever silly joke there was, and I wanted to kiss him too, and really more than that, which was not a straight thing, I know, but also it was true. I wanted to hold him in bed and I wanted our bodies to touch in every possible way, and I needed him to set me free. Only he could do that.

I barely paid attention in calculus, which was perhaps not the greatest of strategies with a test that could determine my future just a few days away, but I was powerless over that. Maybe Rafe was a voodoo doctor. He had me, totally, and I just wanted him to have more of me, to give that away to him, the control that always kept me wrapped so tight inside myself.

The final bell could not come soon enough, and then I had lunch with the team, which was tough, because I kept looking over at Rafe, who was laughing it up with Toby and Albie. I so wanted to be part of that. But I also wanted to keep doing this captain thing, and yeah,

240

there was something to be said for being part of the team. I was liking that too.

My table's lunch conversation started with a competition about whose parents had the best car. Truly. Mendenhall took the lead because his dad had a Lamborghini, and Zack was a close second because his dad had two—count them, two—Porsche Spyders, whatever those were. We went around in a circle, and when it got to me, I gave a comically bug-eyed look, and pretty much everyone cracked up.

"It's funny because he's poor," Zack said.

I shrugged and laughed a little. "Guilty as charged."

"Ben's so poor he thinks Arby's is a five-star restaurant," Standish said.

"Ben's so poor he thinks food stamps are a vegetable," Zack said.

"Ben's so poor he needs a scholarship to go to Natick, and someone has to pay his way to Florida, and he wears a brown jacket from nineteen seventy-five," Mendenhall said, and everyone laughed.

To my surprise, I laughed too. I couldn't help it. "You guys are literally the worst."

"C'mon," Mendenhall goaded. "What do ya got?"

I rolled my eyes. "Mendenhall is so dumb he stares at frozen juice bottles because they say, 'Concentrate.'"

He cracked up a bit. "Lame."

"Mendenhall is so stupid he dyed his hair blond and his IQ went up twenty points."

"Hey, now," Zack said. "Look who's waking up!"

"Zack is so dumb he thinks it's normal to tan until his face is orange."

"No he didn't!" said Steve.

"Steve is so dumb he's friends with Zack."

The table exploded in laughter. "Go Ben!" Mendenhall said. "That's the shit I'm talking about. You take shit too serious. Relax and let that broom handle up your ass go."

Someone—I couldn't tell who—put up a hand for me to high-five, and I stung the shit out of that hand, and it felt great. Some more jokes were passed around as we ate, and then the conversation took a surprising turn.

"What was it like, growing up on a farm?" Standish asked.

I chewed the piece of carrot I'd just put in my mouth. "It's—I don't know. I don't really know what it's like *not* to grow up on a farm."

"Are you going to, like, try to be an investment banker or an entrepreneur or something?" Mendenhall asked. "Like, you don't have it so you want it?"

I wasn't sure if he was goading me or not, so I just said, "Nah. That's not important to me."

"What do you want to be?" he asked.

"History professor."

The guys all looked around, like they were trying to decide if that was funny or not.

"Huh," Zack said. "I guess that's cool."

"It is what it is. What do you want to be?" I asked no one in particular, and the answers came from all corners, rocket fast, and I felt this full feeling in my chest because suddenly I was a leader, and I loved it so much.

I was an also-ran at my afternoon classes, and even at baseball practice I was feeling a little giddy still, so much that Mendenhall even said, "What the fuck, Carver? You on drugs?"

"Your mother and I, we both are," I said, and he gave me a middle finger. It was like I was drunk, in a way. But on good alcohol this time. Not the kind that numbs the pain away. The kind that makes you feel every little thing, good, bad, or otherwise.

Walking back to the dorms after dinner, I realized that I could, actually, have it all. A guy could be serious but sometimes let that wall down. And a guy could joke around even if the jokes were in bad taste, and still go back to his dorm and be himself, and none of it was illegal, and all of it was just so—surprising. I'd never known I could feel this sort of happy buzz down to my toes.

I felt jittery as I walked by Rafe's room. I wanted to knock, but I literally could not stand the idea of him not being there. It socked me in my gut, the possibility that I would not see him. Instead I went to my room, sat on my bed, and held my head in my hands.

I needed to get a grip. But I also felt so freaking incredible that I didn't want to.

I went to the restroom to wash up for dinner. Rafe was in there, doing the same. My heart spasmed.

"Hey, stranger," he said.

Hey, stranger. It was such a Rafe, weird-Boulder-kid-at-Natick thing to say. I sighed and laughed, and even though we were in the bathroom, I pushed up behind him.

"Whoa," he said, moving slightly forward.

"Yep." I moved forward with him, until he was pinned between me and the sink.

"We're in the bathroom," he whispered.

"I'm aware of that." I was fully aroused and my heart was pounding, and it felt so magical and so right and even if Headmaster Taylor himself walked in and said, *Ben, if you want your scholarship and your award, you'll back the heck up and behave yourself,* I would have said, *Screw you and screw that.*

"What is this? Where is this coming from?"

"It's you. It's always been you. I love you, Rafe."

He gasped. "Really?"

"Yup."

"And you thought you'd share this revelation in the bathroom?"

I laughed. "Yup. I love you, man."

"You do?"

"I do," I said, and Rafe turned around, and our eyes bored into each other's.

He gulped. "Right back at ya, big guy. Never loved anyone a quarter as much."

And there in the bathroom, not caring who walked in, I leaned forward and kissed him hard on the lips, and then our lips parted, and our tongues touched.

"Whoa," he said, when I pulled back.

"My room. Stat."

Rafe's eyes lit up. "Yes, please."

During, I found myself feeling the same kind of protective feeling I'd felt for Hannah, and for once in my damn life, I was light as a feather. And then Rafe protected me, and that was unlike anything I'd ever experienced, and wow. There ought to be a law. Oh, wait, I think there used to be one.

And during, I realized that the labels didn't matter, because when two people feel that sort of pull toward each other, it just *works*, and the only label that mattered was that I was in love. Totally, fully, ecstatically.

After, I found myself laughing. Rafe laughed too, and I knew he got it. It wasn't funny, but it was entirely necessary to laugh, like we had to expel more energy that was still pent up in there. And I wondered why people ever stop having sex.

So we started up again.

After again, the laughter had dissipated and we just lay there, exhausted, his head leaning on my bare bicep. I glanced down at his flat chest, where there'd be breasts if he was Hannah, but he was most certainly, definitely not Hannah.

"You're flat," I said, and he raised an eyebrow. It sounded like I thought he had no muscles, which wasn't true.

"Nipples. Why do guys even have nipples?" I asked.

"I know, right?"

"Nipples. Nipples. It's such a stupid word."

Rafe laughed. "Nipples. Nipples."

I laughed back. "It sounds like a clown's name."

"Nipples the Clown."

"He'd wear, like, a nipple hat."

"Look at me, I'm Nipples the Clown."

I crossed my arms over my chest. We hadn't used ours, and I wasn't sure guys even did. How would I know what guys do? I knew Hannah liked being touched gently there.

I said, "I mean, with girls. Sexually, um. And anyway, for girls they're for feeding a child. What do boys' nipples even do?"

Rafe sat up and looked down at my chest. We were both laughing a bit, and then we weren't. I slowly uncrossed my arms.

Rafe brought his hands up to my midsection. And then higher. He placed the lowest parts of the palms of his hands in the ever-so-slight ridges under my chest. Then he gently pressed forward until each hand was cupping a pec. Then his fingers drummed my collarbone, slowly, thumb to pinky, one time. He pressed his hands forward, and when his hands came to rest and the center of his palms came into contact with the little pink lobes, I gasped.

And from that moment on, we never had to wonder what a nipple was for again.

After again again, we talked. A long, long time we talked. I told him every feeling I'd ever had, and he shared with me all his.

"I don't know. I still don't feel like I'm gay," I said.

"What a thing to say to a guy after sex!"

"No, really."

"Maybe you're bi?"

"I feel like I'm more, like, gay-for-Rafe."

He put his hand on his heart. "Sincerely flattered to be a sexual orientation now. Thank you."

I laughed. "I'm just going with it now, you know? All's I know, as Donnelly would say, is that I love you, and you are a boy."

"I am."

We were quiet for a bit.

"I guess I don't really get why you don't think you're bi, though."

"Well, to me bi means attracted to both boys and girls. I'm attracted to girls and Rafe. There's a difference."

He shrugged. "I guess. No. The truth is I don't actually get that, but I love you and I don't need to get that. Maybe someday I will."

"I hope so."

"In the GSA, the guys joke about bisexuality like it's a gateway to gay. Like that's a stop on the train for kids who aren't ready to deal. I don't actually believe that. I think some people are bi, definitely."

"Me too."

"I think it's a continuum."

"Me too," I said.

He lay back down and placed his head in the crook of my armpit. I was sure there were better places in the world to be, but he didn't say anything.

"Is it possible you're just at the gateway of the gateway?"

"I truly don't think that's it, but yeah. Anything's possible."

I closed my eyes, and I didn't have to look to know he had too. So we fell asleep like that, together, like two boys against the world.

35

Rafe's overnight disappearances had been duly noted by Albie and Toby. We spent basically all Saturday in my room, and when we arrived at Albie's room Sunday morning to go to breakfast as a group, Albie and Toby had set up a circle of chairs. They were in two of them, and they wordlessly pointed to two empty seats for us to sit in.

Once we were all seated, Toby pulled a piece of paper out of his pocket.

"You're clearly having sex relations with each other, and that impacts me in the following ways," Toby said.

Rafe cracked up. "Is this an intervention?"

Toby nodded solemnly and continued with his reading.

"One: I would like to be having sex relations, and yet I am not. Two: When you were busy having sex relations, and I tried to walk in on you, your door was locked. This made me think I was unwelcome to be part of your sex relations, which made me feel unwanted. Three: If there truly is something gossip-worthy going on, I would like to know about it."

"Toby makes some excellent points," Albie said, surprising me. "Not about wanting to be part of your sexual relations, because, ew.

But in the fact that there is obviously a good story here, because as we are all well aware, you were boinking last Thanksgiving, and then you weren't, and you weren't even friends, and then Ben had a date to the dance and the date was female, and then this. It feels as if there's something you're not telling us."

I pleaded the Fifth, as there was no chance in hell I would be discussing my personal life with two psychopaths. I may have changed some, but there were still limits. Rafe, on the other hand, upon noting my hesitance, stage-whispered, "Tell ya later" to the guys, who both nodded in anticipation.

As we walked across the quad, Toby glanced over at Albie and then back at us. "Can I be cereal for a second?"

"I don't think so," Albie said. "I think you can either be a shape-shifter and turn into cereal forever, or you will need to remain in your current form. Those are your choices."

Toby ignored him. "I'm actually a little freaked out about coming out as gender fluid. Which I'm pretty sure I'm gonna do."

Rafe said, "It's a lot. Of course you're freaked."

I wanted to ask again: Why come out? It was hard enough being a little different at Natick. Why would a person step into the firing zone by telling the mostly juvenile boys at an all-boys school that sometimes you're a girl?

But also, I knew. He'd already told me. It was just hard for me to wrap my head around it.

"It's the fluid part," Toby said. "That's the part I'm really freaked about. I mean, it would be one thing to be like, 'I'm transitioning, and my name is Tina.' But I'm just telling people that I'm in flux, which is hard. It's putting it on a platter and saying, 'Here's my confusion. Feel free to pick it apart.'"

The wet grass squished under our feet as we walked in silence. The thing about coming out, it seemed to me, was vulnerability. Putting whatever it was that people might judge on a platter. Most of my life, I'd been figuring out ways to armor up, to make myself impervious to attack. That's what we do. Humans. But especially Carvers. Don't put yourself out there. Hold yourself back and protect. Don't be vulnerable. And my mind flashed on Hannah, which didn't feel so good, so I stopped thinking about that.

"I think you're amazing," I said to Toby. "Truly. And if anyone gives you shit, you let me know."

Rafe elbowed me in the side in a gentle way, as if to say, *Thanks*.

Albie broke the silence. "I think it's okay to just say who you are without it being final or something. I mean, none of us are finished products. We change. We keep changing. We won't be finished products 'til the day we die."

That made me think about my dad. I was pretty sure *he* saw himself as a finished product.

Was I?

36

Things went into hyperspeed on Monday of the final week before spring break. I had my big calculus test on Tuesday, which meant an all-nighter and some prayers that I'd do well enough. There was packing to do for break and the trip to Fort Lauderdale, a few more tests and lab reports. My parents were to arrive on Thursday. And then I had my speech on Friday, so long as I didn't screw up the math test too badly.

And after the weekend I'd had, the biggest thing was that I knew who I was. I had Rafe. Maybe I wasn't quite ready for the team to know all my business, or to share it with my family. But at least I knew, and that had to count for something.

In calculus class on Monday, we had a final study session for the test, and in reality I didn't fully understand what Ms. Dyson was saying about formal manipulation of the Taylor series, let alone the shortcuts to computing it. But at least I had one night left to figure it out.

"So starting with this test," Ms. Dyson said, "we're going to do things a little differently. Since we're trying to get you prepared for the AP exam, the test will have more multiple-choice questions than you can possibly answer. I just want you to answer as many as you can, as fast as you can, okay?"

A kid named Cal raised his hand. "Do we need to show our work?"

She shook her head. "Just the correct answer will be enough."

There was murmuring throughout the classroom, and all I was thinking about was how it would feel to not be able to answer all the questions. I'd be freaked out until she returned the tests, which was not what I needed, not with my parents coming and the final touches on my Pappas Award speech staring at me.

I felt these butterflies in my chest as we packed up our bags and left the room, and I tried to talk myself out of them. Yes, if the test was this very minute, I'd probably fail, or get a D. But I had a vague idea of most of the concepts she was discussing in class, and with a good five or six hours of studying, I'd be able to figure it all out. Probably. Ms. Dyson beamed at me as I walked out.

"Study hard, Ben," she said.

"I will."

Heading to dinner, I caught up to Rafe on the quad. We'd been too busy to see each other all day.

"Hey, handsome!" he said.

"Hey. You get your history homework done?"

"Yes, Mother," he said.

"Good, because we have exactly two hours after dinner to hang out. Then it's calc time for me, all night long."

"Sounds like a partay," he said.

"Perchance," I said, and I caught a glimpse of the baseball guys coming out of the dorm to head toward the cafeteria. "Teammates," I said. "Gotta jet."

Rafe rolled his eyes. "Did you just say, 'Gotta jet'?"

"Hey," I said. "This is the new, improved, don't-give-a-rat's-ass Ben. You know. It doesn't take a rocket surgeon to figure this all out."

He cracked up. "Huh. Different. I like it. I'll go find the boys. We will miss you terribly all meal long. Have a wonderful time bonding with Steve Nickelson."

"Other than the fact that he's an asshole, he's basically okay." The guys weren't close enough to hear quite yet.

"Enjoy! Love you."

The longer we stood there, the closer the guys got. I felt a bubble growing in my throat. "Uh-huh. See ya," I said to Rafe, and then I hurried over to my teammates. "Hey, guys. What's up?"

"What up, Carver?" Mendenhall said. "You're gonna sit with us and not your little gay buddies?"

"You're just jealous because gay guys—and straight females, I might add—find you disgusting."

He punched me in the shoulder. "If I'm disgusting, what the hell are you?" he asked.

Dinner was fun, truth be told. We talked about the tournament in Florida. I'd be rooming with Standish, which was fine with me. I just wanted to get down there, get on the outdoor field, and play some ball after all this indoor practice.

When I got back to my room, Rafe was already on his bed, reading. His feet were kicked up on the wall, which he was facing, his body at a ninety-degree angle.

"Did you miss me?" I asked.

He didn't answer.

"Hey," I said.

He didn't answer again.

"Earth to Rafe."

He kicked his feet down from the wall and turned to face me. His eyes were a little red.

"Whoa," I said. "What happened?"

"We need to talk," he said.

Rafe sat on the floor, his back against the bed. I did the same with my bed. We both stretched out our legs, but there was still a gulf of about a foot between us.

"I love you, Ben. I really, really love you."

I didn't like the numb feeling that began to radiate in my cheeks. "I know. I love you too."

"I've never loved anyone close to as much as I love you. But I can't . . . I mean . . ."

"What?" I asked. "You're freaking me out."

He rubbed his eyes. "Before dinner. When you said good-bye to me. I said, 'I love you.' You said, 'Uh-huh.'"

"Oh, come on," I said. "Obviously I love you too. Do I have to say it every five minutes?"

"No. But you didn't say it because your baseball buddies were right there. How did I not realize this was going to happen? Maybe I didn't want to see it, but I need to be loved by someone who is willing to love me . . . openly."

I stared at the bottom of Rafe's shoe. I just sat there for a while.

"Say something, please."

"God. This is so fast. Can't I get a little time to adjust and figure it out? I'm a private person, Rafe. I don't tell everyone my business, and I sure as hell don't want the baseball team to know. I mean, they're idiots. Why would I give them ammunition?"

He crossed his arms over his chest. "You're ashamed of me. You're ashamed to be dating me."

"I'm not ashamed," I said, crossing my arms too.

"Sure you are. If you weren't, you'd be taking me to a dance in front of all your buddies, like you did with Hannah."

"Do I really need to dance with you in public to show you I love you?"

"I've been with three guys in my life. Not a single one of you was willing to date me openly. I'm tired of being everyone's secret, Ben. I want to be loved, proudly. By you. Okay?"

I shook my head. "Wow."

"What does 'wow' mean?"

I shook my head some more. "Are you aware of all the tightropes I'm walking? I'm gonna lose this award if I don't study tonight. My parents are about to come down here, and that's—really stressful."

He frowned. "What does that have to do with me?"

"Don't do this right now, before a test, for God's sake."

"Do what?"

"I can't—you can't keep doing this, Rafe. Pulling me in different directions. You're asking me to be someone I'm not. I can't do what you're asking me to do. You know I'm not about to parade you around. What if my parents found out? My dad would disown me. I just need a little time."

He shook his head. "You know what? It's not like I don't understand that and feel bad for you about it. But. I can't hide that way anymore."

"So what does that mean?"

He shrugged. "It means what it means."

I felt the anger rise into my shoulders. "You couldn't have told me that before I fell in love with you, maybe?"

"I didn't really know," he said. "I didn't really know until you answered 'I love you' with 'Uh-huh.' Then it became real clear."

"Wow."

"Ben," he said. "I told you. I love you. I could see being with you forever. But you don't get to forever in secret. I need more."

"I'm not even sure I'm gay. I'm supposed to come out just because we're dating?"

"You can come out as bi."

I didn't want to have this conversation again. I wasn't even sure I was bi. What would I be announcing, anyway?

He put his head in his hands. He kept them there, and I thought for a second he was crying, but then he took them off and I realized he'd just been thinking. "Could you, like, imagine getting there? Soon? I don't want to lose you again."

I closed my eyes. I tried to imagine discussing Rafe with the entire baseball team. Why the hell would I do that? It didn't make sense to me. But I couldn't say that to Rafe. And I couldn't even tell him a little white lie. We'd talked a lot about lies.

I opened my eyes. "I really don't know," I said, honestly.

He sighed. "You're not ready," he said. "Go find Hannah. Go—I don't know. We'll be, like, besties again. I can't do it. I can't be your dirty secret. Sorry."

He got up and left me sitting with my back against my bed, my legs splayed out in front of me. Each limb suddenly felt like a million pounds.

I wasn't even gonna try to move them. What was the use?

The longer I sat there, the more tense I got, thinking about what I was facing. Last semester, Rafe had come to talk to me about our relationship the night before a history exam. Now he'd done it again with calculus. I was supposed to pull an all-nighter, and that was the last thing I felt like doing right now.

I sat there frozen, thinking about what I wanted.

I wanted Rafe.

I also wanted the award and scholarship.

To get Rafe, I would have to be someone other than me. Because it sure as hell didn't feel normal to me to imagine openly being a couple with him.

To get the award and scholarship, I'd have to study my ass off when all I felt like doing was shutting my eyes and disappearing. I'd also have to give a false speech, because I knew that Peter Pappas wasn't the person the school was making him out to be.

Pappas. He'd been a lot like me, just with bigger stakes. Just like me, he'd tried so hard to make everyone happy, and in the end, no one was happy. Least of all him. It had killed him.

I shook my head hard.

When would I get to stop sacrificing to make other people happy? When would that happen?

And how the hell was I going to forget about everything that was going on, and study for this stupid test?

The answer was, I wasn't going to do that.

I lay down in my bed and closed my eyes, allowing all the sensations in my body and all the thoughts in my brain to pour over me. I was tired. Dead tired of everyone wanting something from me. Myself included. All my life, I'd wanted so much from me, and it was never, ever enough. I was tired of trying, and my brain spun off its axis, and I pictured it flying away like a remote-control helicopter that I couldn't quite control.

After about an hour of this, knowing my future hinged on this night of studying, I finally opened my calculus book. The equations in chapter 11 looked like hieroglyphics. Polar and vector functions put me over the edge, and it felt like knowledge was leaking from my brain. The different symbols all mushed together. I found myself breathing too fast, and my head was beginning to feel dizzy.

I had so much to lose. If I got a C plus or worse on my math test, I could kiss my B average in that class good-bye, and with it, my award and my scholarship, which was pretty much like saying, everything in my life. My parents would be told not to come down for the ceremony, and my dad would be so disappointed in me. And who knew what other college we'd be able to afford, what kinds of scholarships I'd qualify for. No. Not doing well on the test was not an option. Nothing had ever been so important.

I forced my eyes open wide and stared at the book, willing it all to make sense.

It just didn't. None of it.

"C'mon!" I yelled at myself, out loud. "Do it! We're Carvers. We work. We work hard!"

The functions and equations in the book on my lap just stared back at me, smug. Laughing at me. Judging me.

I stood up, enthralled by an idea.

No. No way. Absolutely no way. Bad idea. Terrible idea. That was wrong. That went against everything I believed in. If I did that, I'd hate myself.

But I pictured my dad, shaking his head at me when the news of my grade got to him. I imagined listening to Mike Scalia, the alternate Pappas Award winner, give my speech. Aware that he was getting my scholarship. No.

That was even more wrong.

I took a deep breath, stood up, and took a slow walk down the hall, trying to talk some sense into myself. But there was no sense here. It was a no-win situation.

"Hey," Mendenhall said when he answered the door. "Wassup, Carver?"

"Shit," I said, shaking my head. "I heard you have the test keys?"

He smiled and waved me into his room.

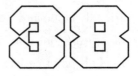

The next morning, I walked in a haze to calculus, where I sat down, unable to look at anyone, and waited for my test.

The multiple-choice answers were chiseled onto my pencil in tiny writing. I'd cheat on this one test, and then, before the next one, I'd get back on track. I even decided I'd get a few wrong so as to not seem too perfect. Nothing to make my grade lower than a B plus, but nothing too good to arouse suspicion either, especially when I went back to not cheating.

After the test, I trudged back to the dorm, even though I had history next. I sank into my bed and let this flimsy blue feeling crest over my head like a wave. I felt utterly unable to handle any little thing, and I just wanted to stay there forever, buried under the current as it rushed over me.

I was now a cheater. A cheater. Me.

Rafe was gone. We were over. And why? Because I wouldn't say "I love you" in front of my baseball team? He couldn't give me a week or two to get comfortable with our new situation?

It felt like he'd burrowed his way into my heart again, and then smashed it. And I'd let him do it. Again. Rafe said we could go back to being best friends, but I didn't work like that. My heart hurt. It actually hurt.

Too much stuff in my brain. Along with the fact that I was now officially alone and a cheater, lab reports were never ending, and there was another one due in two days. History essay, due tomorrow. Undone. Baseball practice later, where I had to be a leader and be tough. My parents arriving in the morning, and they'd spend the day going to classes with me, and I'd be unprepared, and that would be really bad. My speech. It was ready, but it wasn't ready, because I felt like a fraud every time I practiced it. It was a lie.

Too many things.

I lay back on the bed. My dad never missed a day of work in his life. I must be the laziest person in the history of the world. Everybody thought of me as solid and strong, but if they saw me now they'd know the real me. And that was so terrifying that I got under the covers. And then the weirdest thing happened. My eyelids got as heavy as the rest of me, and I let them close, and I let the world disappear. I went to sleep.

My eyes crept open when the clock said 10:17, and I realized it was chemistry class time. I wasn't one to skip classes, ever. As of Friday, I would be the Peter Pappas Award winner. All-around good guy and scholar and athlete. Award winners and all-around good guys don't cheat, and they don't just sleep through the day.

I closed my eyes again, and even though my brain wasn't that sleepy, I willed myself into oblivion.

There was a knock on the door. I opened my eyes. 11:29. It was almost lunchtime.

"Shit," I mumbled, and I stumbled to the door, bleary-eyed.

I opened the door and saw Coach Donnelly.

"You sick, Carver?"

I didn't feel like lying. I shook my head.

"What's up?"

"I give up," I said.

Donnelly stared at me like I was speaking another language. "You give up? What are you talking about?"

"Everything," I said. "I can't do it anymore."

"You can't do it anymore."

I walked back over to my bed and sat down. "Right."

"What can't you do anymore?"

"Any of it. All my life I've been told what I need to be, and I can't be it. It's too much."

Donnelly looked around my room. "I'm reminded of the great philosophical debate about a tree falling in the forest," he said.

This got my attention. "Oh, yeah?"

He smiled, like he was happy to have an audience. "You see, a tree fell in the forest. And then, well, nobody was there to hear it. So the question is, did it fall?"

"Yes," I said. I didn't have the patience to humor him.

"Ah, but how do you know?"

"Because you just told me. A tree fell in the forest."

"But no one was there to hear it," he said.

"So how did *you* know it happened?" I asked.

He looked confused for a second, and then he recovered and said, "Exactly. I might have been making it up. That's the thing, Carver. Alls you gotta remember is, don't believe everything you hear. Maybe somewhere along the way, you believed something that wasn't true. You bought into it, and now it's yours. That's alls I'm trying to say to you."

I stared at him. *Someone should confront Coach Donnelly,* I thought. *Just shake him and tell him to stop. To please stop.*

"Thanks," I said.

"Don't mention it," he said. "And get to class this afternoon, okay? I don't need my star third baseman and team captain getting into trouble before the Florida trip."

He left. I lay back down, and I wondered where Rafe was. He was the one person who would get what I was feeling. Well, Bryce too. But Rafe was my boyfriend.

Wait. No, he wasn't. Shit. Because I was a wuss. Because I was afraid of what people thought.

If I just let people know. If I ran down to the quad, found Rafe, spun him around, and kissed him in public. What would happen?

I laughed. The world would end.

Wait. Would it?

My dad's voice was loud in my head as I lay there in bed, revisiting my problem again and again. *Don't embarrass me, Ben. Stop being so lazy. You're sitting on your ass, wasting your time thinking about a bunch of foolishness. You're being stupid and lazy. Buck up and get to work. We're Carver men. We work. We work hard.*

All my life. All my life I'd heard these voices, and I'd heeded them. I'd railed against myself, again and again. *You're stupid. You're lazy.*

And now I heard Donnelly's voice.

Maybe you bought into something, and now it's yours.

This funny, murky feeling had invaded my head. Maybe, against all odds, Donnelly was right, after all. What if what I'd bought, I'd bought from my dad? What if the biggest purchase I'd made in my life was a soundtrack of negative thoughts about myself that I'd played non-stop? And what if it was, indeed, now mine?

Shit. How could Donnelly be right?

39

At lunch, I sat silently with the team, focused on my ham steak and sweet potatoes. I couldn't possibly joke today, and I wondered if Mendenhall noticed and thought it was about the cheating. It was, partially. Did this happen to everyone who cheated? Steve had certainly seemed pretty stoked when he showed me the A on his test. I definitely wasn't going to be celebrating whatever I got in calculus.

That's when Albie and Rafe entered the cafeteria. I saw them out of the corner of my eye, and this sad feeling pounded at my chest.

Behind them was Toby.

He wore a beige-and-pink pocketed skirt and a white blouse, with dangling earrings, eye makeup, and a little blush on his checks. He'd shaved his legs.

It was hard not to stare at him with an open mouth. Not just because he looked so different, but because it was thirty-seven degrees outside.

The room didn't go quiet all at once, like in the movies. It went quiet in waves, like the volume dropped by half, and then another quarter, and then some more, until everyone was staring at him.

He walked from table to table with a stack of flyers. Rafe and

Albie fanned out to other parts of the cafeteria. Toby came to our table, and Steve said, under his breath, "What the serious fuck?"

Toby ignored it and handed me the leaflet.

It was a head shot of him, made up. It read, ANNOUNCING: THE COMING OUT OF TOBY RYLANDER, AGE 16, AS GENDER FLUID.

Underneath there was a Q&A section.

Q: Is Toby trying to get attention?

A: No. I mean, Toby likes attention, but this is about being true to his gender orientation.

Q: What is gender orientation?

A: Gender is complicated. Some people are male, some people are female, and others feel somewhere in between. It changes. Sometimes Toby feels male. Other times, he's female.

Q: Who cares?

A: I wrote this so that you would understand. You can care or not care. I don't care.

Q: What should I know?

A: You should know that Toby is fine being called a he, a she, or a they. Some people have preferred pronouns, but Toby is happy to be called any of the above, though if she's obviously dressed female she prefers she or they. Also, Toby, who here refers to him/her/themselves in the third person, is not a freak. He/She/They are a human being with feelings. If you hurt his feelings, he will feel sad. Also, if you are cruel to her, you'll get in trouble with the school, which is fully aware of Toby's gender orientation and is fine with it. If you touch them in a violent or inappropriate way, you will be kicked out of school.

Q: What else should I know?

A: Toby knows this is confusing to a lot of people who don't know what gender fluidity is. He gets it, and he'll be patient with you so long as you try.

As I read it, my heart soared, and I couldn't help but smile. It was so—Toby. I felt a little choked up, actually. I wasn't ready for my team-mates to see me cry, but I was ready for them to see me support him. So I said to Toby, "Cool. You be you," and I passed the leaflet to the guy seated next to me, who was Zack.

Noise started up again, and the coolest thing happened. A couple guys started pounding their fists on their tables. It started really softly, but soon it picked up, and I watched Toby put his hands over his mouth, clearly moved by the support. He started crying, and Albie gave him a hug, and Rafe too.

"Fucking crazy shit," Zack said above the din of the table thumps. Our table wasn't doing it. I ignored the comment, walked across the cafeteria to Toby, and hugged him tight. And damned if a bunch of other guys didn't do the same.

40

At practice on Wednesday, I took a lot of shit.

"Yo, Carver, is your friend aware that this is an all-boys school?" Mendenhall said as he warmed up, playing soft toss with Zack.

I shrugged. I was busy throwing with Steve, and I was truly uninterested in discussing the little I knew about gender fluidity with a bigoted idiot.

"He'll get special treatment too," Zack continued. "Just watch."

"Yup," Mendenhall said. "The freaks always get special treatment. Meanwhile, the normal people get fucked, of course."

I held the ball and turned to Mendenhall.

"Are you really serious right now?" I asked.

He shrugged. "Why wouldn't I be?"

"Do you have any idea what privilege is?"

He rolled his eyes. "I'm sure you'll tell me, Professor."

I shook my head. "You're an asshole. You think he's lucky to be gender fluid at an all-boys school? That has to be the hardest thing I can imagine."

"Toby's imagining something hard," Zack said.

I turned to him. "What are you, three? Seriously, guys. Grow up. You think it's easy? I'm sorry, but that's fucking stupid."

"I'm tired of your mouth," Mendenhall said, taking his glove off his left hand.

I punched my glove. "Well, which is it? I don't talk enough, or I talk too much? Make up your mind so I can figure out who the hell I need to be."

"Fuck you," Mendenhall said.

"Fuck you back. Are you ready to practice? You ready to close your mouth and get serious? Because we have a game in less than a week. You in, or are you out?"

And Mendenhall stopped talking, and put his glove back on his hand, and I felt a surge in my chest.

"And by the way: No more talking shit about Toby. I'm not gonna listen to that. Got it?"

No one said anything.

"Good," I said.

Rafe, Toby, and Albie were in my room when I got back after practice. Toby was wearing the same skirt, and he was sitting cross-legged on my floor. His shaved legs smooth as a baby's. Rafe had commandeered my bed, and Albie was on the other one.

Seeing Rafe in my room was confusing. He'd said we could go back to being best friends, just like that. And now he looked all casual, like he'd already made that switch, but I wasn't even close to there. But I was too tired to do anything other than pretend everything was fine. I chuckled. "Make yourself at home," I said.

"I wanted to see this incredible closet you have," Albie said. "I've heard reports but have never had the opportunity."

"I should charge ten bucks per showing," I said.

Rafe jumped off my bed, walked to the closet, and made a big show of presenting it. He slowly opened the door, pulled the string for the light, and said, "Ta-dah!"

"Oh, my," Albie said. "That's intense."

"Laugh it up," I said. "I can see things. And at least I don't have half-eaten candy bars on my closet floor." I nodded at Toby.

He sucked his cheeks in. "Of all days to compare my closet to yours," he said, and Rafe said, "Boo. Leading statement. I'll ask the jury to disregard."

I rolled my eyes. "Subtle," I said.

"Can you guys give us a sec?" Rafe asked.

Toby and Albie nodded and left the room. Rafe sat down on the other bed, and he tapped the spot next to him. I tentatively sat there. My body felt warm, being so close to him again.

"You ready for your parents?" he asked.

"Never."

"Yeah, I'm not envying you. How about your speech?"

I closed my eyes and shook my head. "Ready but not ready, you know?"

"How'd your test go?"

I gave him a thumbs-up and averted my eyes. There was no way I was ever going to be able to tell Rafe about my cheating. That was going in the vault.

"I feel bad," he said. "I shouldn't have done that to you. You were right. I wanted what I wanted, like, immediately. That wasn't fair to you."

He put his hand on my shoulder and leaned the side of his head on top of it. I just sat there and let the feeling of his warmth run through me. Rafe. My Rafe.

"Thanks," I said. "Thank you for saying that. I was really down when you left last night."

"I know. Me too."

"And I know it's not fair to you either. But. Can you slow down, like, a bit? This is — a lot."

"I can," he said. "Love you, Ben."

My facial muscles relaxed. I hadn't realized it, but I'd been tense in my face all day until that moment.

"Love you more," I said, and I turned to face him, and our lips met, lightly, and we stayed connected like that for what felt like forever, and I was home again.

41

Having my parents in my room, the same room in which I'd slept with Rafe the night before, was weird. I kept glancing around to see if there were any signs of Rafe's presence.

"You have this all to yourself!" Mom said, looking at all the space.

"Yep. After Bryce left, they didn't put anyone else in here with me."

"That must be nice," she said.

"Yep."

"And have you made any new friends?"

"Give it a rest, Marlene," my dad said. "The boy's an award winner, captain of the baseball team. Of course he has friends."

It was nice to have his approval, but something about him saying this made me want to correct him. "It's been only okay in terms of all that," I said. "The baseball guys, for instance. We're kind of friends, but I'm nothing like them. I hang out with other kids who I like better."

My dad looked out the window and frowned.

"This is why I didn't want you going to a rich kid school like this. Those kids will smell the stink of the farm on you."

I took a deep breath as I felt his words press down on my chest.

I gave my parents the grand tour. I took them to math class, where Ms. Dyson welcomed them warmly and then gingerly placed a paper in my hands.

My calculus test. A minus.

My heart jumped. And then I remembered that I wasn't seeing an achievement so much as a ruse.

"I told Headmaster Taylor this morning," Ms. Dyson said. "You're good to go, Pappas Award guy!"

I smiled. "Thanks."

We went to all my morning classes. My parents didn't have much to say about them. Dad, for one, seemed a little less — opinionated, maybe? — than usual. Instead of making comments about the ostentatiousness of the campus, he seemed downright awed by the plaques in the hallway of the Arthur Building.

"For each Pappas winner, huh?"

"Yep."

"That's some beautiful wood," he said.

I smiled. That was what I always thought when I walked through the hallway, but I'd never heard anyone else at Natick say it. Maybe that was one really good thing about coming from my family; I never for a second took for granted anything about my education or the incredible institution that was the Natick School.

We wandered out onto the quad after chemistry. It was a reasonably warm day, and I decided to take them down to the waterfront, where we could sit at one of the picnic tables and rest a little.

Toby was out making sun angels on the grass, which were basically like snow angels except there was no snow, and it was sunny out. He was wearing a different skirt and hoop earrings. I'd seen him do this a week earlier, only in men's clothing. I knew my dad would have a comment about Toby's appearance, and I hoped he'd at least be polite and save it for private.

Rafe and Albie were with him, and my heart jumped. I lightly waved over to Rafe, who smiled my way. Rafe was teaching Albie stage combat, which was something he'd done back in Boulder. He'd tried to teach me a few weeks earlier. Stage combat is how actors portray violent acts in movies and onstage. The move he taught me was a face punch, where the puncher actually punches his other hand to make the smack noise, and the punchee whips his head around so that it looks like he's absorbed the punch. I followed the directions, but never really felt like we'd be fooling anyone if we did it in front of an audience.

"So when I lunge my fist at your stomach, you pull your stomach in and grab my fist, and you say, 'Oof,'" Rafe said to Albie, who was faced the other way and couldn't see us.

"You're asking Albie to pull his stomach in? Do you have a crane?" Toby yelled from his prone sun angel position. Albie gave him the finger.

"You should be doing this with Toby. More people want to hit Toby," Albie said. I smiled but said nothing as we walked by.

"Oh, please. Albie, you're way more hittable than I am. People find me delightful. The focus groups we hired found you derivative and sophomoric."

"Jesus," my dad muttered, once we'd passed them. "Them boys play for the other team, don't they?"

I glanced back at my friends, and then I turned away from them and kept walking with my folks.

"Only straight bones in this family," Dad said, and something broke in me.

Something Hannah had said to me came to mind. That thing about vulnerability. *Either you do vulnerability, or it does you.* She'd been right, hadn't she? Because I could pretend that what he'd just said hadn't hurt me deep inside, but that's all it was: pretend.

I stopped walking. I turned to my dad and opened my mouth to speak.

"Has anything ever really made you laugh, Dad?" I asked. "Like, really laugh? Uncontrollable laughter?"

He frowned. "What is this? What kind of question is that?"

"I just wondered," I said, and we started walking again, and I realized there was nothing more that could come out of this conversation. "Never mind." I looked over at Mom. "Hey, are you seeing Hazel again?"

She put her head down, and Dad said, "I think there was a McDonald's on the way in. We'll probably just eat there."

I looked at Mom. How was all this avoidance acceptable to her? And then I thought: *How is this acceptable to me?* It wasn't.

That night at dinner, while my parents were at McDonald's, I sat with the baseball guys, as usual.

Zack started talking about Kyle Guidry, who had gotten into Yale.

"That's you next year," Steve said, pointing to me.

I shook my head, hard. "Nah," I said. "I doubt I'd get in there."

Steve shrugged. "You're that guy. You got that Pappas thing, like Guidry. You're fuckin' perfect."

"Yeah, real perfect, that's me," I said. I glanced over at Mendenhall, who knew the truth about my math test, but he wasn't paying attention.

"Dude's so humble," Steve said.

Walking back to the dorm with all the guys after dinner, I felt like I could vomit up my insides. And there wasn't a person in the world, Rafe included, who could know that I was a cheater. I was a fraud.

That night, as I brushed my teeth and went over my speech for the zillionth time in my head, I looked in the mirror.

What happens if you have everything, but you feel nothing? Because everyone thought I was perfect, and my parents were here, and proud of me, and I was about to give a speech in front of everyone I knew. And then I would be given the keys to everything I ever wanted, a scholarship that would almost certainly allow me to be the first in my immediate family to go to college, and study more history, and maybe become Dr. Carver, which was a lifelong goal. But there I was, in the mirror, blurred by smudged specks of toothpaste and streaks of water, and no less heavy than I'd been that day at the pool with my brother, when sitting submerged on the floor seemed like a normal and fitting place to be.

So I'd been less than honest. Surely I wasn't the first. A lot of the guys on the baseball team—and probably other teams—took the answer keys. It was a means to an end. I'd cheated on one test. I'd never do it again.

Someday I'd be out of this place. I'd be at school somewhere great, and maybe my dad wouldn't get me still, but it wouldn't matter, because I'd be with more people who did get me.

I thought about fear. About how for all these years, I'd been exactly who my dad wanted me to be. And there were perks to that. Sometimes a kind word. But so many other times, nothing, And so much criticism that I believed it. Bought it. I believed I was a screwup, even though I was the first in my immediate family to attend a boarding school, even though I'd been an A student, even though I had dreams of college. I'd gotten so many *Stop that foolishness* looks and *Well, don't get a big head about it* talks that I had taken over for Dad and started giving them to myself in his place when he wasn't around.

I had made sure not to get a big head. I had followed all the rules, sometimes because I was afraid, and other times because I wasn't aware there was an alternative. Groups don't get all civilly disobedient until they realize they've been missing something. That's me. All my life I did the good-son thing, because I didn't realize I had a choice.

I looked in the mirror again. I resisted the urge to clean off the glass with my forearm. I desperately wanted to see myself unencumbered. My true reflection. But I couldn't.

And tomorrow I'd pay homage to a guy just like me, whom everybody loved, but nobody knew. But our stories were different, because I didn't have a Vietnam, and there would be life after this for me. Right? Right?

"Thank you, Headmaster Taylor. And thanks to the Pappas Foundation for this honor. I am humbled to even be considered for this award, and I am beyond grateful for the scholarship that is part of it.

"Even if what I'm about to say means I won't get the award and the scholarship, I am very grateful that it was offered to me."

The audience shifted. I looked out and locked eyes with Rafe. His expression was full of love and compassion, and I smiled at him.

"It's probably not going to surprise you that I've spent a lot of time lately thinking about Peter Pappas.

"All I've heard about him for the past couple years is how brave he was. And I want to tell you: I did everything I could to understand who he was. Partially because I wanted to learn about him so I could pay homage to him, and partially because I'm a big history geek and I like to research things.

"Peter Pappas was, indeed, a very brave man.

"He fought for this country. He gave his life for our country, and that's a kind of bravery I can't even imagine. Could I put my life on the line for this country that I love? I'd like to think so, but the idea of being in a war is something I can't get my head around.

"I read some letters Peter sent to his family from Vietnam. When he wrote about seeing his closest friend get blown up right next to him, I realized that understanding what it feels like to be in a war is impossible unless you've been there.

"And there were other things I read in his letters that made me realize that as brave as Peter Pappas was, he probably wouldn't be too thrilled to know about the award being given in his name.

"Peter Pappas was complicated, like all of us are. When he was at Natick, he was the big man on campus. He was a star on the basketball team and the soccer team. He was a straight-A student, and he had many, many friends. He was in Model Congress. Everybody loved Peter Pappas.

"I'm not sure, though, that everybody really *knew* Peter Pappas. I met his sister, and like her, Peter grew up in a working-class part of Dorchester. I don't know if anyone has ever mentioned that before. When I got the award, I figured he was from a wealthy family. And as I researched, I realized, of course, he wasn't rich. Wealthy kids didn't often go to Vietnam.

"Peter needed everyone to admire him. Especially his dad. That's what his sister told me, and reading his letters, I saw that. Come to think of it, I wonder if a lot of overachievers in the world have that same need to make their parents proud.

"Here's something you didn't know about Peter Pappas: Two years before he enlisted, he was an anti-war crusader. He chained himself to a fence post at a rally in front of the Massachusetts State House. He gave an impassioned argument in Model Congress about how our boys should not be dying to protect a crooked Vietnamese regime.

"His father was an ardent supporter of the war, and Peter hated not being on the same side as his father. So Peter changed his mind to be in line with his dad's opinions, and he volunteered to enlist at seventeen. And then, once he was thrust into the inhuman situation of war, he had a change of heart. I read some of his letters, and he was afraid. Petrified. He wanted to come home. He wanted to live in a peaceful world. That's who Peter Pappas was. But I'm not calling him a coward. He was the opposite of a coward.

"I think that expressing fear was expressing the truth. And it's hard to express the truth when the world wants you to be someone else.

"I guess you might be wondering why I would say all of this. I thought a lot about this, believe me. I'm not a guy of many words, and I'm not one to buck the system. But mischaracterizing a guy who is no longer with us is wrong. Peter was brave, and I do believe Peter Pappas deserves to have an award named after him. But I wouldn't want to be remembered as something I wasn't. Even if the world celebrated my memory. It's not right.

"What I learned, studying Peter Pappas, is a life lesson. It's about the rewards we get when we are who other people want us to be. Peter Pappas decided to be who his father thought he should be. And I'm not saying that being who others want you to be is a recipe for death. That's way too simple. But I do think that when we choose the easy path, where people or society reward us for being what they want us to be, against who we really are, a kind of death occurs. To the soul.

"All my life, I bought this idea that the way to live is to stay quiet, stay serious, even if it means my soul feels dead. I bought that idea, and it became mine. But today, I think the best way to live is like my good friend Toby Rylander, who chooses to be himself even if it makes his life harder in a way, because at least he's alive in his soul.

"I want to be like that. Myself. Even when it's harder. Even when it's inconvenient. Toby has taught me the value of standing up and being seen.

"I thank him for that. And I thank Peter Pappas for that. And—I thank Rafe Goldberg for that. Whom I happen to love.

"Being who you are means admitting when you make mistakes. And recently, I made a big mistake. It probably will mean I won't get this award, but when I think about what my soul would feel like to carry around this mistake all my life, I realize I would rather own up to it and face the consequences than act like it didn't happen and accept the award under false pretenses.

"On Tuesday, I cheated on a calculus test. I had never cheated before. It was a horrible choice. I felt like I needed to cheat, I guess. If I didn't cheat, I would have failed the test, and in order to be the person I've tried to be the last few years—good at everything, with no real weaknesses—I felt like I had to get a good grade.

"I'm sorry for cheating. I let myself down, and I let the school down. I understand that I will get in trouble for it. That's fine. Starting today, I am going to be who I am and stand for what I stand for, so I don't ever have to make a choice like that again, one that goes against my morals, in order to be what people want me to be.

"It's a different situation, but I think Peter Pappas would totally get what I'm talking about.

"Thank you."

As I walked offstage, the lack of applause was palpable. The awkward silence stretched out for what felt like a full minute but was probably just five seconds or so, and I stood in the wings of the auditorium, alone, wondering what was next.

Headmaster Taylor came backstage first. He was shaking his head, clearly annoyed.

"You probably just cost yourself your scholarship, and worse, you may have just cost the school this award," he said.

I lowered my head. "I know."

"Selfish and not smart," he said. "Very disappointed in you."

I didn't respond, and I didn't look up.

"How did you cheat? Where did you get the answers to the test?"

I shook my head. I wasn't interested in involving anyone else in my drama.

"Consider yourself suspended," he said. "You won't be going to Florida either. I'll talk to your parents right now. You'll come back a week after everyone else, and this will go on your personal record."

He stomped off, and I kept my head down. I'd known that could happen. Would happen, even. But hearing that I wasn't going to Fort Lauderdale with my teammates hit me somewhere tender.

Then I thought about Pappas, and that made me feel better. I wondered if there really was an afterlife, and if he'd know that I restored the truth about him. I had to believe he'd be glad I'd done it.

And it occurred to me: All this time, I'd been thinking about how Pappas had believed in something so much that he died for it, and I could never imagine doing that. But I'd just given up a scholarship, probably, part of my future, because I believed in the truth.

Wow. Maybe I finally did find the thing I'd die for.

I only had a few moments to think about that before Rafe tore back the curtain and ran up to me. "Wow!" he said. "That was — unexpected."

I managed a smirk. "Ta-dah! Scholarship gone."

"Maybe. Probably. How do you feel?"

I thought about it. Rafe was smiling at me, and I couldn't help but smile back. "Lighter," I said.

"Lighter?"

I nodded, and Rafe hugged me. I hugged him back, hard.

Then my parents arrived. I pulled away from Rafe, but I kept hold of his hand. Mine shook.

My mother looked a little confused. My father's expression was stone.

"What's this?" He gestured to our connected hands.

"It is what it is," I said. I braced for the verbal assault.

"Let's get going," he said, devoid of emotion, and he began to walk off. "Long drive home."

"I'm not ready," I said.

He stopped walking about ten feet from me, but he didn't turn around.

"I'll wait in the car," he said.

"Dad," I said, quietly. "Come on."

He took a moment, and then he turned and walked back to where I was standing. He spoke very softly.

"How many times do I have to tell you not to embarrass me? And yet you do. I'm embarrassed to be your father."

I looked down. Rafe squeezed my hand.

"You're embarrassed to be my dad?"

"Yes," he said.

We stood there in silence. Dad crossed his arms over his chest. I held on to Rafe's hand, feeling about two feet tall.

I turned and faced Rafe, very aware my parents were across from us. I felt torn between who I was, and who I *was*.

And who was I?

This empty feeling in my chest. It had always been there. And then there was this new thing, light and warm and totally not empty, and it was pressing down on the empty.

I smiled at Rafe, first a small one that matched his sympathetic gaze, and then I looked into Rafe's eyes and I saw him. I saw him. Who he was, and who he was to me. I smiled bigger and truer.

"This is not rocket surgery," I muttered, and he cracked up. Happy Rafe was too much for me to just look at. So I leaned over and hugged him, hard. He gasped into my shoulder, and I gripped him tight.

"I'm not gonna lose you again," I said into his arm, and I heard him say back, "No, you won't."

I pulled away until we were face-to-face, and then I kissed him.

My father cleared his throat. I didn't react. I kept my lips glued to Rafe's. My dad cleared his throat more. *You can clear your throat until your vocal cords are severed,* I thought. *If you want to say something, say something.* But I was through with this not saying stuff. It was just not happening anymore.

I took a full second before releasing our liplock and turning to my parents, who were both staring at us, slack jawed.

I smiled, the warmest, kindest one I could muster.

"This is *me*," I said. "Me."

Me, it turned out, was not something my father was interested in seeing.

"C'mon, Marlene," he said as he started to walk away.

She didn't move.

"C'mon. Let's beat the traffic."

"Stop it, Richard," she said.

"Excuse me?"

"I said stop it. Stop walking away, and stop telling me what to do."

And in the most surprising moment of my life so far, my dad stopped.

My mother took over the conversation, and I felt like my heart was dancing in my chest.

"So, sweetheart," she said to me. "You're homosexual?"

I shook my head. "No. I mean, I don't know what I am. I've always liked girls. But now I like Rafe. I don't think I'm gay, but I like Rafe. Love."

She squinted at me. "I don't get what that all means. Are you a couple with Rafe?"

I nodded and took Rafe's hand.

"Well, then. I always thought Cindy was a bit of a wet blanket. I don't know you too well yet, Rafe. Are you a wet blanket?"

"No, ma'am," he said, smiling, and he walked over to her and hugged her. She put her arm around his neck.

"Well, then, good. I don't want any more wet blankets in this family. God knows we have plenty of those." She looked at my dad. "I also want to let everyone know that I'm selling herbal remedies now."

"Not in my store, you ain't," my dad said.

"Yes, in *our* store. And if not, then someplace else. Seriously, Richard. The world is changing. Stop being so darned wet blanket-y."

As angry as I was at my dad, I could feel what he must be feeling in his chest. *Killer of fun*. It's not a fun place to be, even if you believe it's the right place to be.

And then my dad did it again. He walked away. "I'm not gonna listen to this foolishness," he said.

"Of course not," she said, once he was gone. Then she turned to us. "I don't know that I'm in love with my friend Hazel, but I sure do like her lots. Is that what you guys have?"

I turned to Rafe and swam (and sunk) in his hazel eyes. "Perchance," I said.

Dad took their truck and drove back himself. My mom gave me a little time to pack up and say good-bye to people before I drove her home in Gretchen. She sat at one of the picnic tables by the lake and did her knitting, while Rafe and I walked back to the dorms hand in hand.

Pretty much everybody gawked as we walked by. It was like they were doing the math about all the things I'd said. Some people gave us a "What's up" or nodded. Some people looked and then looked away. No one said anything mean. My guess was that people were too afraid of me to say anything not nice.

Once we got to my room, Rafe threw his arms around me and I threw my arms around him, and we kissed each other for a long time. Part of me wanted to lock the door, but with my mom waiting for us, it felt kinda wrong.

"You, sir, are so getting laid when we get back," he said.

I laughed. "That's why I did it. I threw everything away, and it was all for sex."

He cracked up. "Of course. You sure you don't want to come out to Boulder for the break?"

I sat down on the bed. "I want to more than anything. But I better go to New Hampshire and deal with my dad."

"You and your dad are so different."

I shrugged.

Rafe said, "I guess I see where you get your walking-away habit from."

"Never again. I promise. Never again."

"You love him?"

"He's my dad."

"Well, if you decide you want to come to Colorado, just call. My mom has a shit ton of miles, and I'm sure she'd give them to you."

"That's really nice. Thanks. And I'd like nothing more. Let's just play it by ear, okay?"

There was a knock on the door. It was Donnelly. He seemed different when he came in and saw me and Rafe together. He nodded at Rafe and then focused on me.

"Well, that was quite a talk," he said.

"Uh-huh."

"Headmaster Taylor wanted me to let you know that you won't be coming to Florida."

"I know," I said. "I'm sorry."

"He also wanted me to tell you that the foundation board will be meeting this coming week about this. You might have lost the award. You probably did."

"I'm aware of that."

"Why'd you do it?"

"Because of something you said, actually. You said maybe I'd bought something and didn't even know I'd bought it. You were right, you know. It was time to sell."

He looked between me and Rafe, like he was watching a tennis match. I wondered if he followed what I was saying, or if he even heard it. Maybe it was the first time anyone had ever told Donnelly that he'd said something to them that mattered.

"Okay," he said. "Well. Okay. Have a good break, Carver. I support your lifestyle, by the way. People have the right to choose whatever lifestyle they want."

"There are so many things wrong with that sentence," Rafe said, but I waved him off.

"Thanks," I said to Donnelly. "I support your lifestyle too."

I said good-bye to Rafe, who was going to a hotel near the airport in Boston for an early-morning flight. On the way out to meet my mom, I ran into Mendenhall, who shook his head when he saw me.

"Dude," he said. "What the hell, dude."

I shrugged.

"You left the team in the lurch. That's some selfish shit."

"I wish I could go to Florida. I did what I had to do."

"You're a strange guy, Carver. You gay too?"

I ignored the question and focused on the comment. "You're finally getting it," I said. "I'm a strange guy. And you'll never be a strange guy, which is too bad for you. So maybe we'll just play baseball together and not worry about it, huh?"

"Whatever, dude," he said. "If you tell anyone where you got the answer key, I will ruin your life."

"I won't," I said. "I did what I did. You want to do the right thing, it's on you."

He walked away, and I knew he'd never fess up. He wasn't that kind of kid, and he wouldn't be that kind of man, and that was okay with me. None of my business.

As I drove north with my mom in Gretchen, I was thinking that spring break was going to feel eternal. Two weeks vacation, plus one for my suspension. I had no interest in being up in Alton, but it was the right thing to do — to fix things with my dad, or whatever was like fixing things.

"Are you afraid of what Dad's gonna say about your herbal remedies when we get back?" I asked my mom.

"Nah," she said, but something in her voice betrayed the words. I guess when you've spent twenty years married to someone who treats you a certain way, and you live in a box, it has to be scary leaving that box. "You?"

At first I thought she meant was I afraid of her burgeoning career as an herbalist, but then I realized she meant was I afraid of what Dad was going to say to me.

I sighed. "I don't know."

Mom didn't bring up the fact that I was dating a boy and she'd just found out. She didn't bring up the suspension. I didn't say any more about the fact that she had stood up to Dad for the first time ever, as far as I knew. Neither of us talked about the future, like what was going to happen when we got back to Alton.

"Looks like rain," she said.

"Yep."

"Hope Richard got the cows in the barn. They get persnickety about their food when they're all wetted up."

"I'm sure he did it as soon as he got back."

"How about Czech dumplings for dinner?"

It was familiar. Sometimes, familiar is good.

"Sounds great, Mom. Sounds great."

44

A freezing rain had begun to fall. We arrived back at the farm, and the lack of sound beyond the thump of cold precipitation hit me hard. I was back. This was it. I had nowhere else to go, and I was going to have to face my deeply disappointed dad.

I deposited my bag in my room, and Luke reclined on his bed, playing a game on the same Game Boy he'd had since he was about five.

"Hey," I said.

He didn't look up. "I hear you screwed up."

"A bit," I said.

He didn't respond, just went back to his game.

"Did you hear anything more than that?"

He didn't say anything. I wondered what it would have been like to be here when my dad got back. Did he rant? Was he upset? Any emotion at all would have been nice to see. Anything besides leaving.

"Because if you did, let's just stop this thing where we don't talk about stuff, okay?" I said. "You and me, we're better than that. Come on. Put the game thing down. Talk to me."

He tentatively saved his game and sat up, tossing his dirty blond hair out of his eyes.

"So, um, are you gay?" he asked.

I sat down on my bed. "I don't think so. I'm in love with a guy, though."

"But you aren't gay? That's weird."

"I know. I mean, no. It doesn't feel weird. It feels like the most natural thing. I never thought about guys, but Rafe just, I don't know. I actually had a girlfriend this past month. She was great, but I liked Rafe better."

He threw his legs over the side of the bed and hyperextended his skinny elbows on his mattress. He whispered, "I have lunch with Julie sometimes now. The girl everyone used to call Bulldozer?"

"That's great," I said.

"It's okay."

"Do you like her?"

"I don't know. Maybe. It's hard to come up with questions sometimes."

I didn't really know what to say, and I realized that this was, for my brother, a real conversation. Like when we'd talked in the car after the swimming lesson. That was probably the last time he'd had a conversation with someone in his family. My head hurt thinking about it. I looked at him, and he looked fine. Maybe his was a more right-handed path. Perhaps some people don't feel starved for *more*, the way I always felt when I was growing up.

Maybe that was okay too.

"Tell her things about you," I said.

"Like what?"

"Like things you're interested in."

He shrugged and picked up his Game Boy, and I felt this tenderness toward my brother, who would always be exactly who he was. And that was definitely okay. If I had more to say than he did, I could say it.

"So anyway. I'm suspended for a week, so I'll be around for a while. The worst part is it'll stay on my school record. Good-bye top-level college, I barely knew ye."

"Yeah, but. No school for an extra week. That's awesome."

I didn't say anything, because he'd never get that I actually enjoyed school.

"Meanwhile, Dad is probably never going to talk to me again."

"He didn't say much to begin with, though, did he?"

My brain went *ooooooohhh* when I thought about that. *Deeeeeepp.*

"I love you, surprisingly introspective bro," I said.

He kept playing his game. "I love you too, totally weird older brother."

I glanced out the bedroom window at the barn. Dad still hadn't come out. I'd have seen him. So I waited, all the stuff I wanted to say to him tumbling through my brain.

Dad. I'm not gonna spend my life being the guy who is afraid to disappoint you. I have other things I want to be.

I wished Uncle Max were still alive, so I could talk to him. He'd understand.

Dinnertime came. Still no sign of Dad. I asked Luke to check with Mom, see where he was. In the barn, he came back and told me. I stared out my window, waiting, waiting.

I didn't eat. Dad didn't eat. Luke and Mom had a meal, and when it was over, Mom came in.

"Give it a rest 'til morning, Benny," she said.

"He has to come out at some point."

"You know your father. He's a stubborn old mule."

"This is not okay," I said. "Not anymore."

Mom sat down on my bed next to me and put her hand lightly on my knee. "No. He's got to do better. I know it, you know it. Luke even knows it. Only person doesn't know it is your dad."

I stood up. I didn't have to say anything. Mom knew. I bundled up in layers — T-shirt, long-sleeve shirt, sweatshirt, jacket, scarf, hat, gloves. I walked to the wet room outside the kitchen and put on my boots. Mom followed and watched me in silence. I knew she was rooting for me.

The dark barn smelled bitter. Bitter, chilly sadness, like you could feel it in the stale air. Unmet potential. Wasted dreams. Chicken crap.

Thanks to the moonlight, I could see Dad was in the corner of the chicken stall. Chickens clucked around him. He sat with his knees up, his back slouched against the side of the pen.

I'd never seen my dad just sitting before. Not in a work area, anyway.

"Hey," I said.

His silhouette moved a little bit. He shuffled his behind as if to get more comfortable.

"Dad, it's me."

In the darkness of the barn, I could almost see him shrug. I could feel the air moved by his shoulders' motion. It stung my eyes.

"You gonna just live in here now? Try to wait me out? Three weeks, and I'm not going anywhere."

Still nothing. No words.

"Dad? Are you listening, Dad? I know you can hear me. This ends today. Whatever this is. You can't just walk away and ignore me any-

294

more when I do something you don't like. You either have to talk to me, or — I don't know, but I can't do this anymore. I can't."

Tears now.

"I can't take this. I could take a lot of things, but I can't take this," I said.

I turned to leave.

My dad's crusty voice rose from the chicken coop.

"You're a cheater now?"

"It was a stupid choice," I said.

"I'll say. And you traded away a college education for what? So you could date a boy? What kind of foolishness is that?"

"I didn't trade it away. And anyway, losing the scholarship had nothing to do with Rafe. I'll figure it out. I'll find a way to still go to college."

"And this Rafe boy . . . he's nothin' more than another rich kid."

"That's not true, Dad."

"It is true. And what's worse? You're lettin' him screw you. I don't know what that makes you, but it sure don't make you a Carver."

It took every muscle in my body not to walk away.

I swallowed three times. Four. It was like I was afraid of the sound of my voice.

"I am a Carver," I said. "I'm as much a Carver as you are."

"If you're a Carver, I'll tell you one thing you are. Not gay. That ain't okay. You ain't doing that while living here, you understand? You wanna stay in this family, you'll never talk to that boy again. And you can forget about going back to that school next year. I've had enough of your foolishness."

The words repeated over and over in my brain. *You'll never talk to that boy again.*

This time, I walked away. I'd promised Rafe I wouldn't, but in this case, I was pretty sure he'd be fine with it.

I walked with my head down, away from the barn, away from the house. I took the road toward town, not minding the cold rain beating down on my head, each heavy drop like an assault on my brain.

I grabbed my phone out of my pants pocket. I shielded it from the rain and dialed.

"Hey," Rafe said.

"Hey."

"I'm at the hotel."

"I'm on an abandoned road in Alton, alone."

"You okay?"

"Nah. Is that ticket still available?"

"Yeah, absolutely. Sure. Let me call my mom. You want directions to the hotel?"

The rain around me couldn't touch me. I didn't feel cold. Not anymore.

"Yes, please."

The second time Rafe and I flew to Colorado together was very different than the first.

The first trip, it was Thanksgiving. The night before, he'd slept in my arms. I was freaking out about it a little, and I knew he was too, and then we talked about it. I didn't know then that we were freaking out for different reasons, but that wasn't important now.

This flight felt to me like I was taking a trip away from my life, like maybe losing my mind a little. In twenty-four hours, I'd likely given up a college scholarship, been rejected by my father, left my home, and stayed in a hotel with my boyfriend for the first time ever, and now I was heading to Boulder for who knows how long.

I felt nauseated, and yet goose bumps dotted my forearms. I wanted to scream from anger and sing with excitement and curl up and sleep off the stress.

Leaving Alton had been tough. I went back to my room and started packing my stuff, and my brother watched, and I didn't want to say anything, because if I started talking I might start crying. And then he started freaking out, which was very un-Luke of him.

"Ben? Don't leave. C'mon. You know Dad. He'll be back to normal in, like, three days and it will be like none of this ever happened."

"That's what I'm afraid of," I said, clenching my jaw and measuring my words really carefully so my voice didn't crack.

"You're afraid of that?"

"I'm not *doing* it anymore. Okay? I can't *do* this again. Okay?"

"Where are you going?"

"Colorado."

"Ben," my brother whined. He sounded six all of a sudden, and it hit me in my chest. "Don't go, Ben. Don't go. Please."

"I gotta go, buddy. I'll be back."

"Uncle Max was gone five years. Please, Ben. Don't leave me. Please."

"I'm not Uncle Max," I said, but at this point I was shaking because I couldn't hold the feelings in anymore. "Don't worry."

Then he had an all-out tantrum, jumping on his bed and kicking and pounding his mattress. "You can't do this! You can't go!"

I ran over to him. "C'mon, buddy, hold it together. It's okay, buddy."

"No! It's not okay! This sucks!"

Tears streamed down his face, and I closed my eyes and leaned in to hug him.

He punched me in the chest, hard. His flailing fist clipped me in the sternum; I was shocked, and my body's reaction was to punch back. I'm glad I didn't. I'm so glad I didn't. Instead, I squeezed him harder until he squeezed back, and then I grabbed the back of his skull in my two hands and moved his face so that he was looking directly into my eyes.

"I'm not him. Them. I'm not Uncle Max and I'm not Dad. I'm not running from you, Luke. You have my phone number. We can talk every day. I have to go away because I can't be here anymore and be me."

"You mean gay?"

"No. I mean *me*."

He softened up then, like he understood, in a way, and we got to say a real good-bye. He asked me to call tomorrow, and I promised I would. And I did. This morning. We talked about nothing, and it was great.

Mom was hard too. Or maybe not hard. Just sad. When I walked out with my suitcase, she was in the kitchen, drinking a beer and reading a book about herbs.

"Where are you staying?" she asked.

"With Rafe. Going to Colorado."

"This time of night? No. Go in the morning."

"We have a flight in the morning. I'll go to his hotel at the airport. It's fine."

"It's fine," she repeated, flat. She sipped her beer. "I don't know, Benny. Is it my fault? I should've straightened your dad out years ago."

"It's not your fault," I said, going over and hugging her. "You get why I'm leaving, right?"

"Oh, I get it," she said.

"I love you, Mom."

"Love you too, Benny. Don't get too crazy, hear? And you come back here. You know it'll be okay with your dad."

I didn't know that, but I nodded anyway.

And then there I was, driving and driving, until way after midnight, the roads spreading out in front of me, miles and miles and miles. Country roads, where all you see is the road ahead of you illuminated by headlights, are the loneliest place in the world. Then highways, which were surprisingly busy for so late. Five hours to Boston. It was three in the morning when I got there, and I was more tired than I'd ever been. I had to park in this crazy circular structure, at a skyscraper hotel right in the middle of town. Too tall, too loud, especially for how exhausted I felt.

Rafe came to the door in boxers and hugged me tight, and I just about collapsed into his arms. And this time I had no problem falling asleep.

And here I was. On an airplane. Going to Colorado to—I didn't know—visit? Still tired. Still unsure of everything.

I glanced over at Rafe. Who was my best friend. Who I loved. Who just about three months ago I was so mad at I thought we'd never talk again. And we got past it. That filled me with some hope. Maybe this was just today, with Dad. Maybe things would get better.

Rafe was reading a book called *Two Boys Kissing*. I reached over and pinched him on the neck.

"Ow," he said, continuing to read.

"Do you think things will ever be normal at school again?" I asked Rafe.

He put down his book. "Were things ever really normal there? I had a feeling you were thinking something like that."

"I was thinking about a lot of things. I was actually thinking about how it had been a while since I'd thought about history stuff. World War II. I used to have a constant running monologue, like the History Channel was in my brain. This was the first time I can remember where that all went away."

"Hard to live in the past when the present is so . . . busy."

"It's been busy, all right."

"The cheating thing. That surprised me. Why'd you do it, Ben?"

I was too tired to get into it. "Insecurity."

He nodded, like he got that.

"I don't know. I guess I've never really understood the whole emphasis on 'achieve achieve achieve' that you have," he said.

"You also don't come from a family that has nothing."

Rafe took a sip of his Bloody Mary mix, which, by the way, was absolutely disgusting. "I was thinking about that just now," he said.

"That I come from nothing?"

"No. That you think you come from nothing."

I felt my jaw tightening. This callous attitude about what my family did or did not have really bugged me, but who was I to say something when Rafe's family had footed the bill for my ticket to Boulder, and had offered to put me up for an extended period?

What if Rafe and I got into a big fight? Would I be homeless?

I wiped my hair out of my eyes, and this crazy thing happened. I began to cry. On a plane.

Rafe put my head on his shoulder and massaged my scalp and let me cry, and for once in my life I wasn't my dad, telling myself to simmer down, or man up, or some other way of telling me to be more up or down than I truly was. I just let myself cry, on a plane, in front of people, who weren't gawking, exactly, from across the aisle, but who were definitely looking. I could feel their stares without looking up.

When the tears subsided, I picked my head off Rafe's shoulder and turned to him and said, "I don't know what I have anymore."

And he said, "You have whatever I have."

I said, "What if I never get to go home again?"

And he said, "You'll have a different home."

I wasn't sure that those simple answers did it for me, but they were all I had, and as we flew over Indiana and Illinois, I said, "I'm tired of being afraid."

Rafe squeezed my hand.

"Sometimes I get afraid too," he said. "Like, what if you fall in love with some girl? You are still attracted to girls, right?"

"Yeah, but . . ."

"But what?"

"Relax," I said. "I'm a one-person guy. And that one person is you, and that's all that matters."

"Well, we have each other, so that's something," Rafe said, rubbing my arm.

I looked out the window, and the green squares of farmland below us looked like pieces of a seemingly unsolvable puzzle that were already miraculously in place.

Mr. Goldberg

is a lip kisser. At the Denver airport baggage claim, as we waited for my duffel bag, Mr. G. ran over when he saw us and proceeded to lay a wet one first on Rafe's mouth, and then on mine.

"My sons!" he yelled.

I surreptitiously wiped my mouth while Rafe and his dad were hugging, forgetting that Mrs. Goldberg, who hadn't sprinted over to us, was watching. She gave me a warm smile and a squishy hug into her freckled boobs.

"Thanks for letting me come," I said, holding on to her a bit because I needed the comfort.

"Are you kidding? We wouldn't have it any other way," she said, before planting a drier, more appropriate kiss than that of her husband on my cheek.

As we got on the toll road that would take us north and west to Boulder, I stared at the snow-capped mountains and remembered skiing at Thanksgiving. How Rafe and the Goldbergs had gone out of their way to make me feel at home, and how they didn't seem to think it was a big deal to give me experiences I'd never had. Dinners out at fancy restaurants with cloth napkins? Sure, why not? Rafe would whine about all the different ingredients, as he was more meat and potatoes. Meanwhile, I'd be savoring every new thing I could try. Aioli. Truffle foam. Gastrique this and that.

Rafe asked if we could stop at Smashburger for some lunch, but Mr. G. looked at his watch and said, "There's no t—"

Rafe's mom interrupted. "We'll get you food at home."

"Oh no," Rafe said. "Please no."

Over Thanksgiving, we'd wanted to get something to eat after we landed and Rafe's parents had said the same thing. We'd gone straight to their home, where they'd created a mountain luau–themed surprise party for us. Normally the specter of a repeat would have made me want to jump out of the moving car, but not today.

"You know what? I could use a goddamn party right about now," I said. "Bring it on."

Mrs. Goldberg glanced back from the passenger's seat and said, "Thank you. At least one of you has some gratitude. We did this in half a day, Rafe. Have a little fuckin' grace."

Rafe laughed, not derisively. "Whoa," he said.

"I'm sorry. I just . . . We've spent all morning getting anyone and everyone we can over to the house. It's been a lot, Rafe. A lot."

"Sorry, Mom. You're right. Thank you for throwing us a surprise party to honor Ben's suspension."

I felt a jolt in my chest, but then I looked up and saw Rafe was just joking around, and his callousness made Mr. G. laugh, and soon Mrs. Goldberg was chuckling a bit too. I was thinking how incredibly unlike my life this scene was. I'd loved it at Thanksgiving, and I was hoping I wasn't too much of a mess to love it this time too.

It turned out to be an inside party. Perhaps because it was set up in a day, there was no overriding theme, or at least not an obvious one. What there was, was a playlist that seemed particularly—something.

I'm not a music maven, but as Rafe hugged relatives and his best friend, Claire Olivia, and way more kids than were here last time, I could tell the first song was Elton John. As Claire Olivia and I gave each other the *I remember you* wave and said what's up, a song that seemed to be called "I Am What I Am" blared. After that was that song about rainbows from *The Wizard of Oz*.

"What's with the music?" I asked when I went over to grab some green-looking punch that I later found out was kale-pineapple juice. Ick.

Mrs. Goldberg tilted her head like I was an innocent child. "I made this for you, sweetie. It's a musical trip through gay history!"

"Thanks," I said, thinking, *Thanks?*

"These are songs you should know," she said. "As you come out, you'll find that there's generations upon generations of talented gay men and women who changed the world and paved the way for you." She touched my shoulder. "I am so proud of you, Ben. It's not easy, coming out. Not easy at all."

I was too tired to explain to her that I wasn't coming out as gay, or even bi. Unless she was telling me that there were *generations upon generations of talented gay men* who were otherwise straight until they met her son, none of this was particularly meaningful to me.

"I hear you're transitioning," an elderly woman said in my ear. I recognized her as Rafe's grandmother, who was memorable in that she wound up topless after doing the limbo at the last party.

"Hi," I said, and she grabbed me and gave me a tight hug, and I tried to figure out if she was Mr. or Mrs. Goldberg's mom. It was unclear. "What?"

"They tell me you're transitioning. I think you'll make a beautiful, large-boned woman."

"Mother!" Mrs. Goldberg said. She gave me an apologetic look. "What I said was that you are in transition."

I was so lost. Was this more gender fluid stuff? Where was Toby when you needed something explained to you?

"Well, whatever your gender orientation, I think you're a lovely human being," Rafe's grandma said, leaving me and Rafe's mom standing there.

"That was actually very sweet," I said.

Claire Olivia was wearing what appeared to be a World War I navy sailor's hat on her head. It did not particularly mesh with her outfit: vintage cowboy boots, tight jeans, and a solid yellow long-sleeve T-shirt.

"Please tell me you're staying and you're both enrolling at Rangeview. Pleeaassee! I need my Shay Shay back, and Rangeview desperately needs an out gay couple," she said.

"I, um, I have no idea," I said truthfully. "We just got here."

"Fine, but I fully expect to tag along to every single thing you boys do the next few weeks. Everything but the bed stuff, because I'm not that kind of girl."

"Okay?" I said, just as Rafe came over to rescue me.

"Give him a break," he said, perhaps gauging my bewildered expression. "He's been a Boulder gay boy for, like, two minutes."

She curtsied as a way of apologizing, and we made tentative plans with her to go to a place called the Laughing Goat that night.

When she walked away, I turned to Rafe. "I'm really not comfortable with everyone telling me I'm gay," I said.

He gave me an *Aww, isn't that sweet* look. "You're my boyfriend, no?"

"Yes."

"Then I think you're gonna have to get used to people assuming you're gay. Or bi. Should we tell people you're bi?"

I just looked at him and shook my head. "Can I have a rest, please? Would that be okay? Can I, like, go upstairs? I'm so, so tired, Rafe."

He looked hurt.

"We're fine," I said, sighing. "It's just a lot. I was up 'til three driving. And I have no idea how to do this right now."

He took my arm and led me upstairs. At the top of the stairs, he gave me a big kiss, which half made me happy and half made me want to strangle him. "I love you, Benny."

"Love you too," I said, and I was relieved when he left me alone to take a nap in his bed.

I woke up in time for dinner, and the party had ended, thankfully. I felt sheepish that I'd ducked out, and I hoped the Goldbergs weren't mad at me. I walked downstairs, and the family was sitting around on a cream-colored sectional that was crazy comfortable, as I recalled from Thanksgiving.

"You're up!" Rafe said, and his mom and dad turned and looked. They smiled when they saw me.

"Yup. Sorry about wimping out on the party."

His mother waved her hand like it was in the past. "Come sit down."

I sat on the couch next to Rafe, who put his hand on my leg. I squeezed his fingers and let go, and when his hand lingered, part of me wanted to ask him to move it and I wasn't sure why.

"We have something for you. A gift," Mrs. Goldberg said, and she handed me a wrapped present that appeared to be a book.

"Thanks," I managed. "Wow." I opened it. It was a survival guide for queer teens. I studied the back, or more like I pretended to study the back. Too much, somehow. Way, way too much.

"The coming-out process can be challenging, so we wanted to give you something really good to read that would help," she said, beaming at me.

"Thanks . . ."

"Where's my present?" Rafe asked, pretending to be pissed.

"It's only seeable when the dishwasher is empty," his mom said, and Rafe groaned. She turned back to me. "How did it go, when your parents found out you were gay?"

I knew she was a major advocate for LGBT people and all, but I had to just say it, even if it upset her. I gathered my strength and spoke. "I don't consider myself gay, Mrs. Goldberg."

"Oh. Bi," she said.

I shrugged and looked at Rafe, who grinned at me. "He hasn't landed there quite yet." He lowered his voice and did a stage whisper. *"He's in denial."*

I stood up quickly. "Please excuse me," I said to Rafe's parents, and I headed upstairs. We had the go-ahead to sleep in the same room, but for some reason I went into the guest room and flopped down there.

A few minutes later, Rafe knocked on the door. "Sorry," he said. "You're staying in here?"

"Need some more rest," I said, and I studied the baby-blue comforter and waited for him to leave.

I didn't know what was going on, but something bigger than annoyance was happening to me, and it felt like an explosion, and I was so scared that if I exploded at Rafe, I'd have nothing. The confusion and conflict felt like jitters in my arms and legs.

"Wait. Are you doing one of those walking away things?" he said, his tone sarcastic, like he was basically joking.

"Would you leave me alone?" I yelled. "God, Rafe! Can I have half a day to process that I'm fucking homeless? Without you and your parents telling me what I have to do and who I am? Jesus."

Rafe's eyes got big, and I saw the wound in the crease of his eyebrows. He nodded gently and backed out of the room.

My dad was always fond of saying that everything "out there" was a dressed-up version of what's "already here." By which he meant there was nothing better than Alton.

"You think them Hawaiian people are so special and fancy? Get near one of 'em when they have a stomachache. You'll see what they're made of," he'd say, and part of me knew that was my dad talking about stuff he knew nothing about, and part of me bought into it.

Walking along Boulder Creek the next morning, I realized my dad was dead wrong.

Even with the trees bare from winter, I was pretty sure the creek running through the city was the prettiest place I'd ever been. The sound of the water tumbling over rocks calmed me, and in the distance I could see the Rocky Mountains, which were so much taller than anything we had back home. The sunlight peering through the brittle snow-covered branches lent warmth to the scenery, like you could taste the hot chocolate waiting for you.

That was never the case in Alton. For me, anyway.

Rafe's house was less than a mile away, so we hiked over and strolled along the frozen creek. We didn't say much at first, and I knew I had some apologizing to do from the night before. A squirrel flashed by our feet, chasing God knows what.

"I'm sorry," I said.

"What for?"

"You know."

He stopped walking. "I accept, but I kind of want to hear why you're sorry."

I started walking again and he stayed with me. "I'm sorry for being nasty to you last night. I don't know why I'm mad, to be honest. I have no idea."

"I guess it's a lot." His gloved finger touched mine, tentatively. I wrapped my hand around his and we kept walking, stepping carefully over downed branches and huge roots.

"Yeah."

We walked some more, and I realized other things were bothering me. All my life I'd let those kinds of things go. But here I was, doing all sorts of things I didn't do.

"You know, it really did bother me when you made that joke. The one about denial," I said.

"Huh?"

I stepped over a mud puddle. "Your mom was asking if I was bi, and you whispered real loud that I was in denial."

"I was joking."

I stopped walking. "I get that. But do you get that I'm not in denial? I feel like I've told you a hundred times already that I don't think I'm gay or bi beyond you, and every time, it's like you don't absorb that."

He stuffed his hands in the side pockets of his purple jacket. "I just—I feel like you're me, but a few years earlier and with parents who don't accept you."

"Yeah, but I'm not," I said.

I could hear him exhale dramatically. "Well, you're definitely not straight in bed with me."

I looked out at the mountains, fixating on their snowy caps. "That's not what I'm saying. I'm saying that I'm Ben, and you are Rafe, and we are not the same, and you don't know what my future is just because you came out a few years ago. Okay?"

Rafe didn't say anything, and part of me was worried that it was too much, that I was being too contrary and that he was going to just walk away from me. But then I thought about the baseball team, and how maybe it was okay to speak your mind and disagree, and not every argument had to lead to someone, well, leaving.

We started walking again. "I also think you don't get privilege," I said.

"Oh, come on," he said, and our jackets rubbed together, making a hissing sound.

"No, I really don't think you understand. Like, you don't get how lucky you are to have parents who accept you. And on the plane, when you corrected me. I said, 'I came from nothing' and you said, 'You *think* you come from nothing.' I don't know if you understand how aggravating that is. When I was growing up, if we didn't have a chicken to process and we were out of eggs, we might not eat that night. Do you get that?"

"I don't think you get what I was saying," he said, and I could hear the defensiveness in his voice. "Being poor isn't nothing. You still have parents."

"Yes. But having no money is still having no money, and you have no idea what it's like to have literally forty-three dollars in my pocket until June, and no way to get more. Do you get that? How you have a safety net and I have none? How fucking scared I am that you'll just drop me again, and I'll be stuck out here with nothing?"

We walked side by side in silence. I could feel his simmering anger. And then, as we walked farther, it was like the snow dissipated the bad feeling. Maybe he finally heard me.

"Sorry," he said. "Am I a horrible boyfriend?"

I cracked a smile and squeezed his hand. "Nah. You're just Rafe. Which is pretty great, and totally worth putting up with the fact that you don't always listen."

I could feel him bristle a bit next to me. "Thanks."

We walked some more. Water scurried down the creek, which was nearly dry.

"I guess there's one thing I don't understand," he said.

"Shoot."

"What do you mean you're homeless? I mean, you weren't kicked out. You can go home."

I knew what he meant. I'd been thinking the same thing. It wasn't as if I couldn't go home, and I knew that there were plenty of kids out there who literally couldn't. Yet at the same time, I *felt* homeless. I couldn't explain it. I tried anyway.

"I don't know. It's a feeling. Like I don't exactly know where my home is. I don't think you get that. I don't think you get—"

"Get what?"

I stumbled a bit over a particularly high tree root. "Never mind."

"Ben, you can say stuff to me. My parents and I actually have arguments and live to tell about it. No offense."

I chuckled. "None taken. I've noticed that. It's weird. I'm not used to it."

"I know."

"I guess . . . I guess the truth is I'm a little mad at you."

"Mad at me? What did I do?"

"It's not what you did. It's what's happened since I've known you. In six months, I've gone from being an A student and a standout in two sports to being—this."

"I know you're not pegging your cheating on knowing me."

"No," I said. "Not at all. I'm talking about being confused about who I am and what I want. Unsure where my home is. Having a dad who thinks I'm worthless."

"Well, I think *he's* worthless," Rafe said.

"You sound a little like your mom sometimes," I said back.

He exhaled and said, "I'm not sure that's such a bad thing."

"Maybe not."

"So you're mad at me."

"It's not rational, but maybe."

Rafe stopped, gave me a quick kiss on the cheek, grabbed my hand, and then we started up our walking again. "Don't stay mad too long, okay?"

I squeezed his hand and smiled a little. "Okay."

At dinner that night, Mrs. Goldberg had fashioned herself a huge white ribbon that read, MOTHER OF THE FREAKIN' UNIVERSE. She was wearing it over one shoulder and across her chest and torso.

I thought it was hilarious. Rafe thought it was nauseating.

"What can I say? I suddenly have two sons. My heart is full!"

"Oh my God. I'm so moving in with the Carvers," Rafe said.

I said, "Yes! Next on Fox: *Parent Swap!*"

I'd never lived somewhere before where you could just say whatever was on your mind at the dinner table. And suddenly I was taking it maybe a little too far.

"I would totally watch an episode of Rafe trying to milk a cow," I said.

"I could milk a cow."

"I'm sure there are aspects of our canoodling that could translate," I said, and Mrs. Goldberg laughed. Mr. Goldberg made a sour face.

"Okay, then," Mr. G. said. "In other news . . ."

"Did Ben just make Dad uncomfortable by being too out there? Did that just happen?" Rafe asked.

I chewed and chewed and chewed my tofu. I didn't mind the taste of the stuff, but the texture left a lot to be desired. I knew Rafe felt the same way, but when his parents believed in something — that tofu is food of the gods, for instance — there was little chance of changing their minds.

"Can we talk about something serious?" Mrs. Goldberg said. "Or would you rather continue to freak out my surprisingly prudish husband — who certainly wasn't such a prude back at Oberlin when — "

"Mom!" Rafe said. "Yes, please. Something serious. Anything but that."

She smiled. "Ben, you're perfectly welcome to stay here and enroll in Rangeview." She turned to her son. "And, darling, we can re-enroll you. If you feel you're more safe and more comfortable here, we can figure it out."

I studied the table in front of me. Suddenly the saltshakers in the shape of Buddha and the lilac butter dish changed before my eyes. They became palpable to me. Not like I couldn't touch them before, but now that touch would change meaning. I could live here? Could I? Would I?

Rafe's stare brought me back, and we shared a wide-eyed look. I wondered what he was thinking. I wondered what I was thinking. I simply didn't know.

"Of course, if you boys continue to see each other, we might have Ben stay with the Caseys. Just so there's a bit of normalcy for you both. Dating and living together so soon might be a bit much, don't you think?"

It was all happening so quickly, and I couldn't put it all together. Me, living with Claire Olivia's family? What would happen with mine? Would they cease to be my family? That thought stabbed me in the side.

It was all too fast. All I knew was how I felt today. How was I supposed to know how I'd feel in two weeks, let alone two years? And staying here? That felt—well, it felt like something that would become a thing in my family. Like Uncle Max going away. Luke would not like that.

"You look flummoxed, Ben," she said. "Can you share your thoughts with us?"

I really wasn't sure I could. I opened my mouth but no words came out. I tried again.

"Thank you," I said. "You're so nice, and you know what? I kind of love you."

I glanced at both Mr. and Mrs. Goldberg, and watched them share a sweet smile that felt incredibly intimate. They knew each other so well. Someday maybe I'd share looks like that with someone. Maybe even Rafe.

"I think I need to go back to Natick and finish what I started, though. And at some point I think I'll need to go home and work things out there."

Mrs. Goldberg gave me a proud smile, and that made me smile too.

"Thank you for the offer. Really. It means a lot to me."

She said, "Also, I want to talk to you about PFLAG. I'd like for you to come to a meeting. It may really help with this coming-out process."

Mrs. Goldberg was waiting for me to respond. I looked from her to Mr. G., who at that very moment was looking at me with more affection than my dad had in a lifetime.

"I know you don't get this," I said, "but I'm really not gay. I don't feel like that."

Mrs. Goldberg sighed. "Jesus. I feel like I just had this conversation with Rafe."

"I'm not," I said. "To me, gay means attracted to boys. I'm attracted to one boy. I'll take gay-for-Rafe, but if I'm being honest?" I took a deep breath. "I really feel like I'm straight."

"I think perhaps you're not ready to come out," Mrs. Goldberg said, spooning some cauliflower onto her plate.

"Aren't these labels up to me?"

"I know your generation is different, and I know I shouldn't be labeling, but I must say this is a perfect example of bisexual invisibility."

I looked Mrs. Goldberg in the eye. She was a beautiful person, an individual. She spoke her mind. She let me speak mine. That, to me, was beautiful.

"I love your son. Isn't that enough?"

She pressed her lips together in that *Isn't that sweet* way. "I suppose it is."

I grabbed for Rafe's hand. "This is my person. That's all that matters."

Rafe squeezed my hand.

"To me, straight and gay and bi are just words. None of them really feel like me. I'm Ben, you know?"

"Nice to meet you, Ben," Mr. G. said.

"I'm Ben and I like World War II history and I grew up on a farm and I play baseball and I'm an introvert and I'm gay-for-Rafe."

Mrs. Goldberg smiled that beautiful smile at me.

"All those labels are just — I think the world is more comfortable if it can put you in a box." I was thinking about Toby and his left-handed paths, and how by coming out as gender fluid, he had really gone hard left, which takes more bravery than I have, I think. And I was thinking about what Hannah had taught me about vulnerability, which I guess means opening yourself up to being hurt. And really the kind of courage Toby showed when he chose to follow his own path was a perfect example of being vulnerable.

"If you live outside a box, everyone gets all freaked out and tries to put you in one. No offense," I said, looking at Mrs. Goldberg.

She shook her head. "None taken. You're teaching me something."

Rafe said, "I kind of remember us talking last semester, and you saying something about how you'd thought a little bit about guys before."

"Have you had fleeting thoughts about girls?"

Rafe crooked his neck. "Sure."

"That," I said, pointing. "That's me and other boys. I'm a human being. I'm curious about lots of things. But no, before you, Rafe, never before had that really occurred to me in a real way. Never, ever. And God forbid you dump my crazy ass, my next person? I think it would be a girl." I thought about Hannah, and I felt a pang of something in my chest.

Rafe's parents shared a look.

"It's going to take us a while to sort this out and understand it," Mr. G. said. "Just know we love you precisely as you are, okay?"

And in that moment, I realized I knew exactly what it felt like to come out.

Dad,

I'm writing this because I'm still new at this whole expressing myself "foolishness," as you would say. I'd like to get to the point that I could trust myself to say it all in person, but I'm afraid the words would leave me and I'd be standing there, needing to tell you something but not knowing how.

You are a good provider, Dad. I know you pride yourself on that, and you have provided for me and Mom and Luke. I appreciate that more than you know. Unlike some of the other kids at Natick, I appreciate every single thing I have. I do.

You're also a really difficult father to have. I've never said that to you before. I've never said most of the things I think to you before, but now I will say them. Or write them. And you can read this or not read it, but at least I will have said/written it all.

You always say, "Don't get a big head about it" anytime I succeed in anything. Dad, I think I can safely say I have a teeny, tiny head by now. You taught me it wasn't okay to have pride in myself or belief in my ability, and I am angry that you did that. That was bad for me.

You also taught me that my voice wasn't important or necessary. The fewer words the better is how you are, and I don't know if that's really who you are or not. But I know it's not actually who I am. I like to talk and be talked to. I like to express ideas and talk about them. I'm not afraid to disagree, and another crazy thing that's happening now is that I'm becoming not afraid to get angry. That was always so hard. I don't know why.

I do know why, actually. I lied there to spare your feelings, but I need to be honest here. It's hard for me to get angry because you taught me to walk away from conflict. You taught me to stay on the outside of any situation and look in, and the biggest problem with that is that your life becomes devoid of situations. I think the thing I've learned this year is that life is basically all about the situations, and I want to have a life. I don't want to avoid everything just because it's uncomfortable or hard. I want to live!

I don't know exactly what happened with you and Uncle Max, but one thing I do know is I'm not him. I know you worry that I am; I can feel it all the time. What Max and I had in common is that we're sensitive. I know. To you that's bad. To me that's good. I like people who are sensitive.

I don't think I'm gay, by the way. I think I'm in love with my best friend, and he happens to be a guy. It's confusing for me too. I wish we could be confused together. But you don't like to be anything with anyone, and I can't fix that.

The Goldbergs have offered to let me stay in Boulder

and attend school here. But I have parents and I have a brother and I go to a good school. I am grateful to have each one of those things. I'm grateful for you, Dad. I love you. Even if sometimes I don't like you.

So I'm not staying here, as wonderful as Colorado is. I'm coming home to you and Mom and Luke after spring break, and boy, do I hope things will get better between us. And then I'm going back to Natick, because you and I both know that I deserve a good education, and you're not going to take that away from me because I'm not who you want me to be. That doesn't make sense. You're gonna have to get over that.

I cheated. I was as surprised as you were when it happened. I didn't think I had that in me. I don't like that it happened, and I will work my very hardest to make sure it never happens again. If the Natick School will give me a second chance, I sure hope you will too.

As I said, I hope things improve between us. But even if they don't, I can promise that I will speak my mind and be who I am, even if you don't want me to be. Because, Dad, I have the right to exist.

Love,
Benny

"Hey," I said, when Hannah picked up.

"Um. Hey."

"I just have three things to say to you. Can you just listen? Please?"

She sighed. "Go."

"Okay. First, I'm sorry. I didn't think I was leading you on, but looking back, I should have been more aware. I think whatever I was feeling for Rafe was so tied up in denial that I didn't know how strong it was. Not an excuse, just saying I'm sorry. Two, for what it's worth, not only was I attracted to you, Hannah, but I actually like you. Like, I value your opinion and I valued your friendship. So, you're basically a hot girl who is also extremely interesting, and you deserved better treatment. Third, if you ever, ever decide that you're interested in a friend who values who you are on the inside, I'm here. I mean, not right now, because I'm suspended and in Colorado because my dad apparently no longer has a son, but I will be here. For you."

She laughed a little. "Well. I'm guessing there's a story there."

"Suffice it to say that when you try to be everything to everyone, sooner or later you cheat on a math test and then admit to it in a speech in front of the whole school."

She laughed a little more. "Yup. That's what tends to happen. I'm not hugely, antagonistically angry with you anymore. I'm not sure I'm up for seeing you, but maybe someday? We'll see. You're with the Rafe guy?"

"Yup."

"Okay, then," she said. "Yep. Not ready to talk about that."

"You actually changed me," I said.

She paused. "Do I want to hear this? About how I changed you? Is this going to hurt my feelings?"

"No, not at all. It was that stuff about vulnerability. I think I'm definitely one of those people whose dad taught him never to be vulnerable, and that totally screwed me up. I'm trying to learn how to do it now. So thanks for that."

"Huh," she said. "I can live with that."

"I'm glad."

"Take care of yourself, Ben Carver, okay?"

"You too, Hannah Stroud."

Rafe claimed he could teach me to swim.

"I don't know, Rafe. I was told once that I have the buoyancy of a, I don't know, a really un-buoyant thing," I said.

He responded, "Nice metaphor."

We went to the Colorado Athletic Club in Boulder, which was basically the nicest place I'd ever been, yet Rafe acted like it was a nuisance to walk through. I would never get used to that sort of callousness, but that was a whole different plate of Czech dumplings.

As we got changed in the locker room, I looked over at Rafe and saw him. Not, like, his body. Just who he was. And that made me smile. He was a good person, and I knew now I could trust him. With my life if I had to.

"Thank you," I said.

"You're extremely welcome," he said, slamming the locker shut. We walked toward the pool. "What for?"

I threw my towel over my naked shoulder. "I'm grateful for you."

"Aw."

"No, really. Maybe all this stuff wouldn't have happened had I never met you, but on the other hand, none of this stuff would have happened."

He laughed. "You speak in riddles now."

"I just mean, I'm glad, is all. You helped me be me."

"Wow. Thanks," he said. "That means a lot. I'm grateful for you too. Before you, I had nobody beyond my parents who knew how awesome I was."

"Such a narcissist," I said, and he stuck out his tongue.

Rafe dove in, and I got splashed a bit. Then I gingerly took the steps into the shallow end. The water was lukewarm, which surprised me. I sat on the top step and adjusted to the wetness on my lower body.

"C'mon. I'm gonna teach you to swim," he said.

I shook my head. "Nope. No, thanks. I'm fine going through the rest of my life without swimming. There are some things I'm good at, and this is not one of them."

"C'mon," he said, coaxing me off the steps. "I'm here, and I'm going to teach you to float. I won't let you sink."

I tentatively walked toward him, as if the water were my enemy. Rafe just looked at me, bemused. He crossed his arms and picked his feet off the floor and treaded water, making it look easy.

When I got to him I was up to my chest. He turned me around, goosed my butt, and put his hands on my back. Slowly I allowed myself to lean back onto his hands. I picked my feet up off the floor and held my breath, sure I'd go under, that I'd be too heavy for Rafe to carry.

I wasn't.

He was holding me up!

Then he took me out a little deeper, and soon he was treading water while holding me. I saw the 8 FOOT sign, and I thought, *Wow.*

324

All that had happened in the last few months had changed me, changed my body. Taken weight off my shoulders, that sort of thing.

"Take that deep breath. You'll see. It'll keep you afloat."

I took a deep breath. I held it. My face sunk under the water. My body began to as well.

"Holy hell, what the heck is wrong with your body?" he said as he struggled to keep me up.

I started to thrash my arms. I could hear him repeatedly saying, "Relax, relax," even though my ears were submerged in the water. Rafe was keeping me afloat by treading as fast as he could, kicking underwater and waving one arm like an angry ferret. Still, we slowly began to sink.

"Well, this is unpleasantly ironic," I said, water seeping into my nostrils as my nose and eyes submerged.

"I . . . You mean . . . coincidence," Rafe said as he attempted to pull me toward the shallow end. I heard every other word, as my ears were now underwater.

I didn't mean coincidence, actually, but there was no time to explain the irony — that I'd just learned to tread water in the world, and now I was drowning.

A funny thing happens when you're drowning and a person attempts to drag you to safety. You fight. Instinct. I thrashed and kicked, and I saw his face go under and he raised himself up momentarily and then went under again, and I thought of that scene at the end of *Titanic*, and wondered which of us would be barely alive on the piece of wood from the ship, and which of us would be dead.

I had a guess. And truly, I'd rather it went that way. If one of us was going to die, let it be me. Not Rafe. Though best would be if we both lived.

"You're gonna have to save yourself, or tread 'til I can get some help or a kickboard," Rafe said, his breathing labored. "In a second I'm gonna let you go. Okay?"

I didn't have time to say okay, though I meant it. *Okay.* We shared a final eye contact and I thought, *Not now. Please not now. When things are finally happening in my life.*

He let me go, and just like in New Hampshire, I dropped like a stone. I hit the bottom.

But this time, I bounced up. Maybe I had a little extra spring in my step. I don't know. I bounced up once, almost to the surface, and the second time I hit bottom I bounced up high, and then I just moved my arms and got myself to the side.

I grasped the side and clung to it, never so thankful to be holding on to something.

And as I held on with all my might, and Rafe instructed me to pull myself along the ledge to the shallow end, I realized: I saved myself. Rafe didn't. He helped, but I was the one who figured out how to swim my heavy body to safety.

ACKNOWLEDGMENTS

So many to thank . . . Great appreciation to:

The hundreds upon hundreds of fans who took the time to email or message me on social media about your absolute need for a sequel. This book wouldn't exist if it weren't for you!

Marty Cornelissen and Kim Moore for showing me Alton, New Hampshire, and life on an Alton farm. Sorry for all the ridiculous questions and thanks for your patience!

Patrick Jackson, the original "Are you in, or are you out" slam poet.

My great beta readers, Joey Avalos, Kameron Martinez, Anthony Isom, Josh Horton, and Logan Moreno. Your enthusiasm and smart comments really helped.

Brent Hartinger, my writing buddy, who is always there with the kind and useful critiques that save me from being boring (bye-bye, hazing plot!).

Erin Jade Lange and Amy Dominy for the smart critiques.

Lisa and Matt McMann and Tom and Joy Leveen for the wonderful support and friendship. Love you all.

Kail Overstreet and all the wonderful people at TYME and Just Us at the Oasis Center in Nashville, who helped me understand gender fluidity better than I had before. I'm still learning, and I hope I did you proud!

Mike Graham, who helped me turn things around when I was struggling, and who introduced me to the ideas of Brené Brown. When Hannah talks about a woman who writes about vulnerability, she's referring to Brown. To read more about these ideas, I strongly suggest Brown's *The Gifts of Imperfection*. And to Dr. Brown, who fundamentally changed me for the better: Thank you so much for all you do.

My loving family. My father, who is always there with a (tragically bad) idea; my mother, who is my biggest fan; my sister and brother, who love me as I am and encourage me to keep going forward; my Karen and Sam, and even Finn, who should never have garnered the name Cousin Oliver; my Mabel and Buford, whom I love so dearly; and my Chuck, the original Ben, who is my life.

My Scholastic family. My editor, Cheryl Klein, who repeatedly had to ask, "Is that what you think 'repressed' means?" You soften out my roughest spots and magically seem to bring out my best, every time; Arthur A. Levine, for your encouragement and friendship; Lizette Serrano, Jennifer Abbots, Lauren Festa, Tracy van Straaten, Christine Reedy, Emily Heddleson, Michelle Campbell, and Antonio Gonzalez. You are the best team possible, all of you!

And to everyone out there who is on a left-handed path. If it was easy, everyone would be doing it. Keep rumbling with your truth. You are all extremely badass.

ABOUT THE AUTHOR

Bill Konigsberg is the author of *The Porcupine of Truth*, which won the Stonewall Book Award for Young Adult Literature and the PEN Center USA Literary Award for Children's/Young Adult; *Openly Straight*, which won the SCBWI's Sid Fleischman Award for Humor; and *Out of the Pocket*, which won the Lambda Literary Award. He is the Writer-in-Residence at the Piper Center for Creative Writing at Arizona State University, where he coordinates the Your Novel Year online certificate program. Prior to writing novels, Bill was an award-winning sports writer and editor with the Associated Press and ESPN .com. He lives in Chandler, Arizona, with his husband, Chuck Cahoy, and their two Labradoodles, Mabel and Buford. You can find him online at www.billkonigsberg.com and at @billkonigsberg.

This book was edited by Cheryl Klein and designed by Nina Goffi. The production was supervised by Rebekah Wallin. The text was set in Fairfield LH Light, with display type set in Adobe Acropolis and Avenir. This book was printed and bound by R.R. Donnelley in Crawfordsville, Indiana. The manufacturing was supervised by Angelique Brown.